ATTACK OF THE ROM-COM

Martti Nelson

**HUMORIST
BOOKS**

New York

First Printing: 2023
ISBN 978-1-954158-22-1

Humorist Books is an imprint of *Weekly Humorist* owned and operated by Humorist Media LLC.

Weekly Humorist is a weekly humor publication, subscribe online at weeklyhumorist.com

110 Wall Street New York, NY 10005

weeklyhumorist.com - humoristbooks.com - humoristmedia.com

Cover design by Marty Dundics
Book editor: Brian Boone

To my best friend since middle school, The Amazing Freedom Kim. Her love, support, and propensity to curse those who would subdue us has shown me what bosom friendship is.

I write books about incredible friendships among women because I know first-hand why they make life worth living.

Zuwiekis forever!

CHAPTER ONE:
WHEN SOPHIE MET TIFFANI

I stumbled off the Zipper Shaker Widow Maker ride and reached to steady myself on Jodie. Which did not work whatsoever, so I landed on my butt with the grace of a drunken llama. "Suck it, ride," I groaned as the world spun around me. "Sophie Sweet makes the widows around here."

Jodie Edwards, my best friend on this whole godforsaken planet, doubled over with laughter and not vomit. Advantage: Jodie. "You sure about that, Barfy? You literally went green on the last bend. It looked so cute on you, though." She crouched to pinch my cheeks, which earned her a swat.

"Screw off, Buffy."

"Barfy and Buffy ride again! At least you didn't vomit on my socks like when we were 16."

"It is an honor to be yakked upon by the great Barfy." I tried to say it with a flourish, but burped instead. Like a lady. "And I had that ride right where I wanted it."

"You sure? You're even pastier than usual."

"Hey, that's 'Mayonnaise American,' thank you very much."

Clutching my belly, in a super tough and not-at-all pathetic way, I managed to stand. I forced air in, past the vinegar French fries, around the chili dog, straight through the fried pickle—all of which stayed down, ha! My eyeballs almost focused in the same direction, and one of them managed to goggle Jodie, fresh as a daisy after being shaken like a go-go dancer's ass. How did she do that? "What's next? If you say the Spinner Winner Chicken Dinner, I will stab you."

We grinned at one another. Every Halloween, we adventured to the Gator Riviera, Florida, Autumn Carnival, a tiny affair where you risked your life—and lunch—for grubby fun. We grew up in this one-stoplight berg, later moving to Miami, but could not resist returning north to our hometown festival and its many stomach-churning traditions.

"Let's get you some water," Jodie said.

She took me by the hand and led me toward salvation. Or death. Either way, I trusted her.

"Huh. I thought you were gonna argue and try to eat something else disgusting." Jodie leaned me against the concession stand like a pair of skis. "One water, please."

"And a cheddar corn-dog muffin," I added.

The concession lady nodded. "Got it."

"No!" argued Jodie.

"Yes," I counter-argued her argument. "Cheddar corn-dog muffins are good for a sick stomach, right?" *Deep breaths, Sophie. Barfing is for losers.*

"Uh-huh," replied the concession lady. "Better put butter on it. To settle everything."

I managed to crack a smile. "Scientific. I like that."

Jodie pulled her own face, which she did often with me. I chose to take it as a compliment. "Fine," she said. "But at least sit while you eat your gastrointestinal bomb. I don't understand how you do it."

"Internal organs made of barbed wire."

"Scientific. I like that."

We sat at a picnic table. Jodie made me drink water before eating any of my food-medicine. She looked around and took a huge inhale of air. "This place always smells the same. Gasoline. B.O. Scrub pine. Hey, Barfy— remember the year we snuck out to come here because your dad had grounded you?"

"And I got into a war of words with that horrible man with the seven bratty kids."

Jodie lit up with a gorgeous grin. She could illuminate the whole town with that wattage. Some poor fella nearby stumbled for staring at her, the stunning Black goddess powering the carnival all by herself. Her deep-brown skin shone like…like a sapphire in the night time? Ugh, I was bad at words and crap, but wow. My poor, abused stomach unwound a bit.

She laughed. "The big one tripped you, then the other ones ground gum into your hair because you wouldn't let all seven of them cut in line… Wait, what were we in line for?"

"Fried butter!" Oh, yeah. I could giggle about it now. At the time, however, I would have happily committed seven little acts of murder. Also while giggling, let's be real. The evil queen in *Snow White* was a woefully misunderstood heroine. "You gave me an awesome pixie cut—mostly even and everything." She'd performed her act of mercy-barbering in the middle of the night so my dad wouldn't realize we'd gone out. Heh—I like to tell myself I'd been cool about the whole thing, but when Jodie had cut off my pretty black curls, I nearly cried. *Cried.* Like some kind of *person.* It was one of the few times Dad yelled instead of just shaking his head and ignoring me because a daughter of his "shouldn't look like an ugly boy."

I shuddered at the memory, my mouth forming a tight line. I cleared my throat. "You did a perfect job on my hair, Buffy."

"Of course, I'm amazing. The expression on your dad's face the next morning…" Jodie opened her eyes so wide that they damn near shot across the table. "That man was not equipped to handle you or your perfect pixie."

I chuckled through a tight throat. "He didn't *want* to handle me. Still doesn't." Ugh, after that cut, he'd demanded I wear a bunch of makeup, and dresses, to emphasize his idea of what a "daughter" should look like.

Even now, swiping on mascara felt like trying in vain to please a crappy dad who'd ignored me 99% of the time.

The muffin sat in my mouth like a rock. My heart sorta went…black-hole-y whenever I thought of him or my mother. Like it was being sucked into an invisible void from which no light escaped. I forced down the muffin. My parents had been ill-suited for each other. Ill-suited for me. They'd wanted to birth the sparkling, ideal child, whoever the hell that is. Not sure she exists, but she sure ain't me.

A gentle hand turned my chin. "What's that face?" Jodie tilted her head and did the cute thing she did—she pushed her bottom lip under the top. "Your stomach acting up still?"

"No, the butter medicine is perfect. I just --" I squeezed my eyes shut. "Do you think if I'd've been the perfect kid, that --"

"You stop right there!" Jodie shot off her bench, came around, and bumped my hip to scoot me over. "First, you are the perfect kid. Adult. Whatever. Secondly, *nobody's* perfect!"

I blinked. "What?"

"Sophie, your mom would not have been happy if you'd have gotten straight A's and made hats for the poor and…and…fed soup to indigent cats."

I blinked. "What?"

Jodie waved her hands. "I don't know what perfect people do. Point is, she was unhappy with your father. He was miserable with her. Instead of coming to their senses and getting divorced like normal folk, she pulled a disappearing act, and he took it out on you with his silence and disapproval. Classic transference. Probably. I read that on the internet."

Whoa. My brain spun anew with the force of these truths. Usually, I worked hard not to remember any of this stuff because it made the black hole beckon, cold and hollow. I tipped my head back to stare at the stars, yet they formed a gray mass. Time to shove the painful stuff way, way down. Ugly feelings were why I'd left home at 17 for good. Out of sight, out of existence, right?

But Dr. Jodie was on a roll. "...and your mom! Not even a phone call on your birthday. You didn't deserve their emotional abuse! Sure, you're a little wild and mouthy and made of barbed wire, but those are wonderful things."

I shot her a sideways look. That's not what those kids said when they'd stomped Hubba Bubba into my bangs.

Jodie squeezed my shoulders. "You're generous with the people you like..."

"You," I said.

"Yes, and I appreciate that." Jodie's brown eyes burrowed underneath my armor. "There is no more loyal friend than you, Sophie. You don't deserve to be depressed about the fact that your parents are assholes. I said what I said. Assholes. Now—eat your disgusting buttered hot dog bread."

I did as Jodie ordered, and her reassuring grin made the dark, feathery edges of the black hole recede. About the only place I'd ever behaved was at Jodie's house. Her parents housed me when I couldn't cope with my unbearable home life anymore; they were so supportive of Jodie that I got abundant cast-off affection. It was nice. A smile burst out of me; I took a bite to cover it. Okay, more than nice. Jodie's family had given me my first and only glimpse of parental love and stuff. I could breathe with Jodie.

"Thank you, Dr. Jodie," I said through muffin. Huh. What useful advice had I ever given Jodie? Ah! I taught her how to punch without breaking her thumb. Not that she ever had to punch. Not around me, anyway. "I'm sorry I'm not good at this—the advice...feelings, uh..."

"Talking?"

I grunted and shrugged.

"No, you are not. But later, you'll win me a dirty stuffed animal prize, and we'll call it even."

"I'll probably steal one."

"Thanks, girl."

I laughed and finished my snack. Mmmm... butter. I licked my lip, reaching for a glob with my tongue.

"You missed." Jodie snapped a photo.

"Hey!"

"New phone background, thank you." She chuckled like an adorable super villain. "Feeling better?"

I nodded. My hand shot out to grab hers on the rough wooden table as I met her gaze. "Thanks."

Her eyebrows rose. "For what?"

A million warm and fuzzy emotions I refused to name because I was too cool for them crowded into my chest. They didn't seem tight, like a panic attack, more like being tucked into soft blankets with a purring cat. Or beach sunshine on your face. How did people express this kind of stuff without sounding like a soap opera? Jodie was my world. My bosom friend, as Anne of Green Gables would say, not that I got sappy like that. It's just…she was the best person I'd ever known.

I tucked my hair behind my ears and changed the subject to something less terrifying. "Thanks for the cheddar corn-dog muffin."

I put my thumb to my nose and wiggled my fingers at her in our sacred gesture of friendship. Maybe not-so-secret, because a little girl nearby cracked up and joined in. Jodie returned the compliment, and we grinned like dorks. In this circle, when your best friend wiggled her digits in your face, she meant, "I love you." And I did.

Jodie snorted. "I'm not saying 'you're welcome' for buying you the muffin. You'll probably barf it on me after the next ride."

"You're welcome. What will our next adventure be, boss?"

"Gwendolyn the Fantabulous!" she announced, most fantabulously. "I am so painfully single I keep cruising straight girls at South Beach drag shows. I need her reassurance I won't die alone."

"You'll never die alone—Barfy will stick to Buffy like a crusty barnacle. Forever."

"That's hot." Jodie hauled me to my feet.

We started toward "the psychic's" tent. The only thing that old bat Gwendolyn could promise was that you'd be parted from your money in exchange for fake fortune-telling, but I readily agreed. Gwendolyn—an old Russian white lady who could've been 50 or 150— was hilarious, and always shared her vodka, offered in a skull-shaped shot glass.

"Should I tell her that I never did run away to become the world's first stripping astronaut?" I asked.

Jodie gasped, clutching her bosom like an Austen heroine. "Don't be so cruel! I've concocted a whole story about how my career as a spy for the Kremlin is proceeding apace. See?" She fished in her pocket, then lifted something over her head.

I busted out laughing. "Wow. That is one amazing eye patch."

She posed from side to side, the red sequins of the patch glinting with intrigue. "I am Kremlin spy-ski!"

"How did you lose your eye, comrade?" My turn to snap a photo of this dork.

In an epically atrocious Russian accent, she said, "Baking accident. I try to put file in Matryoshka doll cake for to break partner out of gulag."

"Oh!" I applauded her performance. "Because Gwendolyn predicted that you'd be a baker who made dirty cakes in the shape of male body parts."

"Da." Jodie screwed up her face. "Swing and a miss with that one. I'm a boob cake girl."

"You can cake my boobs any day."

"That's very reassuring."

I took a deep breath, the nip in the air settling my swirling brains with each inhale. The blinking carnival lights flashed rainbows across our path, and everything was right with the world. Me and Jodie—that's all I really needed. Plus game code. I sat on my butt for hours commanding computers and building worlds of violent fun. In a game, I was God.

Ooh, maybe I should add a skeevy carnival to my game! Imagine the battles my heroine could fight in a scary, decrepit setting like this—perhaps with an eccentric psychic as her nemesis.

I flung an arm around Jodie. "Why do so many of our conversations eventually turn to tits?"

"What else is there to discuss?"

"Buffy—asking the important questions."

We arrived at the psychic's tent, a purple and pink eye-assault painted with shooting stars, fading crystal balls, and mystical shapes borrowed from miscellaneous religions. The "open" sign had been flipped our way, so I tossed back the flap and went straight in. "Gwendolyn!" I called. "Show me my sexy future, baby! But if you say 'ballerina,' I will riot."

Jodie collided with me in the tent. "Whoops, sorry, eye patch."

Gwendolyn was not in the front part. It smelled different. I blinked to adjust to the darkness and took a sniff. What was that?

"Chanel Number Five?" Jodie guessed. She lifted her eye patch. "Look, Gwendolyn got a decorator."

A pink velvet couch sat where Gwendolyn used to keep her dusty collection of stuffed Victorian birds. And her table, with its entirely non-magical crystal ball, was gone, replaced by a kidney-bean shaped one. A goofy orange armchair sat across from the sofa. Strings of lights bobbed and weaved from the tent supports, flashing yellow and pink in a candy-coated seizure.

"You're here!" piped a voice from behind us.

We jumped as one to see—

"Who the hell are you?" I asked. "Where's Gwendolyn?"

The human cupcake tossed her long, black hair and laughed, her face breaking into a gorgeous smile. Definitely not Gwendolyn—this lady was young, tall, and East Asian. Kinda had Gwendolyn's curves, though, and stood full-figured in every right way. Gorgeous. "She retired to Cleveland. Horrifying, right? Ha-ha!" She wobbled forward on the tallest hot pink heels I'd ever winced at. "I'm Tiffani the Psychic. And my angels tell me you super-duper need my help."

"Nope." I turned to leave, as I was entirely allergic to silly sorority sisters.

Jodie grabbed my arm. "Stop! I want a reading." She tore off her eye patch, and then ran her hands along her fade, the way she did in front of all pretty ladies. "Hi, Tiffani. I'm tragically single, and I want to know if I'll meet anyone decent." Jodie winked at me, for Tiffani the Psychic's first test was—what sort of date would she recommend to the enthusiastically lesbian Jodie?

"Yes! Come. Sit. Both of you." Tiffani smoothed her ridiculous scarlet caftan, bedecked with glittery gold stars, and perched on the orange chair. "The veil has lifted, and I can see *everything*."

Jodie wanted this, so I sighed and let my BFF lead me to the offensively pink couch. Gotta take one for the lady who'd let you barf on her—that's a life lesson right there. The one and only time I'd dared to vomit in front of my mother, when I was six, she'd smacked me upside the head. Ugh, the perfumed room made my nose burn.

"Kombucha?" Tiffani offered a jar of brown sludge, at which Jodie readily nodded.

I blinked. Tiffani batted her giant eyelashes. I grimaced.

Tiffani poured some brown stuff for Jodie, and then put on a serious face. "Here, hold on to me."

"Jodie."

"Jodie." They held hands, and Tiffani closed her eyes. "Mmmmmm," said Tiffani, *mystically*. "You're such a sweet person! Awww, I love that. My angels tell me you enjoy girl bands from the eighties—that's sooo cute."

Jodie wore a Go-Go's T-shirt.

"Oh, yes," Tiffani squeaked. "I see romance in your future. Super romantic romance." She paused and said with wide eyes. "True love."

With a gasp, Jodie leaned forward. "Who?"

I slumped, crossed my arms, and let out a snort. Silly Mcbubblegum would now crash and burn.

Tiffani's shining dark eyes bored into me. "She's someone unlikely." She cocked her head. "Did I get that right? *She?*" Smugly, she flicked her gaze to a grinning Jodie. "My angels tell me everything! Especially

Happizzez, I just looooove her. She's the one who filled me in about Lizzo becoming a huge star who wears a lot of corsets. But Jodie, neither you nor your ladylove have realized that true, everlasting passion is floating in the ether, ready for you to reach out and grope it!"

Jodie waggled her eyebrows, and then elbowed me. "Really? What's her name? Hair color?" She leaned forward. "Bra size?"

"Every conversation," I murmured.

"Priorities," replied Jodie. "And please describe Lizzo's future corsets."

The psychic smirked. "Revealing her identity would be too easy! Also…" Tiffani pressed her manicured fingers to her temples. "My angels say…you're going on several trips. One—you're at a wedding with a beautiful woman. She's wearing white. *You're* wearing white, *awww*. I see a lot of fashion in my visions because clothes maketh the woman looketh cute. Oh! Another journey will be to a historical village. In Plopshire, England. With horses, butter churns, mud, and whatnot." She shrugged. "Old timey things, ha-ha! It'll be sooo great, though. Plopshirewill change your life."

"Really? I'll churn butter?" Jodie pursed her lips to one side. "Do I have to?"

"Romance cannot happen without butter!"

It was the first thing Tiffani said that made sense.

"Plopshire." I barked out a laugh. "Plop. Shire. Your angels have a lofty sense of humor."

Jodie threw me *a look*. "Unlike you?"

Tiffani blinked wide eyes. "Now for your friend!"

With a jerk, I avoided the psychic's grasping hand. "I am not spending my hard-earned money so Glinda the Sparkle Witch can talk a bunch of woo-woo at me." Ugh, why did this Tiffani irk me this much? Gwendolyn babbled nothing but bunk, too. Yet Tiffani invoked "angels"—that sort of thing would get her far in Gator Riviera, where churches darn near outnumbered people. I leaned back and crossed my arms. "Yaknow, Tiff, if you just wanted to lie to people, you should join Congress."

"I probably wiiiilllll." Tiffani said it with yawning vowels and a wide smile. "I'd run on a platform of love for everyone. Wouldn't that be amazing?"

Was this chick for real? Perhaps I'd died from vomit overdose after the last ride. My eyebrows rose to the heavens. "So that's it? Jodie will get true love and some mud in Poopshire, that'll be 10 bucks?"

"Twenty." Tiffani shrugged one fancy shoulder. "Jodie, I guarantee you love, within the month, or your money back."

Jodie whooped and clapped.

"But!" Tiffany took a long, dramatic pull of her tea. "This one. The rabid one," she flicked a long finger toward me, "must let me do a reading."

I smiled. "Finally, you got a prediction right."

"My reading?" Jodie asked.

"Rabid."

That earned me another elbow. "Do it for me," Jodie said. "She'll do it. Hold hands like a nice girl, Sophie."

I growled like the monster I was; Tiffani grabbed at me anyway. *Do it for Jodie.* After all, Jodie was a ride-or-die friend. Always loyal, always reliable, always forcing down my Doritos Surprise, which was the only thing I cooked.

The secret recipe, passed down from my brain when I got drunk and watched *Cutlery Corner*, contained Doritos, cheese, ground beef, spaghetti, and Nerds candy. It was *fantastic*. To sophisticated palates, anyway.

Unlike Tiffani the Psychic. What a load of Diet Cool Whip this woman was. Her performance was Oscar-worthy. Tiffani hyperventilated, swayed like an inflatable air guy at a discount tire shop, and squeaked sort-of sayings, like, "A stitch in time saves wine." Finally, she stared at a candle until her eyes crossed.

I shot daggers at Jodie, who proceeded to laugh at me shamelessly. The hussy took another picture! Just when I began to giggle at the ridiculousness, the lights went out.

"Oh, damn," murmured Jodie.

In the dark, Tiffani said, "I see…for you…the color pink! A pink dress! Aw, I looove pink."

"Hell," I muttered while gnawing on my lip. "I'm in hell."

Tiffani's voice dipped to ominous levels when she said, "This isn't even close to your personal hell." The backlit outline of Tiffani cupped her ear to listen to…nothing. "Your hell is inside your own head—what with your soul-shattering self-doubt and feelings of inadequacy as a byproduct of your abusive childhood."

"Excuse me?" I went hot everywhere at once, losing my words to the inferno. I couldn't seem to spit out anything else. Like "I hate you" or "pink is ugly, you horrible ball of cotton candy."

So Tiffani kept right on blabbering. "I see that you're a Scorpio."

Jodie whispered, "Yes, she is."

Ugh! I hip-checked Jodie to get her to stop helping Tiffani. What on earth was the woman talking about? Feelings of inadequacy? I did my best to never have feelings in the first place! Which proved the orange armchair psychologist wrong. This room stifled me. I itched everywhere, but on the inside.

The psychic spared a minute to quote more nonsense ("All that glitters is mandatory!"),then, she announced, "I see…the letter R. And a C!"

I pulled the leather jacket off my throat to catch a damn breath. "How about the letters F, U --"

"Sophie Sweet!" Tiffani boomed. "The angels have peered into your soul, and we know!" She slammed the table. Jodie and I clutched one another. "That you do not believe in love. Which is a real shame, because love is eeeeverything!" She pointed at me. Dramatically! "For instance, whatever happened to Earl?"

Jodie gasped. Like, full-on, hand-to-her-heaving-bosom gasped. "She knows about Earl!" she squeaked. Leaning forward, my bestie growled, "I never liked Earl."

"And I dumped Earl," I informed Tiiiiiifani. Who knew his name for some reason. Fuck, my heart thumped in my earballs. Why had I dumped Earl? Oh, yeah, he'd wanted to love me and live with me, couldn't have that. He'd been a much better guy than Regina had been a girlfriend, and yet I'd clung to Regina like cheap plastic wrap. I shook off a shiver. "He wasn't my forever person, if that person even exists."

"Oh, they do."

With the smirkiest smirk I could smirk, I said, "Because there are so many amazing couples who last 50 years. Yup! Sure."

"That attitude? That's why you're miserable and lonely and pathetic, ha-ha!"

I shot to my feet. "Hey!" I stumbled over the kidney table and flailed until I flopped backward to the couch again. "I am not miserable, or *pathetic*, you glitter-bombed, fake-ass grifter!" How freaking dare she? "Turn the lights back on! See, Jodie, *this* is why I carry a switchblade."

"How did you know Sophie's last name?" Jodie asked. "Scorpio?" Her tone soured. "And Earl."

A finger snap sounded, along with a "Ha-ha!" The twinkle lights resumed their bopping journey across the tent. Jodie gasped.

Tiffani perched there, her smile stiffened with so much dippy superiority it brought me to an absolute boil. Beads of sweat erupted at my hairline, and I—I—

Oh, come on! As if I'd allow some ridiculous stranger to come at me, insult me, degrade me, and call my shitty childhood shitty. Then *giggle* at it.

"Nice trick, Hermione Houdini." With a sneer, I shot to my feet again. "Quick—what's my cat's name? Or maybe you could pull a rabbit out of your Liberace hand-me-down."

Tiffani clutched her pearls. Literally. "This caftan is Dior! Now you're deflecting your overwhelming isolation into attacks on me. That'll be $20."

"Are you delusional? Do you actually believe you can read my mind? Oh, I'm frowning at the most absurd person I've ever met, therefore I'm psychologically damaged. You must give the same reading to everyone who stumbles into the tunnel of love, eventually."

"No, I do not. But Happizzez enjoyed that joke." Tiffani rose like a debutante and slid her curtain of hair off her shoulder. "The more you retreat into yourself, you cantankerous turtle, the worse your life will get. How many lonely nights shall you suffer? How many disgusting corn chip casseroles will you burp over? Please open your heart to love. I mean…it's love! What's not to love? That's an actual saying, ha ha!"

Jodie had the friggin' gall to laugh, so I sailed past her on the way to the door.

"Sophie!" Tiffani turned me by the elbow. "By hook or by book, romance is coming for you. And my angels will make sure you don't run away from it. Ordinarily, I'd just let you die alone, but I like your friend."

"Aw, thanks!" Jodie positively tittered.

I threw back my head and cackled, sure now I was being trolled. "OooOOooooh! Psychic Barbie is gonna force me to Tinder! I'll make sure to leave a window open for your kidnap squad of angelic romance commandos. Jodie, remind me to wax tonight." I sauntered out of the tent, away from the stifling stench of perfume and bullshit.

The cold air slapped my sweat dry and lifted the fog from my brain. I stopped there, eyes pressed closed, willing the red in my vision to dissipate before I—

"You owe me 20 bucks." Jodie joined me, her tone nicer than her expression.

"You paid her?" I flapped my arms and starting walking. "You paid her to say that my childhood made me sad."

"Your childhood did make you sad."

I missed a step. "Childhood screws everyone up!" Gross, why were we dwelling on this stuff tonight? My face went all weird and numb from the sheer volume of garbage emotions trying to shoot out the top of my head. I balled my fists. "You realize Tiffani basically read a horoscope, toggled the lights, and fed you rot tea, right?"

"Says the lady who makes Doritos Surprise."

"You love Doritos Surprise." I dragged Jodie toward the beer stand.

"Because you said you'd never talk to me again if I didn't eat it. By the way—*corn chip casserole?*" Jodie began jumping along. "Come on! How could she know that repulsive detail about you?"

"Oh, poor, sweet, gullible Jodie. This is why so many of your girlfriends keep your clothes after you break up."

That made Jodie turn around mid-skip. "You're buying the beers, jerk."

I waved my arms. "WoooOOOooOOO! The angels tell me a drink that starts with B is in your future!"

Yup, she flipped me off. I deserved it.

Later that night, after apology beers, we retreated to my place for another annual tradition, the post-carnival sleepover.

Jodie turned off the bathroom light switch as she joined me in my adjoining bedroom. She was wearing her hair natural nowadays, shorter on top with a cute fade on the sides and a semi-circle hard part. After using a spray bottle to wet her hair, she used a head massager to work coconut oil into her scalp. Mmmm, the smell was so nice. So Jodie.

She said, "That lady Tiffani gave me the chills. Happy chills, if that makes sense."

"Because she was gorgeous." I ran to get a necessary component to our sleepovers—one of the silk pillowcases I'd bought especially for her. "You'll believe anything a hot lady has to say."

I fluffed her new-and-improved pillow, and then pressed play on *Bride Wars.*

Not for the first time, I shook my head at the fact that I actually deigned to watch rom-coms. For Jodie. *Only* for her. No matter how unpleasant. No matter how Kate Hudson. She loved that crap so much, who the hell knew why. It's not like the sexist heroes made of plastic were appealing to her.

But the ladies were beautiful, no doubt, no doubt.

I grabbed a fistful of Nerds to go with my gallon of boxed cabernet, the only way to get through a war of brides.

She leaned over to her bedside table and grabbed her hair bonnet. "Excuse me, I don't believe *anything* a hot lady has to say. I'll believe *most* things a hot lady has to say. I believe you, don't I?" All finished with her crowning glory, she snatched the box of candy away from me.

"Aw, shucks." My black cat, Satan, jumped on the bed to join in the group cuddle. He plopped on my belly and proceeded with his hoarse purr. They say cats help with stress relief; I probably would have burned down something by now if not for him. Hail Satan! I even had a huge shoulder tattoo of this little goober—Satan, growling at my enemies. And I'd given him saber-teeth, which I know he appreciates.

I dragged him up to lay on my chest face-to-face to me. "Who's my sweetie evil kitty? You're my sweetie evil kitty! Yes, you are." I put my forehead to his, and his motor-boat noises hit full throttle. "My snuggly baby kittykins, I love you so much, yes, I do. Yes, I do!"

Jodie near fell off the bed giggling. "I'm gonna send Tiffani the Psychic a video of you and your one true love, Satan."

I had to laugh. "Has anything been more true in this world?" Ugh, I shook my head. "At least Gwendolyn never pretended to be real. That's what pisses me off the most about *Tiffani.* Who probably spells her name with an I.'" *Hmmm.* "Two I's."

"The sign of true malevolence," Jodie agreed through the crunching of Nerds. "Hey, where are your nail clippers?"

I waggled my eyebrows at her. "Got a hot date?"

I was rewarded with a cartoonish wink. "Why do you think I'm here?"

Well, then. I gave the lady her nail clippers. There aren't too many people I'd let clip in bed, but this was my Jodie.

My Jodie, my friend who would not let things go. "Sophie…she knew about Doritos Surprise. And that you're a Scorpio. And your last name! And *Earl.*"

"That's because…um…the horrible woman found a way to see my driver's license." I got a weird yawning in my belly. Probably Satan's kneading. Or the ulcer shoved down my throat tonight. I drained my wine to drown the ugly feelings. And the good feelings. Feelings in general could suck it.

Jodie crunch-crunch-crunched her candy. "How would she have seen your license?"

"When she turned out the lights with her remote control or whatever."

"Because it's so easy to pick pockets and read licenses in the pitch black."

I opened my mouth to argue, but nothing came out. How the hell had Tiffani done that? Maybe more wine would tell me. "Whatever. Good luck with her grift, I guess."

Jodie scooted closer and put her head on my shoulder. I leaned into her warmth, her safety; this was the first time in hours my muscles melted. The coconutty smell of her hair loosened my shoulders. All that childhood talk had left me unmoored, and I squeezed my eyes shut against the crashing memories.

"I think Tiffani's right," Jodie said. "You're going to meet the person of your dreams. Maybe at work, amongst the game nerds. You two will scream at one another about *Silent Hill* vs. *Resident Evil,* and then make mad love in the broom closet!"

"Is that your psychic vision, oh mysterious Buffy the Clairvoyant? Because I would never suffer a date who talks smack about *Silent Hill.*"

"Obviously." Satan abandoned me to head-butt Jodie, who obliged him with cuddles. "That'll be 50 bucks."

I did not pay up, but I was exceedingly free with the candy and wine and cat, like a true best friend.

I attempted an act of sleep, yet my brain kept cycling to the "psychic." How dare she babble about my childhood? As if she knew me? And what about her obsession with loooOOoooove. Of course love is the only thing a woman should be interested in, right? Ick. Jodie and I were both professional women—me, a coder, and Jodie, a high school physics teacher. We didn't need romance, we had brains and ambition and each other.

Besides, dating was a disastrous occupation—a torture chamber full of small-talk land mines and slobbery first kisses. I shuddered and clutched the blanket tighter, because "opening up to people" was the freaking worst. Just the idea made me want to hurl more than the Widow Maker ride.

Why would anyone choose to spew emotion and weakness far and wide? After all, no matter how much you cry and scream and beg, Mom leaves anyway to get away from the slow death of female domesticity. I pressed my hand to my chest against a wave of winey heartburn. As soon as my father transferred all the "woman" stuff in the house to eight-year-old me—cooking and cleaning and scrubbing and lying to bill collectors—I suddenly didn't blame Mom for leaving anymore. Too often, dudes didn't want a real human being, but a bang maid, ick.

And when you date ladies…they were more confusing, as they seemed to need a level of emotional sharing I could not bring myself to give. I leaned a little more toward women in terms of crushes and lusting and more lusting, but when I got the "What are we?" question, apparently running away was a bad response. Not an unclear one, however. How on earth could I know what "we" were? I didn't know what I was!

Maybe I needed someone who didn't identify with either binary…butno doubt I'd find a way to disappoint them, too.

Contemplating emoshuns made my head hurt even more than Jodie's snoring. I turned over and punched the pillow into submission. Love was trust, and trust, a trap door ready to drop you at any moment.

I stretched and shrugged the whole bizarre night off. I'd never have to look at the sentient Pepto bottle ever again. Tiffani and her angels could go to hell. Heh—I would meet her there, preferably with a pitchfork.

CHAPTER TWO:
SOME KIND OF DREADFUL

weet. Sweet! Are you sleeping?"

I came to with a gasp and sat straight up, crust in my eyes. Cobwebs in my brain. Gym teacher in my face?

Coach Cummings leaned close enough that I could savor the stale coffee breath shooting at me. "It's volleyball time. No, I do not believe that you're on your period. You were on it last week. And the week before that. And the entire month of February."

What? I pushed myself off the cold, wooden floor of my high school gym. My terminally pasty legs goose-bumped under short shorts. Short orange gym shorts. No. What? "Maybe my uterus is haunted," I whispered from memory. The kind of memory that gives you the sweats late at night. "I should go to the ghost-o-cologist."

The class around me giggled. Oh, God, there was Ben Woodbine, Gator Riviera's wedgiest bully. And Tracie Willes! Who merely called me short and ugly, which was a wonderful change of pace from being accurately referred to as "white trash."

An elbow to my other side swerved my attention. Jodie! Thank God. Relief flooded me, as it always did with my bestie, and my shoulders fell. Now, I could face them all.

"You have to dodge volleyballs like the rest of ush," Jodie slurred through her braces.

Oh, no. No, not the braces! I lifted a hand to my own mouth—with its food-filled, metallic grill. Dammit! So, I was what? Sixteen? A forever decade ago. "This is a dream?"

Bam! I slammed backward, my head bouncing off the free throw line. Pain exploded across the back of my skull, and for a moment, everything went dim. Dear Tracie had smashed me with a volleyball right in the mouth. I managed to push myself off the floor. Yay, warm blood in my mouth.

Jodie jumped up to yell at Tracie, and Coach Cummings stepped between them. Tracie didn't get in trouble, of course. That might have to do with the fact that I put a plastic cockroach in the coach's coffee every time she forced me to do a sport despite my perpetual fake period. And one time a real roach. In a pinch.

With a shiny grin bedazzling her freckled face, Jodie helped me to my feet. I cracked a smile knowing that I had my ally in this extremely lucid dream. Wow, the reek of the abandoned sneaker pile, enhanced by desperate teenage armpit, could wake the dead. Shoes and voices squeaked as gawky kids dove for volleyballs. And my mouth freaking throbbed, the taste of blood pooling there, giving me a rancid stomachache. *Like last night.*

Ohhhhhh, this was a fried pickle dream for sure!

Maybe I should eat healthier?

Nah.

I let Jodie lead me to the side of the volleyball net to await our dreaded turn. The last time I'd been forced to play, I'd ended up with a concussion and a coach laughing at me. Why had that been allowed? Just the memory shifted my pulse into overdrive, pounding like panic and perspiration and a stew of teenage angst.

I picked at my fingernails until they stung. Screw high school. Double screw the girls who mocked Jodie for being out and unafraid.

A rush of pride rolled through me, and I put my arm around my freaking awesome friend. I remembered how tough Jodie's teenage years had been. Gator Riviera was about thirty years behind the rest of the world, and its general "fear of the other" was as painful as it was clichéd. How was Miami only an hour down the highway?

Yikes, these teen hormones ping-ponged through my body from horror to glee and back to horror again with extra horror on top. My boobs started to sweat because of the mean kids. Or the gym stench. Or was I the stench? I took a subtle whiff of my --

"Hey, Sophie."

I dropped my arm. Deigning to speak to me was Channing Angelopoulos: captain of the football team, prom king his freshman year, and the guy usually meanest to me in the halls.

Yup, that smell was me. Dammit. Perhaps I could weaponize my odor.

"Screw off, sports ball Ken." I swallowed a mouthful of blood. Ugh, gross. And the blood was awful, too. "I'm not in the mood for a hilarious joke about which trash dump I'm from."

He tousled his blond hair; a spontaneous sigh burst from the equally blonde Tracie. The pair were like a gymnastics recruitment poster from the USSR.

"Uh, yeah," Channing said with a grin. "You're from Ponce De Leon Avenue, I remember."

I blinked in pure amazement. "Wow. Have you thought about being captain of the academic decathlon team, too?"

"Um." He furrowed his wide brow. "Yeah, maybe! Anyway, so you wanna go to prom with me?"

Tracie released a stream of shocked screeches, like that of a jealous monkey wearing too much self-tanner.

I laughed. "Why the hell would I do that?" I cocked my head. "Are you drunk? ...Am I still drunk?"

"Is that a joke, Channing?" Tracie asked. "I have a poodle if you're looking to date for LOLs. She's prettier, I promise."

Jodie swept a leg, like she'd learned in karate, and down Tracie went, right onto her Juicy Coutured butt.

"Girls!" Coach shuffled over. "Don't fight," she barely urged.

"So, Sophie, lemme take you to prom tomorrow," Channing said. "Cuz you're pretty hot. When you shave your--"

"Nope!" I grabbed him by his T-shirt to shut him up, but then froze. His shirt was orange, same as our Gator Riviera High School gym uniforms. Yet that wasn't the name emblazoned across his enormous chest.

It read, "Déjà Vu Senior High School."

I took a step back, my hands shaking as they dropped his tee. My face went numb. My lips. My brain. "This is one weird-ass dream."

"Sophie Sweet!" squawked the loudspeaker. "Sophie Sweet to the guidance counselor's office!"

Jodie took my arm. "You okay? You're really pale." She started to drag me away. "She sayshyesh, Channing. And now, darn, we have to miss volleyball to go to the office."

Coach blew her whistle. "Edwards, they didn't call you."

"But if I don't go, she won't go. You know how she ish." With that, Jodie ran us both out of the gym and into the much less stanky hall. "I want to punch Tracie Willes in the freaking fascscshhe."

Oh, no. It must be pretty soon after she'd gotten the braces; her speech had suffered for a while. My poor girl had hurt so much because of those tiny metal torture devices.

"I thought she washsh dating Channing? Who *asked* you to *prom*!" Jodie skipped along the orange and lavender linoleum floor, her Afro puffs bouncing, spit bubbles escaping through her braces. "Your stock just went up, Barfy! It's always A+ with me. Or however stocksh are rated."

Still rubbing my head, I followed behind in a daze. This was what I got for mixing beer, wine, Nerds, and a box of really old jalapeño cheese crackers I dug from the back of the cabinet. My guts churned—the way they'd bubbled the entirety of high school.

Jodie had been my saving grace. We'd met the first week she'd moved here from Atlanta, when I found a group of girls slap-fighting her underneath the football bleachers. Since they were some of the same folks who routinely terrorized me, my fists intervened. And my overbite. So freaking satisfying. I'd walked away with bleeding knuckles and a new friend for life. I may not look like much, but I will never back down once the fight starts. Duking it out for Jodie always calmed the monster inside my brain and gave me a…glow, or something. Even when I lost. We were like twins, with our braces and freckles, although she wore them better for sure.

I giggled to remember our slogan: *Misfits of a feather hide in the toilet during lunch together.*

I stopped short to grin stupidly at her, like the high school dork I'd been. Was. Whatever.

With a flourish, Jodie held the office door open for me. As a thank you, I put my thumb to my nose and wiggled my fingers in the sacred gesture.

"After you, Barfy, darling," she said, returning the wiggle.

"Thank you, Buffy, darling. Y'all called me?" Heh, my country vocabulary was back—along with my zits. I shouldn't've scratched at that pulsating one on my chin, ow. The ooze started to slide, like my self-esteem. Sixteen-year-old me had not yet discovered the wondrous world of clay masks. I dipped my chin to hide the carnage.

"Yes, Sweet, thanks so much for doing me the honor of actually showing up." The office administrator loved me. "I have something for you." He slid a box from under his desk and set it on top. With a smile more akin to a snarl, he reached in with hairy knuckles and threw something at me.

I ducked as several flopping somethings smacked me upside the head. "What the hell?"

"Language!" he screamed, throwing more somethings at me.

Ha! Caught one! My fingers closed around rubber, and I burst into a cackle. "Thanks, Bob!"

He actually stomped his foot. "My name is Louis! Take your stupid snakes, you witch!"

Chuckling, I dropped to the dirty carpet to gather my friends—the many, many rubber snakes I'd hidden all over Bob's desk. And briefcase.

And car. And basement, one memorable Christmas Eve. Oh, wow, I'd forgotten how fun I used to be. It was an important reminder that you're never too old to laugh. Or hide rubber snakes to scare jackasses who call you Pizza-Face Sophie even though they are adults who shouldn't be bullying children.

In fact, I loved snakes so much, I'd gotten a scarlet king snake tattoo that wound from my hand all the way up my arm to my shoulder and down part of my back. Scarlet and me—two venomous Florida natives who scared the normals. Ungrateful Bob should be delighted I never left him a real one, but would he thank me?

My colorful collection of snakes in my arms, I didn't try to contain my glee. Finally, this dream was getting good! Joy ceased the churning of my stomach, and I gave Bob my sweetest face, batting eyelashes and everything. "Thank you for my snakes. Buying in such volume was getting expensive."

The horrible man's expression fell as he realized what he'd done.

I presented a gorgeous blue and yellow specimen. In a squeaky voice, I said, "We'll sssssssssee you later, Bob!"

"Get out!"

"I hear and obey." I turned to leave.

"Wait, shit."

"Language!" hissed Jodie. Because of her braces, and also the snake, she cracked like a whip.

Bob ducked and screamed, and I was pretty sure steam shot from his ears. From the floor, he ground out, "The new guidance counselor wants to see you. I guess she's the optimistic sort."

"Ha-ha," I replied.

"Ha-ha!" rang through the office.

A chill shot down my spine, and I shook my head, which refused to turn to see—

"Hi, Sophie. I'm Tiffani the Guidance Counselor!"

Jodie dropped her snake and fluffed her puffs. "Ooh, she's pretty."

My eyes bugged from disbelief. "Don't you recognize her?" I whispered.

Jodie's eyebrows rose. "No. She's new. I would remember her, my future wife."

In slow motion, as if in a horror movie, I faced the psychic. My snakes fell from my arms. "You," I ground out.

"Yes. It's meeeeee!" Tiffani clasped her bosom, clad in baby pink tweed. She wore a baby pink headband. Baby pink stacks of bangles. And a baby pink –

"I'm here to help you, Sophie."

"Can you help *me*?" asked Jodie.

"Of course, Jodie!" Tiffani pulled my protesting ass into her office.

Jodie whispered, "She knowsh my name."

Once the door closed, I groaned, "Why are you in my dream? Ughhhh, I want to wake up now, please."

Tiffani flipped her hair. "Oh, sweetie! You're not dreaming."

I pressed my fingers to my temples, which throbbed with new gusto. "I spy…with my little psychic eye…the number three." I stuck out my thumb: "One." My pointer finger: "Two." Grinning, I released my middle finger straight up: "Three!" She should loooooove my middle finger—it had tattooed sparkles on it so the people I flipped off could enjoy the magic of the experience.

"Ha-ha, you're so very funny. It's one of your…qualities." Tiffani sat behind her desk and clicked her baby pink nails on the Formica. "Now, I have an important question to ask you." She cleared her throat. "Why would you do that?"

"Huh?"

"Your hair. Your curls are amazeballs, and you cut them off. Is it a perm or natural?"

I ran a hand through my hair. Ohhhhh, this was my post-Hubba-Bubba haircut. "The curls are all natural, thanks to Mom. Good talk, I'm leaving."

Tiffani stood. "You have a lot of things to thank your mom for, right? Like your fear of emotional attachment?"

"Do not talk about my mom!" Teenage adrenaline shot through my limbs, and I whipped around the desk to get in her face. Well, in her chest; Tiffani towered over me. Like my mom. My mouth went dry, and I spat, "Stop with your psychobabble! Ugh, why am I dreaming about you?" I slapped myself. "Ow! Damn shit fart!" Stupid braces, holy crap, that hurt! Tears burst into my vision. I wanted to scream! Why was I not waking up?

Tiffani took me by the shoulders as a stupid tear escaped down my cheek. "My angels told me, and I agree, that you need a safe environment to work out your fears, which are ruling your life, Sophie. Solitary nights. Bitter thoughts. Surly attitude. You need a lesson in true love before you get premature frown lines." Her face lit up like a demented neon sign. "And there's noooooo better way to learn about love," she squeaked and giggled, "than in a rom-com!"

"What?" Ugh, another pointless tear fell, but Tiffani held me too hard for me to get rid of the damn thing.

"You're in my rom-com." Tiffani cocked her head. "*Starring* in my rom-com, I should say, you lucky lady."

"Are you drunk?" The room started to spin. "Am I still drunk?"

"You're the heroine of high school hijinks, congratulations! And the plot has already begun. Channing Angelopoulosasked you to prom, right?"

I recoiled; Tiffani held on. Her nails dug into me, as did her searing gaze. A wave of panic buckled my knees, but she held me up.

She leaned down, down, nose to nose. "Sophie, you desperately need the help only I can provide. Therefore, I'm gifting you your very own rom-com so you can learn to live in love instead of fear. Ha-ha!" She blinked her giant lashes. "You thought you were in hell before, remember? *Remember?* Well," Tiffani's perky little face hardened, "how's this one, Kate Hudson?"

I screamed.

CHAPTER THREE:
MY BIG FAT GREEK TWUEWUV

ran. But in a tough-girl heroine kind of way.

I didn't run away from Tiffani. I would never. I ran toward…being away from this waking nightmare that made me feel sweaty and rank and like a tax audit had barfed in my mouth.

Jodie caught up with me at the bottom of the school steps. "What was that? You screamed, bolted from the office, screamed some more, knocked down a freshman hall monitor, and now we're outside, ditching class, I guess?"

Ugh, not even ramming a hall monitor had helped. I gripped Jodie's shoulders. "Slap me."

She reared back. "What? Are you ill?"

"Hit me!" I grabbed her hand and flung it in my direction. It flopped down again, as if to say *WTF?*

"You *are* ill." Jodie leaned in, her eyes huge. "Period for real?"

Oh, FFS, fine. I hit myself. Ugh! Pain, braces, blood all over again. I squeaked a squeak of frustrated agony and stomped on my foot. Argh! Again. *Stomp!* Again! Shit. I fell onto the sidewalk, pain colliding from eight places. More useless tears rushed in.

I screamed and raged and damn near pitched a toddler tantrum on the sidewalk. Still—*I did not wake up.*

Jodie kneeled down beside me. "Do I need to call 9-1-1? Sophie, you're scaring me!"

"I--"

I gazed into her eyes, and my tears fell. What the hell was I supposed to say about Tiffani the Psychic/Guidance Counselor? Or about our last *10 years of life*, that were, apparently, gone? The absolutely *only good times* in my life had been wiped away by that horrible woman. No wonder I screamed!

Deep breaths, shit, deep breaths. High school had absolutely suffocated me like an 800-pound gorilla that called me worthless. My brain-monster burst to the fore; she needed to burn down the school with Tiffani inside it. But Jodie wouldn't approve of anything even close to that. So...I cleared my throat and somehow wobbled up to stand. "Yeah, let's just...just skip class."

Jodie cocked her "Ugh, Sophie" hip. "And the whole hitting yourself thing? We're gonna ignore that?"

"Yup." I cocked my "Don't question me, Jodie" eyebrow.

She heaved an elaborate sigh. "Fine. But you're buying me frozhen yogurt for my trouble."

The doors to the school flew open, and Channing Angelopoulostrotted through them like a magnificent horse, the wind in his mane and everything.

I greeted him. "What now?"

He laughed. "My parents are out of town, and --"

"You're throwing a pre-prom party, like in every high school rom-com ever," I finished for him.

"How did you know?" he said. Commence more flirty smiling. At me. For some reason. He flashed the same smile when he punched books outta nerds' arms in the hall. "You have to come. Jazzy, too.Both of you."

Jodie's eyes bugged out so far, it's a wonder she didn't lose one. "Do you legitimately think my name is 'Jazzy'?"

Channing's gaze went wide. His mouth dropped. The sound of the ocean emerged.

"Nah, that was a joke," he lied, after much too long of a pause. "Anyway, you have to come. You're my prom date, Sophie!"

With that, he cantered down the sidewalk—not toward the school, not toward the parking lot, just…into the neighborhood.

Jodie craned her neck. "Where is he going?"

I squeezed my eyes shut. "This sentient potato is who I am supposed to be excited about? This is my *twuewuv*?" Who was I asking? Jodie? The universe? Tiffani, whose taste in twuewuv was sucky-wucky?

Jodie shrugged, put her eyeballs back in their holsters, and started toward the parking lot, where her 1984 Camaro Z28 spent its days. A hand-me-down from her mom, it was the coolest thing about either of us.

"I don't know about twuewuv," Jodie said. "But maybe he'sh good at making out."

"Ah, okay. The plan is to assault him with my braces. Love it." If I drew blood, maybe I'd become a vampire like I always wanted. Not the "glittery and mopey" kind, but a "ripsout throats with a grin" type.

"Well, duh!" She started hopping and skipping along, and stole a smile from me, dammit. "First, frozhen yogurt. Schecond, Channing's party. Third, shleepover at my place, where we shall tell stories about our first ever cool-people shindig!"

I climbed into her silver-with-accents-of-rust car and again reminded myself to breathe. For, in true Han Solo fashion…I had a baaaaaaaad feeling about this.

* * * * *

That night, for my official debut in a John Hughes film, I dressed the part of Frowny Outsider Girl Who Hates Everyone. How I managed such an attitude was a wonder. Black jeans, black tee, black leather jacket, black hair, black expression. Jodie looked like the good angel to my bad one in her baby blue sundress and wedge heels.

Before we even got to the front door of the enormous Florida Beach McMansion, with elements of shell and sinkhole, Channing ran out of the house to meet us. Why was he always running? Practice for a shampoo commercial casting?

"Hi, Sophie!" he said, raking a hand through his blondness. "I knew you'd come! I told the guys, didn't I?"

The guys appeared behind him, as if summoned by the power of the bro-code. They had names; I didn't care to learn them. Rest assured, they matched one another in extreme height, linebacker weight, and whiteness.

"Wow, she really did come," said Dude #1. "Er…and with her friend."

Jodie held out her hand. "Jazzy'sthe name."

"Whoa, I knew it!" Channing congratulated himself by clapping Dude #2 on the back. "Come on in. We have tons of beer and stuff. We can talk about the prom and how she's totally going with me, guys!"

The brollective cheered.

I grabbed Jodie's arm and started toward the door. "I need a cocktail." I'd needed a bathtub full of them since the carnival. Truth be told, booze was the only reason I'd come. In this past, I didn't have my fake ID.

Jodie gasped. "We're not going to--" GULP"drink?"

"As long as you stay away from Midori sours, you'll be okay." Midori sours led to questionable taste in ladies in questionable bars in questionable beach cities.

I found the kitchen right away and grabbed a bottle of pinot noir and a tray of cookies.

Channing galloped into the room, colliding with Jodie in the doorway. "Uh, that's my mom's wine," he said over her head.

"Nice, it probably won't taste like garbage." I handed the cookie tray to Jodie and followed a current of teens to the back, where the pool sparkled. I found a couple of extremely lavender wicker chairs, woooooow, and whipped the wine open like a woman 10 years ahead of her time.

Channing stopped in front of our chairs and watched Jodie and me pass the bottle of wine. "Um…so…you like wine?"

Glug, glug. "Yup. Very good, Sherlock Homie."

Jodie tittered. And then she snorted.

That was fast. I yanked the wine from her. "That's enough, my dear."

"Well…" Channing began, swaying side-to-side and flapping his arms. "I'm gonna take off my shirt and do cannonballs. Wanna watch?"

"How could anyone say no?"

The poor boy seemed not to have any sarcasm-dar whatsoever, for he grinned and whipped off his T-shirt. His bros joined the half-naked melee, and they all splashed like it was the beginning of a gay porno. Not completely unappealing, so I did wanna watch.

"Hey, Sophie!"

I looked around for the source of the female hey-ing.

"Hi there, Jodie!"

Jodie cringed—she knew the source. I handed her the wine bottle; it seemed like the right thing to do.

"Ohem gee, you guys came!" Tracie Willes sauntered over to our wicker whiledraggingan aluminum lounge chair behind her. "Glad to see you didn't feel the need to dress up for us, Sophie."

Well, *TRACIE*, some of us didn't have rich parents buying them the latest in tacky mall trends. Not that that satisfied Tracie, nooooo, for I was 99% certain she'd stolen my favorite purple jacket in kindergarten class. My *only* damn jacket. Florida doesn't get that cold in the winter, but colder than a T-shirt and second-hand jeans covered.

I took back my damn wine; it seemed like the right thing to do.

"Go away, Traschshie," said Jodie, loud and firm. Oooh, she was at the perfect amount of inebriated—the IDGAF level, with no vomiting.

"But I'm here for girl talk about the prom." Tracie sat much too close to me. I leaned away, lest my skin crawl right off its bones. My nose burned from her odor, sulfur with notes of strawberry and nail polish remover. "I'm thinking…makeover!"

Oh. Okay, I saw where this was going; I'd seen this movie against my will several times.

High School Hijinks, the Plot:

- Dipshit popular people form plan/bet (blan) to embarrass gorgeous unique moody girl

- Douchey popular boy asks gorgeous unique moody girl to prom as a joke

- Gorgeous unique moody girl says yes despite her lived experience

- Gorgeous unique moody girl gets makeover/takes off braces/grows 12 inches of hair

- She's hot?!?! Duh, it was right there in her name

- Douchey popular boy falls in twuewuv with gorgeous unique moody girl because he nearly sees her as a person now

- But! Dipshit popular people's plan to emotionally stunt gorgeous unique moody girl proceeds apace

- The secret blan is revealed

- MANY TEARS

- Douchey popular boy expresses twuewuv using his words like real man

- Gorgeous unique moody girl tells douchey popular boy she wuvs him back because the patriarchy is a helluvadrug

- The end

- Of her

"Sure, Tracie," I said with a smile. I knew my part. I'd played a rat in the *Pied Piper of Hamlin* in second grade. I was the loudest rat of them all!

Her nostrils flared. "*Good.*"

"What?" Jodie took a drink of wine.

I'd explain the plot to her later. "Let's meet at your house tomorrow, Tracie, and you can definitely give me a makeover for prom." By tomorrow, I would wake up. Right? Ugh, why was I holding my breath? *Right?* Right. Just because a Frappuccino named Tiffani said I was in a rom-com didn't make it real. For that was impossible; also: She sucks. Better to just go along with this nonsense now in order to drink more wine.

"How fast does your hair grow?" Tracie asked, her eyes widening in horror at my lack of long, flowing tresses.

"Twelve inches overnight."

She cocked her head and blinked. "Um…" Pasting on a grin, she continued, "Oh, that was a joke, right? Very funny! See you tomorrow at one. Do you know where my house is? It's the huge beige one three doors down."

"Which one?" I asked.

"With the koi pond in front."

"Which koi pond?" asked Jodie.

"With the statue of Neptune spitting into it."

"Oh!" WTF, I had forgotten about the cookies! I shoved three into my mouth and proceeded to spit crumbs all over Tracie's cheerleading costume, which she was wearing to a party at night for some reason. "The koi pond with Neptune that also has flamingos standing in it, or the koi pond with Neptune that also has garden gnomes frolicking in it?"

Jodie and I had spent a lot of time walking the neighborhood laughing at the horrible houses before arriving at this one, whose koi pond featured a six-foot mermaid with salmon-colored nipple shells.

Tracie's mouth went pinchy, but her adherence to the mean blan could not be broken. "Ours is the flamingos one. They were very expensive and from Italy."

"*Molto* bonehead," I said in perfect Italian. "I'll be there with bells on. Or maybe a prom dress, I'll see how I feel."

She bared teeth at my joke and left.

Jodie burped. "I like wine and cookiesh."

"And you will for many years," I assured her. I stood. "Okay, my part in tonight's Act I is finished. Let's --"

"Hey, Sophie!" A wet, shirtless Channing ran up to me. I stared at his pecs while he spoke. "Want to watch me chug a case of beer?"

"No."

"Want to sit in the hot tub with me?"

"Before or after all that beer?"

His brows collided as hard as his brain cells. "Then...want to take a walk with me?"

"No."

His poor, handsome face went slack; he had not considered the eventuality of a "no," much less multiple ones.

"Ugh." I slumped into the chair, stole the wine from an already drunk Jodie, and started in on the cookies again. Mmmmmmm, just a whole pile of chocolate shortbread. Classy shit. "Let's sit here, and you can blather on as necessary to fulfill your blan. Jodie is staying, though."

"Jodie's sleepy." She started messing with the lever on her purple wicker. After a moment, the seat back fell away, depositing her horizontally. "Whoa!"

Channing's nostrils flared. "Fulfill?"

"Yes, tell me how you've always secretly liked me, even though we travel in different circles. I'm different and interesting, and you can't help yourself. Right? You know, the chocolate cookies pair well with the fruity pinot noir. Your mother is cleverer than you look." I took a gander at the many plastic Greek-ish sculptures and began to form a hypothesis that Channing had been magicked to life from one of them. Maybe a different one could be my twue luv? That mermaid over there was one hot sea hag.

Aw, I'd confused the fellow too much. I sighed and put on the most "heart eyes emoji face" I could genetically manage. "Anyway, prom will be way magical for us, and we'll totally fall in love, dearest Channing. Hear that, Tiffani?"

Jodie poked up her head to search around. "Is she here? Maybe in a bikini?"

Poor Channing. I'd stolen his dialogue. He said, "Yeah, I --" He looked to his friends, and several Dudes came running. They stood there, a row of linebackers against an offense who knew the game better than they did.

"Come on, Jodie. Let's get outta here." I stood and yanked her to her feet. We'd walk home—this town was not large—and battle Tracie tomorrow at prom. Maybe I could—

No! I would wake up in my own bed in my own time tomorrow. Because otherwise, Tiffani the Psychic was magic, which was one thousand percent impossible.

Jodie looked one way, then the other, then slid the rest of the cookies straight into her purse.

I asked, "Channing, you got a to-go cup for this wine?"

"Isn't a bottle already a to-go cup?" Jodie asked.

"Take a lesson, Channing." I pointed at Jodie. "That is how you make me fall in love with you."

CHAPTER FOUR:
WHAT WOMEN DON'T WANT

yawned. I stirred. Jodie snored. I laughed to be back in real life after one helluva"I had the craziest dream about Tiffani the Psychic." Jodie got an elbow to her ribs. "Let's go get pancakes. My fried pickle needs food friends."

Something lodged under my back. I reached to yank it out—Piggy Bear. Jodie's stupid stuffed animal. How she loved this scraggly thing. Wait…I examined Piggy Bear closer in the dark. She was fresher than usual. Less old and matted.

Oh, hell. My stomach knotted in on itself. I examined the room more closely. Jodie's parents' house? *When* was I?

"What fried pickslesh?" Jodie slurped through her braces.

I bolted straight up. No. No! This was Jodie's *teenage* bedroom, with its many posters of Rihanna on the wall. "Fuck! Fucking fuck shit fuck fuck fuck!"

"Hey, hey, hey!" Jodie's mom burst through the door. "Language, Sophie. Keep the fucks in single digits, please." She grinned the same mischievous smile she'd gifted her daughter. Her hair wrap shook as she giggled. "Jodie, rise and shine, sweetie. Dad's making eggs Benedict."

"Oh, no," Jodie groaned.

"What day is it?" I flicked an eye crust away.

Mrs. Edwards cocked an eyebrow. "Saturday. How does a teenager not know it's Saturday?" She started to come into the room. "What did y'all get up to last night?"

"Nothshing!" Jodie said with a definite croak. "We'll be out in a --" *burp* "minute."

Ooh, that burp carried the bouquet of pinot noir and cookies and evil. "Five minutes," I amended. "Teenage girls, you know."

"Mm-hmm." An unconvinced mom closed the door. Slowly. Then, she poked her head in. "And I'm sure the eggs will be delis—fine. So, no commentary!"

"I'm gonna barf," Jodie groaned as she weaved to the bathroom.

She had her own connected bathroom, like in a movie. I'd sighed with wonder over it at 16, which was apparently now.

Why was I still here? Er, now. Then?? *Why whywhy?* I broke out into yet another rank teenage sweat and ran to help Jodie.

Damn, teenage Jodie was a lightweight. Truth be told, adult Jodie was, too, so I dutifully kept her head wrap from falling into the toilet while she barfed up a lung.

"I'll never drink wine again," Jodie groan-lied.

"I'll never go see a psychic again," I groan-truthed.

We cleaned up Jodie and ate eggs Benedict. Or eggs…something. Jodie's dad thought he was a chef the way I thought I was Chris Pine's girlfriend. That was the only explanation for eggs over a slab of burned bread (maybe) with a lumpy green sauce (maybe) over top. The lumps were crunchy.

The Edwards' Chinese Crested dog, Schatzi, didn't seem to mind.

After we faked breakfast, Jodie and I laid on her bed in a dark bedroom. "I've got to tell you something," I began. "But I'm going to need your assurance that you will believe me, no matter how whackadoodle it sounds."

Even in the darkness, I saw her lift a listless hand to her nose and wiggle her fingers.

I took a deep breath and pushed my hair behind my ears. Well, I meant to. I kept forgetting I possessed very little hair. "I have been trapped in some sort of…alternate reality in the form of a rom-com, thanks to a pushy psychic named Tiffani who wears way too much pink."

"Counselor Tiffani?" she asked, her voice perking. "She'sh so pretty."

I gritted my teeth. "Er, yes. In reality, we, you and I, are both 26 years old, living on our own in Miami, being awesome and happy. This is not real. Not anymore. It's—it's the past."

She sat up, the icy washcloth on her forehead plopping into her lap. "Wut?"

"None of this happened in high school." I turned to my side and set my head on my hand. "I never went to prom with Channing. We, you and I, went to prom as friends, wearing tuxedos, and we threw water balloons at anyone who made fun of us. Well…we'd planned the balloons but didn't get to toss them. It would have been amazing, though. We did dance and have a great time." Except for the people who said nasty things at us out of the sides of their mouths. I'd managed to throw a piece of cake at Tracie. I sighed over the memory, because barely any frosting had gotten on her dress.

Jodie's eyebrows hit her baby hairs. "What?"

"Okay, *I* filled the water balloons with barbecue sauce and you begged me not to. The rest of my point stands." I ignored her squeak of alarm and fell back to stare at her ceiling, which had those little sparkles in it. So fancy! "I'm trapped in a rom-com invented by a cupcake. Because *apparently,*" my hands clutched into fists, "I need *luuuuv.*"

"But—"

I flung an arm over my face. "You said you'd believe me."

Jodie sucked in and released several loud, deep breaths. Doubt? Barf? Who can say? In the end, she patted my shoulder. "Okay. I believe you. I have to admit, " she slapped the washcloth back to her eyes and held it there, "you going to prom with Channing schounds way less plausible than you using a dance to antagonize people in order to throw barbecue sauce balloons at them."

Tears burst from me, and I rolled over to hug her. "Thank you!"

"Are you…crying? Oh, heck." She shook her head. Water slithered down her nose. "We're trapped in a rom-com," she said with wonder. "Because of sexy Tiffani!" she said with horniness. "Are you okay? I've never scheen you cry like this, not even when that weird alligator lady in your trailer park stabbed you with a fork."

"I stand behind my decision to set her baby gators free." I sniffed. "But I'm ashamed of my loser liquid."

"It's okay to cry, Sophie."

Oh, no—she was so hungover, she made no sense. Weepery was nothing more than manipulation; I learned that shit early. Cry at the teacher? She still let Tracie snap rubber bands on my face, and then everyone called me "Salty Sophie." Tears made Dad go fluorescent red and throw me out for a week because I got my first period and "Don't ever try to manipulate me like your bitch mother did."

Crying made every situation worse.

Jodie continued, "Besht thing to do is make a plan. Wait --"

"What?"

Jodie slowly pushed up on her arms. Her washcloth splatted to the bed. "Are my—I mean, in ten years, are my parents…"

"Totally fine!" I assured her. "Great, even. Happy, together, successful. Total dream team. You see them and your siblings often, and you all love each other so much that it's a little irritating."

"Thank God." She released a long breath and managed to wind herself into a cross-legged position.

I sucked a great glob of snot into my nose and matched her. "I don't know what to do about…magic psychics, neither of which exist."

"Oh, she exists." Jodie nodded, her first smile of the day emerging. "She's magic for sure. And she literally told you that you're trapped in a rom-com?"

"She called me…" I swallowed bile. "Kate Hudson."

Jodie gasped.

"I know." I wiped a tear away. "She said I need to learn about love, so now I'm in a rom-com."

"Seems like in a rom-com, you'd just learn about internalized misogyny and slightly curled white-lady hair."

"That was solid."

"Thank you."

We fell back, for everything was too much. I blew out a breath. "Okay, so: rom-com. I guess I'm supposed to get into embarrassing situations, strip during a big business meeting, achieve a makeover, and…fall in love with Channing Angelopoulos? Then end it all with a blissful lobotomy."

"You might need the lobotomy before you fall in love with Channing."

Beep boop. My cell phone. I leaned over the bed and fished it out of my bag. Ugh, WTF was this tiny flip phone? This thing had barely been worth stealing. The past was the worst! "Oh, good, Tracie is texting. Time for my makeover. She says to bring my prom dress and heels and bag."

Jodie said thoughtfully, "It seems to me the sooner you start, the sooner we return to real life. Do I have a hot girlfriend in the future?"

"Nope, you're single and lonely."

She heaved.

I reassured her that she'd never die alone while she threw up breakfast, and then we made plans. I would need a prom dress (not a tuxedo, dammit), heels, and a fancy evening bag, but I was poor white folk and could not afford such finery.

To the Goodwill! The better to choose the ugliest dress possible. I would go to the prom, but I wouldn't make it easy on them.

When we got there, Jodie objected to the ugliest-dress-possible plan, even though I'd fed her a bag full of Krystal burgers to make up for the "eggs" "Benedict." Ungrateful.

Jodie's Questionable Thoughts on the Ugliest-Dress-Possible Plan

- An ugly Goodwill dress from 1972 might not give Channing a boner, my entire reason for existing in this, er, existence. As a result, I would never achieve the "love" necessary to return to my awesome life of not being a poor white folk.

- It smelled like moth balls and Jean Naté.

Sophie's Awesome Thoughts on the Ugliest-Dress-Possible Plan

- An ugly Goodwill dress from 1972 would be awesome, as long as it revealed enough boobs for Channing not to care about the horrid pastel flower pattern, but not enough boobs to cause attempted groping.

- Tracie would make many screechings about the ugly dress, which would be hilarious.

- Jean Naté isn't so bad and would probably air out if I hung it outside my trailer.

In the end, Jodie gave into the ugly dress from 1972 because I looked hot in the halter neckline. Also, it was freaking hilarious, with a giant ruffle around the boobage and at the hem. I would be her phone background for a long time. We also found a sci-fi book from the 80s about a dude named Blowgort who shot lasers from his penis, which we cackled so hard about, it cured her hangover. Science!

Laughing with Jodie about Prince Blowgort and his royal ability to vomit poison gas made me feel better than I had since…well, since before Tiffani the Psychic. This had been the best part of my life thus far at the time. *She* had been.

Jodie had been my first real friend, honestly. For some reason, my school chums didn't like the surly girl in ill-fitting hand-me-down clothes who told them to go to hell. In second grade. Nobody wanted to switch lunches with me, since half the time, my 7-Eleven plastic shopping bag was empty.

I shook off these memories with a curse to Tiffani the Jerkface. There was a reason I'd left this crap behind. The idea that returning me to the worst time of my life would put me in a romantic mood was ludicrous.

I sagged against the metal Goodwill bookshelf, sweat shooting down my spine.

"Hey, hey!" Jodie pulled me into a hug, strong and warm.

I clung to her like she was an island in a sea of goofy psychic magic.

"Aw! Prom dress shopping, I looooove it!"

"No!" I yanked myself away from Jodie...and friggin' Tiffani? *Why?* "Are you stalking me? Go away!"

Tiffani's head cocked. "I'll always be here for you, Sophie, ha-ha!"

Today, her ridiculousity was truly inspired. She wore a hot pink shorts-onesie, off-the-shoulder, with such short shorts that the old fella behind her ran into a wall. Her long hair shot from a high ponytail, bedecked with a nightmarish hat-thingie made of feathers. An entire parrot's worth of red and pink feathers. And her face glittered like a disco ball.

Jodie nearly shoved me out of the way to get closer to Tiffani. "First? *I'm* always here for Sophie. Shecondly, how dare you look so amazing, could you teach me?"

"Thank you."

"You gotta be kidding me," I muttered.

"Manager?" Jodie turned the plastic tag pinned to Tiffani's chest. "Wait, you're manager of the Goodwill *and* the school guidance counselor?"

"And a psychic. Idle hands are the cat's pajamas."

"What?"

Tiffani pulled Jodie into a hug. Jodie did not resist. I ground my teeth.

Jodie turned her head, nestled on Tiffani's chest. "You're telling me the truth!"

I flapped my arms. "You thought I was lying?"

"I thought maybe your dad left too many paint thinner cans open in your trailer again."

Well…okay. The last time Dad had done that, I'd written my magnum opus, which turned out to be the word "marshmallow" 8,000 times. All of them beginning with the letter "b."

"It's a super-duper good thing I'm here," said Tiffani the Psychic-Guidance Counselor-Goodwill Manager. With two long, white, bedazzled fingernails she picked up my prom dress. It apparently alarmed her so much, she damn near fell off her heels and grabbed a shelf full of Precious Moments knockoffs for support. "This will not do. You're trying to inspire loooooooove! Not bed bugs."

Giving Channing bed bugs would damn near be worth having them again.

I pushed the shopping cart into her glittery legs and started walking toward purses. I saw a straw number with the word "Acapulco" embroidered across it that would mismatch my dress perfectly.

Tiffani click-clacked behind me in a zig-zag pattern. Why the hell did she wear those shoes if she couldn't walk in them?

"Sophie!" she called. "Let's get you a real dress! I have an American Express Black Card, and there's a Nordstrom in Fort Lauderdale."

"No!" I tossed my new straw tote, with a gorgeous purple stain on the back, into the cart and headed toward checkout. "If it's true love, won't Channing adore me no matter what I'm wearing?"

"No." She shook her pretty head, and her hair whipped like it had its own wind machine. "That's not how it works at all! Don't you read men's magazines? Oh, also, we're going to need makeup to cover those icky tattoooooooos. A giant snake and some weird demon-cat do not send the correct message."

Jodie caught up to me. "That was rude. And watch out—last time someone called Sophie's tattoos 'unladylike,' she got their face inked really small on her ass. The clown version of their face, anyway."

I cracked up. It was true! That manager at the BBQ Bonanza had quit after that. Start shit, get immortalized as a drooling clown, I always say.

My bestie shot a sour look at Tiffani. "You're not a very good guidance counshelor, are you?"

Tiffani released a series of giggles. "Silly, I'm amazing at eeeeeverything!"

I laughed. More like, I cackled. "Well, lady who is amazing at accurately repeating aphorisms, I have to go be amazing at getting a makeover from a sociopath now." Then I laughed again because of literally everything. And also because I'd remembered the part in Prince Blowgort's book about the time he sexed up an entire harem with his three robot penises, one of which could talk. "Come on, Jodie, we got some cheerleaders to go mock."

We declined Tiffani's offer to drive us in her hot pink leopard print Range Rover (*wow*) and made our way to Tracie's place. I tore the price tags off my discount haul and steadied my racing heart. Ugh, why was I nervous to see Tracie? I was badass Sophie. She should be afraid of me!

But I wasn't a badass game designer with an impressive collection of leather jackets yet. I was poor, zitty, and not even cool enough to be queen of the losers. Ximena was queen of the losers; she had clear skin and a new MacBook, the jerk.

My stomach sunk further, into my decrepit motorcycle boots, to see Tracie and her evil cabal standing on the porch when we arrived. Lying in wait. In a firing line. The smile on that chick's face was that of a reedy hyena, all teeth and mockery.

Jodie clutched my arm. "We don't have to do this."

"Yes, I do. I have to go through the steps of this game show to return to my awesome life. At least…awesomer than this." I turned in the seat to face her. "But you don't have to come. This is my burden."

She unclicked her seatbelt. "Oh, no. I'm coming. If only to be your witness to the police after the melee."

I snorted, my head falling onto the seatback with a *thunk*. "I apprec--"

"Sophie! Get out here!" Tracie screamed. Jodie and I jumped as she banged her fist on the passenger window. "We're going to try our best to make you look like something other than a dollar store box of tampons!"

The sliver of vanity that had not yet been punched out of me withered and died. Damn.

"Let's do this, I guess." Jodie squeezed my hand so hard I yelped. She didn't let go. "What's the signal to throw nail polish on her and run?"

"I don't have nail polish."

"Ummmmm," Tracie began, intelligently, "can you two losers come in already? The mosquitos are eating me alive."

My best friend fished in her Goodwill bag and grinned when she held up her prize. "I bought nail polish at Goodwill. Some sort of peach they discontinued in 1979. May or may not already be infected with legacy toe rot."

Bang, bang, bang! Tracie continued attacking the window, her rage-filled cheeks now mottled like a fresh bruise.

Fuck, she looked like everyone in this town when dealing with me. My teachers. My father. His church. I lost my breath.

Ugh. My dad's nightmarish "church." Basically a loose collection of weirdos and abusers who formed a 14-person strip-mall congregation. Every eight months or so, they'd try to "fix me," and they all looked like Tracie. They preached about "goat-demons," which had sounded hilarious to me. If I were a demon, I'd want to be a snake-demon. Or a dragon-demon.

Funny, Dad had never defined what "fixing me" entailed. Sure, it could have been the getting in trouble at school, my evil tongue, the fistfights, or the fact that I pooped at the Arby's down the street because I refused to chisel the filth out of the trailer's single bathroom like a good female.

Probs it was the bi thing, though, even though I never officially came out to him. The congregants loved to throw holy water on me while I played a video game in the back row, but sometimes, if I was truly bored, I fell to the floor and flopped around so they felt they were getting their holier-than-money's worth.

See, I wasn't not all bad.

Tracie continued screaming, her spittle painting the window like a Jackson Pollack. Jodie said something, but I didn't hear what?

A pit of pure terror spit acid into my stomach whenever I even thought about telling Dad I wasn't straight. That was the beginning of the black hole. Or "ulcer" as the fancy doctor I ignore calls it. I swallowed a lump even now to know that Dad would have 300% shipped me off to a reeducation camp if he'd known for sure, so I kept my smarmy mouth shut until I ran away for good. And today—could he ship me to the desert to gay-die even now?

Jodie shook me. "Sophie! Is it a mom-emotion emergency?"

I shook my head.

She nodded. "Dad-emotion emergency."

"Desert," I whispered.

Her face went hard like a diamond. "You know very well, he will send you away over my, my mother's, my father's, and our dog's dead bodies. Also, my cousin is a marvelous attorney. You're okay, Sophie." She rubbed my arm. Tracie took to kicking the car. "You're okay."

I licked my desert-dry lips. "Did I ever tell you, they love to preach about demons? I'm a demon, of course, but they have determined I'm not a goat-demon." Deep breaths, Sophie. But darn it, I'd never beheld an actual goat-demon; I guess I didn't do enough nude midnight dancing in the forest.

I laughed, short and hollow, fuck, and pushed open the door of the car. Better to stand up like a woman and face the demon horde. And also stop thinking about all this awful crap yay.

Now, in Tracie's house, I finally saw the mysterious creatures for the very first time—goat-demons!

The Cheerleading Squad

- Nevaeh—Captain Goat-Demon, red of hair, pale of face, very uppity since they corrected her overbite

- Tracie—Vice-Captain Goat-Demon, blonde of hair, tan of face, succubus on the weekends, evil on the daily

- Kellseye—Regular Goat-Demon, a.k.a. The Eye of Kells, She of the Flaming Sky Eyeball in Blue Mascara, brown of hair, orange of face

Once we got inside Tracie's Florida-fancy foyer (muddy beige for days!), she made a grab for my Goodwill bag. I held on for dear life and wrestled it away from her clammy hooves; nobody would part me from my hideous dress! Not even a Vice-Captain Goat-Demon.

"My parents are in Jamaica—we can do whatever we want," said Tracie, gigglingly, the gleam in her eye like a warning beacon: there would be no witnesses.

She shuffled us into the living room, where she'd placed a chair in the middle of a tarp. I reared backwards, right into Jodie, who caught me and held on with panic claws.

"Tracie," I began, all the warnings in the world in my tone, "if I see one pair of scissors or buzz clippers, I will end you."

Her smile slipped.

Yeah. "Anything you do to me today, I will revisit upon you tenfold. Meaning, if you and your coven shave my head, I will shave yours 10 times. I'll follow you through your life. Starting a new job? Chop, chop! The day before your wedding? Bald as a cue ball. I will sneak into the maternity ward and shave you, your kid, the poor dipshit who married you, and your OBGYN!" My nostrils flared. "Got it?"

Her eyebrows came together so hard, you could hear the thud.

"Um…you're so weird, Sophie," Nevaeh said. "Why would you think we're going to shave your hair off?"

Kellseye kicked a small black case under the couch.

"Maybe I'm just paranoid," I replied. "And vengeful. So. Very. Vengeful."

We stood in silence. Jodie's grip on me tightened. The grandfather clock ticked.

I released my held breath and reached into my Goodwill bag. "Let's get this fun girl bonding over with. Where can I change?"

Tracie pointed down a hall.

Jodie leaned close. "I'll watch them while you go. But do what we talked about before you change or pee or anything."

I nodded and hurried to the seafoam green bathroom, featuring mirrors bedecked with seashell frames. And a big shell sink, also in seafoam.

Oh, Florida.

No matter! Time to do my super awesome secret spy shit I learned from the internet.

Super Awesome Secret Spy Shit I Learned From the Internet

1. Turn off the lights

2. Fish the empty paper towel roll from my bag and hold it up to one eye

3. Grab my flashlight and beam it right next to the roll

4. Scan the bathroom for the white reflection that will glint off a camera lens

Jodie and I experienced sinking twin feelings that Tracie might try to record incriminating video of—holy crap, what was that? I flicked the lights back on to investigate the glint, which came from the shower.

That. Horrible. Vice-Captain. Goat-Demon! There, duct-taped to her shower head, was a spy camera, an inch-and-a-half or so, pointed toward the toilet. The bathroom wasn't big, so I expect you'd get a lovely view of anything happening there.

I texted Jodie with my ancient flip phone: YOU WERE RIGHT! SPY CAM @ TOILET! I LIKE ALL CAPS TEXTING!

Jodie to me: THAT POOP BUTT FACE! WHAT ARE YOU GOING TO DO?

Jodie to me: ALL CAPS IS THE BEST

Jodie to me: LOOK FOR MORE, SHE MAY HAVE BRIC-A-BRAC

Jodie to me: SORRY I MEANT BACKUP

Jodie to me: STUPID AUTOCORRECT

I couldn't even summon the level of rage this stunt of Tracie's deserved because my BFF was smart and amazing and hilarious. Naturally, I followed her advice, but only found the one bric-a-bracamera.

What to do?

Bang, bang, bang! went the door. "Sophie! What on earth are you doing in there?"Tracie asked through laughter. "Do you need air freshener?"

My teeth ground against each other like they were eating her face. No wonder she thought it was hilarious. She expected to post my pooping video all over Facebook in the next hour.

Well, then. Let's not disappoint a goat-demon.

"Tracie, I'm so sorry. I --" my voice broke, and I sniffled like Meryl Streep. "Do you have any more toilet paper? Oh, God, the humanity!" I threw myself against the closed door, and she yelped. "Please send Jodie in to help me. I'm so embarrassed!" I wailed to shake the house down. "Why…why did I eat those three egg-and-hot-sauce burritos for breakfast?"

Oh, the giggles from the other side of that door. Evil, the lot of them.

I pressed my hand against my mouth to stifle my laughter. My shoulders shook with it, and I fell to my knees with the force of my delight, which zinged through my body like the first cold beer of the weekend. Finally, this was fun. I was glad she'd planted the camera.

But what to do with it?

A knock sounded on the door. "Sophie?" Jodie asked. "You need me?"

Always. I cracked the door and released a shriek. The cheerleaders crowding Jodie stepped back. "Help me, Jodie!" I yanked her in and slammed the door in Tracie's face.

"Oh, my God, she can't even poop alone!" Tracie hollered to uproarious cacking.

"Is that what lesbians do?" asked Kellseye.

Jodie peeked out the door. "Yes. Yes, it is." She slammed it again, and then fell against it, laughing. With a grin, she covered her eyes. "Are you really pooping, or just buying time?"

"Time. You're welcome. Look at the shower head."

She revealed one elevated eyebrow. We shimmied past one another, and she stood on the tub edge to examine the lump taped to the pipe. "What the heck?"

I shimmied-switched with her again, climbed onto the side of the tub, and picked at the tape until I could unwind it.

The door shook with bangs. "Hurry. Up!" Tracie screamed. Then, she kicked her own door.

"Ugh! I'm allergic to eggs!" I screamed.

"Hold on to the toilet!" added Jodie. "Don't fly off!"

I laughed so hard, I had to cover my mouth.

Jodie shrugged. "That should buy us a few more minutes. And maybe an exorcism."

"Do you think it'll be free? My dad's church wants to do one on me, but they want to charge him $500, which he keeps trying to negotiate down. It's hard to be evil and poor."

Once I got the camera off, I made sure to give it the middle finger before I tossed it into the toilet. Next, I removed the black cap from one of her hair products and taped it to the shower head. If you didn't study it too close, nothing appeared amiss, so I crossed my fingers that she wouldn't actually notice until we'd left.

I flushed the little camera, where it would hopefully clog their pipes. Tracie's parents might be innocent in all this, but then again, they did raise a Vice-Captain Goat-Demon.

"Come on." Jodie lifted my ugly dress. "Time to suit up."

"Aye, aye, cap'n." I wiggled into my gorgeous/ugly (or "gugly" as sophisticated people say) prom dress and pranced before the mirror in a celebration of its gugliness.

Jodie danced behind me in the mirror. "Amazing. You look like one of Dolly Parton's poor relations." She gave me a zip-up.

"One of the ones she doesn't like, so she doesn't toss them money." Of all the poor relations I might be, Dolly's would be the absolute best. "Actually, Dolly would give everyone cash, wouldn't she?"

"Duh."

Unfortunately, I could not hide in the booby-trapped bathroom forever.

My stomach fluttered with nervous energy when we emerged. I squashed my stupid feelings and put a hitch into my voice. "Oh, my goodness!" I collapsed into Jodie's arms. "I must sit after that ordeal."

The Goat-Demons clicked their forked tongues in glee, no doubt anticipating the horrific, yet hilarious, tandem pooping video Jodie and I had birthed.

Jodie led me to the living room and pushed me onto a beige sofa so I could do my best impression of a gugly quilt made by grandma. Well, not my grandma. My grandma's greatest creations were her piles of cigarette butts on the front porch of her ramshackle 1920s house. One of them had been two feet high before collapsing.

Tracie and her other apocalyptic horsewomen surrounded me. Jodie ducked and covered on the couch to avoid their claws.

"Umm," Nevaeh began. "Wha --" she paused to giggle and elbow her comrades. "What are you wearing?"

Uproarious laughs! I ground my teeth and closed my eyes. Damn, I was 10 years past this crap, but still—my heart thumped, my pits leaked, my stomach retreated, and my brain downshifted into teen-mode. Ugh, here they came—*feelings*! Teenage feelings, the worst kind, unless you counted adult feelings. Gahhhh! I was ugly! Pointless! I'd die forever alone, misunderst--

Jodie squeezed my hand proportionally to the amount my eyes narrowed, and soon, my face had de-numbed. She kept hanging on, silently telling me to make nice via every squeeze.

I tore my hand away; I'd behave. "It's my prom dress, Nevaeh. See? It's long and crinkles when I walk, like I'm a fairy fucking princess." Their maws opened, maybe to speak, or perhaps to release the darkness from within, so I kept talking. "Let's make me over now. I want to be pretty, like…" I took a long, steadying breath and whispered, "you."

Little did they know, I'd meant Jodie. My heart swelled like a barbecue-filled balloon every time I looked at her. She'd considered herself so unattractive at this age, but oh no. Not by a mile. Her skin shone in the light, clear and perfect. Cheeks still sported a ton of baby fat—adorably so. She'd hated those "chipmunk cheeks," as she'd put it. In a couple of years, her cheekbones would *kaplow!* everywhere, and the result would be stunning enough to make me sweat in my gugly dress at just the memory.

Back to today. Er, yesterday?My "compliment" made the cheerleaders' faces go haywire. First, shock that I'd apparently called Nevaeh "pretty." Next, a grimace, for they wanted to crap all over my choice of gown some more. Then, a forced smile, for they needed to keep me here in order to perpetuate their evil, if simplistic, plot upon me.

This whole thing was so cliché; really, I ought to be friends with the cheerleaders. A buncha chicks wearing sexy short skirts and screaming all the time about beating up their enemies on the field of valor? My kinda people.

Kellseye yanked on my forearm, the better to pull me toward the Chair of Doom. I craned my neck to see Jodie, but Nevaeh jumped between us. They both shoved me down. I had to squint—the grins on their faces blinded me with creepy whiteness, like that of a frozen zombie king.

"What shall we do with this?" Tracie said, two of her fingers holding a piece of my stubby hair.

"I—" I began.

"That was a rhetorical question!" she screamed. I winced and went left, she held on to the right. My neck crunched. "We're giving you extensions."

My jaw dropped. "Who is the 'we' in that sentence?"

Kellseye held up several bedraggled lengths of hair.

Blonde hair.

Behind me, Jodie burst into laughter.

I sniffed, determined to not let these devil-goats see me sweat, although I was surely ruining this dress. Once I'd moved out for college and left my father behind, I'd actually gotten some health care, and some much-needed prescription deodorant. Sexy, huh? The only reason I'd gotten braces at this age was because an orthodontist's kid had clocked me in the mouth with a medicine ball during gym, and I'd threatened to sue.

Yet that was long ago. Or far into the future. Today, I was just a sturdy peasant lass who sweated too much in the face of her sworn enemies.

"Great!" I said for the benefit of the cameras Tracie surely had in this room. In for a penny, in for a pound of flesh. With a shaky breath, I said the most disgusting thing I'd ever uttered:"I can't wait to be blonde."

Jodie squeaked.

Wow. I'd said that without letting out a single "fuck." Was this what heroes felt like?

The demons tugged my head. They yanked my ears. They scraped my skin and pinched the roots and chanted demonic hexes. Or maybe that was just cheerleader gossip. Sounded the same to me.

My BFF inched her way around to the front of me, seemingly without the notice of Winkin, Blinkin, and Succubus. She slapped a hand over her mouth at the sight of me, which gave me so much confidence.

All too late, they were done. Tracie declared, "My God, you look better."

"Anything would be an improvement," added Kellseye.

"Are you referring to an alternate spelling of your name?" I asked her.

"Huh?"

My mouth crinkled in disgruntlement. It was almost no fun when they couldn't understand the insults. My head certainly understood the insult of what they'd done to it; even sight unseen, my whole damn scalp throbbed.

Nevaeh appeared in a puff of smoke before me, and I reared away from the smell of sulfur. "Now for the makeup!" She whipped a brush back and forth. "What did you bring?"

I blinked. "Um…"

A screech reverberated behind me, continuing like a siren until it woo-woo'd to my front. "I'm not using my makeup on you!" Tracie yelled. "You would infect it with your disgusting skin!"

My eyes shut, as if they refused to allow themselves to convey the fact that her jab had actually hit a tender spot. Yeah, I knew I was ugly as hell. In high school. Not today. Right?

Could I invoice Tiffani the Psychic-Guidance Counselor-Goodwill Manager for the ulcer medicine I was too cool to buy?

Kellseye ended her buzzard-circling of my chair. "Ladies, I got some makeup at the drug store." She held open a plastic bag for her fellow goat-demons, and, looking inside it, they whinnied and barked, and I don't know what noises goats make.

Jodie leaned over and peeked inside the bag. The face she pulled told me everything. Apparently, prom would be a costume party for me, wherein my disguise would be "18th century prostitute for clown fetishists."

I sighed. "Wonderful. Put it on. What value does a rom-com heroine have if she hasn't been made over and assimilated into a Revlon ad? After all, zitty bitch never won fair hero. Our guidance counselor told me that."

Their eyes got so wide, my intestines twisted, wondering if they were actually about to acid-burn me.

Tracie dragged a chair to sit knee-to-knee with me. "Stop making that face! I'm not going to hurt you."

My body rebelled so hard, I tipped the chair. Jodie caught me. "Who brought up hurting?" I asked in pure squeak-syllables.

"Shut up and let me do what I can." Her eyes almost popped out with the force of their somersaults. The gleam in them went from snarky to gleeful, which couldn't be a good sign.

Behind the group of demons, Jodie gestured to me that she was going deeper into the house. She dropped dramatically and crawled to the hallway, like a Navy SEAL storming a hostile beach. Cracked my ass up! Which made Tracie yell at me.

I prayed that salt was being added to toothpaste tubes, and hair remover to shampoos.

My nemesis spackled some cold, wet goop all over my face with a sponge and then made an interpretive dance performance out of taking it to the garbage since "your heinous, greasy disease skin has ruined it." She jabbed me in the eyeball with a mascara stabby thing not once, but three times. And also a fourth time in the ear? The time spent painting my cheekbones probably meant they could be seen from space, and my right eye literally hurt from the pressure she used to apply a color they refused to let me see.

After way too long, and much too much throbbing on my head's part, the cheerleaders took a step back to survey the damage. And take photographs. Of course.

I swore with every fiber of the hair they yanked from my scalp, I would mail dildos inscribed with "eat a dick" to every single one of their places of work. The packages would be full of glitter. As soon as I got to my future life again.

Nevaeh whispered to Tracie. Kellseye whispered to both of them. All three peeled their faces off to reveal lizard women! That would have been interesting. Instead, Tracie dug through the drug store bag again to reveal...false eyelashes. They were *blue*?

Nope. I stood and yelled, "Jodie!" Enough. Enough, enough. How the heck was *twuewuv* going to magically come into my life when, apparently, the plan was to remind me of every horrific teenage emotion I'd ever denied having? "We have to go now. Thanks for the, er, makeup and..." I held a piece of blonde hair in two fingers, "this?"

"It's not time for you to leave yet," Tracie said, her face awash in slack-jawed protest. "You still look horrible."

"Hey!" Jodie zoomed into view and planted herself between me and the goat demons. "She does not look horrible! Except—Kelly green eye shadow? But that's your fault."

Nevaeh shrugged. "Green eye shadow is very in this year."

I said, "You'd be more believable if the other two Assketeers weren't laughing."

"Well, you can't leave. You have to be here at five."

Slowly, and with great dread, Jodie and I turned our heads her direction to ask, "Why?"

"Just—" Her eyes went wide. "That's when the limo comes."

Jodie grabbed my arm. "We're leaving."

I planted my stubborn feet.

Her eyebrows lifted to the heavens. "Come on. This is bullshit, and you know it."

"I have to stay," I whispered. "If I don't, I'm stuck here, in the past, with skin like a defective pizza and hair the color of pissed-on Florida sand."

"Don't care, I am not allowing this."Her adorable face went hard. "You will never make it into a limo at 5p.m., you understand that, right? They will throw you into a pool filled with vomit, or chain you toa meth den's radiator, or toss you off the roof and call it a sorority hazing."

"What are you two lesbians whispering about?" Tracie laughed at her very clever jab.

"Why, yes, I am a lesbian." Jodie stood to her full (short) height and stared her down. Er, up. "What is your point?"

The three goat demons flapped their mandibles, emitting uncertain clicks.

My bestie grabbed my hand and yanked me from the bowels of hell. Into the outside bowels of hell, a.k.a. Florida. "Whatever you do," she called as we ran, "don't look in a mirror."

I immediately wanted to look in a mirror.

"Don't you dare immediately look in a mirror," she said, shoving me into the passenger seat of her car. She slammed the door, the goat-demons almost on her! Whew, she made it into the driver's side and locked it before their tentacles reached the handle. "Stop!" She tore her purse, and the compact within, away from me. "We are getting some cherry limeade, then we will go to my place to remove whatever nonsense they have put on your head."

She fished up one of the extensions and felt around my scalp.

Ugh, spikes of pain shot through my head. "Can't you just snap them out?"

"They—they *glued* them."

"What?" I raked my fingers through the painful mess, only to find that, yup, this mess crunched under my fingers. It was glued to my actual hair. "Nooooo!"

The goat-demons, in a semi-circle on the lawn, cackled as the skies opened up above them. Splat, splat! went the rain on the windshield. I reminded myself that they had not actually caused the heavens to weep; that happened every day at 3:30p.m. in the state that is, technically, a swamp and not"land."

Some might think from my jokes that I hate Florida.

Jodie started the car and slammed on the gas while I flailed for my seatbelt. "I need this out of my hair!" I gasped, tugging as I did so. Which stung more, so I elevated to caterwauling. "Why weren't you watching?"

She huffed a sigh. "You are having a traumatic moment, so I will forgive your rudeness. I wandered off to snoop the house when they were distracted. Did you know that Tracie uses prescription deodorant?"

My hands dropped, for I did not want to commiserate with Tracie in any way, shape, or form. "Yeah…that's unfortunate. That stuff can really chafe."

"What?"

"What?"

Jodie continued, "Anyway…" she fished in her purse. "I stole it."

"Really?" I took it from her—wow, this was brand-name pharma crap. Heh-heh. "What other wonders does your bag hold?" I reached to explore it, and she slapped at me.

"Patience." Jodie tucked in her lower lip and dove back into her bag one-handed. "Let's see…oh! Here." She held out a towel wrapped around…golf balls?

"Stolen towel?" I asked. She nodded. It was salmon pink; we were doing them a favor. "Ooh, bon-bons! Here." I fed her one, and she made the appropriate yummy noises.

"Godivachocolatesh," she announced. "I left one in the gold box— some crunchy thing nobody likes."

Mmmmmm coconut! "I love you."

"I know. There'sh more!" Eating really gave her problems with her braces, my poor honey. Yet, she bravely continued searching through her bag for stolen booty. "Here—" She tossed something lavender in my lap.

My brain exploded. "Oh my God."

She nodded. "She did it. All those years ago, she damn did the thing!"

Tears—rage tears—sprung into my eyes to clutch this small bundle of cloth in my hands. My mom bailed on us when I was eight years old. Before that, life hadn't been too bad; she and Dad had fought like cats and other cats who hated the first cats, but at least I'd been clean and fed. Our last good Christmas, my mother had bought me a lavender jacket. Some Hot Topic thing, nothing expensive, but it featured red and pink flames flicking up from the bottom and the sleeves.

I had loved that jacket beyond all. It was badass and unique, and I would wear it like armor whenever they'd fight. So, every damn night. It made me feel…maybe how Wonder Woman feels in her bracelets. Pain comes at you, but you swat it away with your lavender flame-arms.

One day at school, it had been stolen from my cubby. I'd sobbed all afternoon, all night, all week. And gotten screamed at for having lost it.

Well, here it was. My tiny little lavender flames jacket. In Tracie Willes' house.

Tears glomming my voice, I whispered, "Where did you find it?"

"In her closet. Hanging in the very back." She put a loving hand on my knee. "I remember you telling me that story, about the jacket."

I nodded, but couldn't speak through a closed throat. It'd meant the world, that jacket. The loss of it had been as devastating as the joy had been euphoric. Not to mention that my mother slapped me when she figured out it was gone. Ugh, my throat tightened in on itself. Sometimes I'd wondered if my loss of it had been the final nail in the coffin of her life with us. She'd left at the end of January, soon after.

"Tracie Willes," I whispered. I swiped away a tear. "She could have anything she ever wanted. Any clothing, any device, any car. And she took my one thing."

Jodie shook her head. "She's rotten to the core."

I put my hand over hers because she sounded like she was about to cry. "You know, we were friends then, me and Tracie. I had…friends then."

"You have friends now."

"I have *friend* now." I kissed her hand, loud and sloppy. "And you're all I need." Determined not to let this revelation ruin my second prom date with Jodie, I blew out a long breath. *Shove it down with all the rest, Sophie.* "Did you find anything else? Is she a secret drag king? Damn it, I'd like her better if that were the case."

"Alas." Jodie pulled into the drive-through to get cherry limeades with a side of cheeseburger. For strength. "I did leave Tracie a nice message."

I perked in my seat.

She giggled and said, "I wrote 'lesbians rock!' on her bedroom mirror. In the ugly, old nail polish."

Hahahahahaha! "I love you!"

"*And*…I got an interesting recording."

These words of hope straightened my spine further. "Go on…"

"When you went to the bathroom…" she trailed off, her fingers to her lips.

"Yes. Yes?"

"Yes, I'll take two cherry limeades, two cheeseburgers, two of your biggest fries, two onion rings, two tater tots, and two of any other thing you have made of potato."

These words calmed my rageful soul, currently blinking red and purple as it fought to escape out of my butt. I nodded as Jodie patted my head gently. She pulled around the corner to pay the people for the potatoes.

"They outlined the plan," she said casually.

"Huh?" I pulled down the sun visor, but Jodie slammed it on my fingers. "Ow!"

"No mirrors!" She pulled forward. "So, the plan is—thank you! Can we please have ketchup?"

Drkjfhkldahflhfahrufhaieurhf.

While we got the food and pulled away, I went ahead and found the videos on Jodie's phone. I didn't have a fancy smart phone in this, my hell, because we were too poor. Cradling bona-fide technology—even 10-year-old technology—in my grubby little hand was like a cool breeze upon my soul, which stopped trying to butt-escape. My fingers tingled, even.

There it was—Jodie must have propped the phone against something, because a sideways coven of goat-demons appeared. I made a face. An enormous faceyface.

Jodie giggled. "Yup, ew, gross."

Ew, gross, indeed, for their mandibles flapped and their claws clacked as they outlined their evil plan.

Evil Goat-Demons' Pom-Pom Plan

- *"Carrie"* me at prom

- That's it, that's the plan

I waved my arms. "Wait, wait. So I've been cursed back in time; forced to endure whatever blonde plastic is affixed to my scalp; made to dance, at a dance, with Doofus McGhee, who I am also supposed to love for some reason—and on top of that…I shall wear a crown of pig's blood? Why even make me a blonde if they're just gonna pour Babe all over it?"

"Is…is that the worst part to you?"

"Kind of. I mean…" I pulled a faceyfacey face. "*Blonde.*" Sure, many women made blonde work—my mother was blonde—but we don't choose our allergies.

Jodie nodded as she pulled into her driveway. Home at last. She grabbed the many bags of potatoes and climbed out of the car. "Well, let's get my video on Facebook. Those chicks are gonna be *ruined!*"

"Ha-ha!" said someone too bubbly. "No, you can't do that."

I started and turned. And cursed. And balled my fists. And wondered how this silly woman in the 10-inch high heels kept sneaking up behind me. Perhaps that was the true magic of Tiffani the Psychic-Guidance Counselor-Goodwill Manager. But why didn't my evil eye tattoo on the back of my neck warn me? "Get off my lawn!" I hollered.

Mrs. Edwards hurried down the front stops. "My goodness, Sophie! Your guidance counselor is here to speak with you, and she most certainly does not have to get off *my* lawn." She was a clone of her daughter, lovely and sweet, usually wearing a flowy jewel-toned caftan with her close-cropped black hair. She was the kind of mom who came around with actual cookies and milk at a sleepover. The kind who slipped lunch money into my pockets when I wasn't looking. The pockets she'd washed because a baby alligator lived in the trailer's outside washing machine, and I didn't have enough money for the laundromat.

Guilt slapped me like a cold fish, and my face went hot. "Sorry, Mrs. Edwards."

"It's okay. So…somebody did your makeup, huh? It's…" Her face went through the Stages of Horror: denial, terror, bargaining, castoff embarrassment, and lying. "Looks great." She gave me a shoulder squeeze. "And that is one groovy outfit, child. I hope you brought enough for everybody."

"Enough ugly dresses?"

Laughing, Mrs. Edwards said, "Of course." She liberated one of the fast food bags and sniffed at the top. "Tater tots."

"I got you." Jodie grinned at her mom and hurried inside. We all followed.

Once inside the foyer, Mrs. Edwards picked up one of the "strands" of my new "hair." "Um, you know, I have actual professionals we could call regarding the tragedy that has befallen you this day. Never really saw you as a…this."

Me, neither. Not ever. My shoulders fell, knowing that even if we did call in the big guns, I had negative two pennies to pay them for their expertise. "That's—it's okay. Thanks, Mrs. Edwards."

"I'll fix it! I looooove doing hair," declared Tiffani, in an entirely new outfit. Gracing us now was a different pink onesie-thing with a hundred black and white tassels swinging from it. "Mrs. Edwards, your house is adooorable! I love the wall color. It's such a happy hue, and you know what they say—be it ever so humble, there's no place like a home with Tiffany blue balls. Because I'm Tiffani, get it? Ha-ha!"

Mrs. Edwards stopped short, her eyes opening wide. "Uh…sure. Well, I'll just steal some tater tots and leave you to be…counseled." She gave a little head shake on the way out of the living room.

See? Mrs. Edwards knew what was up.

Tiffani clapped. "Sophie, you look amazing as a blonde."

"No."

"Oh, come on. You know it looks so natural on you!"

I shot her a dirty, dirty look, because I did not know any such thing.

"Potato cake?" Jodie offered to Tiffani in hushed tones.

"Ha-ha! No, I don't eat white foods." She whispered, "Starch." Tiffani made a horror face and patted the seat next to her. "Come, Sophie. I will fluff up your hair while we talk and…do something with your makeup. I don't think that other girl has a future in the beauty arts. Jodie, I'm afraid this is a private session."

I bolted to my feet. "No!"

But traitor Jodie shoved a cheeseburger into her smiling mouth and headed toward the exit post-haste. "Have funshsh!"

I scanned the room for weapons. DVD player. Drink coasters. Jodie's spelling bee trophies—yup, those would be my go-to. They featured a winged victory person whose metal feathers would be sharp.

"I'm proud of you, Sophie."

Uggghhhh. I sank sideways onto the couch opposite her.

"You are giving this whole thing a chance." One of her ankles rolled in her enormous shoes, even as she sat there. "Look at youuuuuu! You're wearing a prom dress, sort of—it's terrible, and we will change it—and you've been made over."

One of the blonde things on my head slid to the floor, and Schatzi attacked it. I closed my eyes and imagined myself as a dog three stories tall. I'd bite every evil in the world, starting with—

"Sit up and let me admire your marvelous new coiffure."

Nah.

She closed the distance between us and dragged me vertical by the wrist. The horrible woman ignored the clear frown emoji I wore on my pimply face and kept talking.

"I'm proud of you for really embracing Channing and the love journey I have begun for you!" She clapped. Again. For real. "Let's fix this hair."

Yank. I squealed from the shiny new pain shooting down my scalp, yet there was no time for protest. Tiffani whipped my head back and forth like I was Willow Smith.

"Now, it may sound silly, but I know you can be loved in a huge romancey romance way."

Wow. Thanks.

"We just need you to open --" *yank* "your --" *yank* "heart!" YANK!

"Stop it!" I scooted away from her, crab-style, sideways and furious. "Lady, they're gonna Carrie me at prom. That's the plan. Channing doesn't love me. Tracie straight up hates me. And I feel like the poor pig who's losing its volume of blood isn't all that fond of my ass, either."

FFS, my head throbbed. I pressed flat palms to it, but the extensions felt…different. Not stringy and patchy anymore.

I pushed past her wobbly knees and made my way to the mantel, which had a huge mirror above it. "What the what?"

I looked like friggin' Dolly Parton. If Dolly were significantly uglier and poorer and pettier. Great cascades of blonde hair, in a totally different blonde color than that of the demon-goats, shimmered around my face. This hue made me grit my teeth; it was the opposite of everything I'd ever chosen for myself, damn her.

And whoa: "Where did my zits go?" The exploded crater from this morning, which had been leaking hazardous materials all day, was just plain gone. Mascara lined my lashes, and gloss plumped my lips, and they were both appropriate colors for the human face.

Tiffani the Magician teetered behind me and put her hands on my shoulders. "Woweeeeee! Look at you."

"Look at *me*? This isn't me!" Ugh, I wanted to slap her, but I stalked to the far side of the room instead. Mostly because I thought Mrs. Edwards would be disappointed in me if I pummeled the guidance counselor.

I turned to take her on, blood pounding in my ears. "None of this is me! Why are you doing this? True love will come from me changing who I am, going to prom, and having pig's blood dumped on me? I musta missed that very special episode of *The Bachelorette*."

"I got you a dress." Ignoring my intelligent, angry points, she picked up a garment bag from a chair. Where the hell had that come from? She thrust it toward me. "Something more appropriate for a dance than the Von Trapp children's curtains you've chosen."

I threw the bag behind me. "What is *wrong* with you?"

Tiffani pursed her lips and narrowed her eyes. Yes, this was the real her shining through—a lot smarter than she projected in pink. "Nothing, sweetie, but thanks for aaaaaasking. I'm supremely well adjusted." She clasped her bosom. "Sophie, you need to learn to open your heart, no matter how difficult the circumstance."

"Lady…" I squeezed my eyelids against the swell of rage stiffening my every muscle. "I've had enough hateful circumstances in my life to fill a…. to, to… it's a lot. My mother abandoned me, then my father did. He did it while in the same house, which was somehow worse." The black hole section of my soul gaped, threatening to suck the rest into it. The pull nearly dropped me. "This house --" I spread my arms wide to indicate the Edwards'. My hands shook. "Was the only...only place where anyone considered me a human person at this time. But sure, force me into the clutches of every pubescent shitheel who wants to destroy what little pride I've managed to throw together."

Screw her. I turned on my heel and started toward the door. "You know, Tiffani the Psychic—you needn't work so hard to break me down. It's not a long-distance trip."

I opened the door to find Jodie there, a potato cake in one hand, an empty glass in the other. I had to laugh. "Have you solved the case, Nancy Drew?" I asked.

Her eyes went wide for having been caught. "Have a potato! What the heck has happened to your --" she leaned in, her jaw going slack, "everything?"

Mrs. Edwards zoomed by, then stopped short. "Sophie!" After blinking so many times I thought it was a stroke, she held my face. "Sweetie, that guidance counselor of yours might ought to be Elizabeth Arden. That blonde looks like it's growing out of your head! You really pull it off."

My face went numb. "No, I don't!"

"You always know how to take a compliment, Sophie." She paused and settled onto one hip, just like her daughter. "Does your guidance counselor always carry around a lace front? Damn, she did your eyebrows?How—oh my God, I didn't even notice your braces got taken off!"

My tongue slid over my teeth. So smooth!

"You are gorgeous," murmured Jodie.

I giggled. Or tittered. Or another woman noise. Whatever it was, it unballed my fists, and the hole in my soul shrank to a livable level. "Thanks. I—I...I mean..." *Giggle.* "Errrrruhhhh." *Giggle!* "Potato me."

Jodie slapped it into my palm. "You got it. Wow, the tater tot bits won't even get stuck in your braces. That'sh elegant."

"Well, my work here is done!" Tiffani click-clacked to the foyer in her best impression of a giraffe on Molly. A grin of satisfaction smuggedher mug. "You know what they say, the roots of all evil are the ones you don't touch up."

I would've torn her head off with my fangs, but they were coated in potato. It was not elegant.

At the door, Tiffani turned. "Open your heart, Sophie. The possibilities are endless, like breadsticks. Which I don't eat because they are a starchy white food. No offense, to you as a white person, or the breadsticks."

"None taken. Hey—" I placed a smile on in order to ask her, "Can you, um, make Jodie's braces go away, too? The poor thing can barely eat. I mean, she's got a whole tater tot stuck in those things, and she served her sentence the first time around."

She pursed her lips. "Done. Byeeeeee! See you at prom!"

I threw the bolt behind her, even though I suspected that locks would not slow the least of her roll. A squeal sounded from the living room, so I hurried in there to find Jodie staring in the mirror. "Sophie!" She grinned.

"Yesssss! You deserve some magic, too."

We jumped up and down together exactly the way we had when we'd been freed from our grill-prisons the first time. Man, it unknotted my shoulders to see her happy.

She bounced to the garment bag. "Have you looked in here? This dress is gorgeous!" Her squeals went all kinds of girly. "She brought this for you?"

I sighed.

"Okay, okay, " Jodie draped the open bag across the back of the sofa. "I know your '70s dress is a mashterpiece of pastel horror, but this one…" the bag rustled, and a swath of filmy maroon fabric frothed out, "is amazing! You have to wear this." She grinned so hard, the walls buckled in on me. "You'll be beautiful!"

"I… "Ugggggghhhhhhhhfuuuuuuuuck, I wanted to argue. To yell, to scream, to tell her I didn't give two shits about being "beautiful" for these awful high school people. Instead, I sagged in defeat. I could tell Tiffani to screw off, and hopefully would again, but not Jodie. Not when she was looking at me like she looked at Victoria's Secret catalogs and made my brain go all sideways.

Apparently, I was going to be a pretty, pretty blonde princess wafting around in a cloud of red just to make Jodie happy. Hey, at least the pig's blood would match the dress. Unless…

Okay, sure, I would make an appearance at prom. Sure, I'd wear the big red Cinderella dress—I was a poor scullery maid, anyhow. Yet Tiffani hadn't said a damn thing about being obligated to participate in a discount production of *Carrie*.

"Jodie, let's go to your room. We have an evil plan to…plan. Evilly."

She cradled the pretty dress close, her eyebrows rising. "Does it involve revenge on Tracie and her crew? Because the recordings I had on my phone of the cheerleaders are gone."

Tiffani. *Grrrrrrr.* At least Tracie didn't have blackmail video of me from her toilet.

"Yes, we will have our revenge, after a decade of waiting. For me. And for you. Not that you're aware of that. You know what I mean."

She pointed toward the heavens and struck a dashing pose. "Avengers, let's get revenge! Or…let's mess 'em up, Avengers!"

Look at that—we almost had a catchphrase.

CHAPTER FIVE:
TO ALL THE BOYS I'VE DESTROYED BEFORE

Jodie and I, the "let's avenge the revengers avengingly" crew, showed up at prom bright-eyed, bushy-tailed, and itchy as hell.

"Stop wiggling," Jodie whispered. She pried my digging fingers out of the neckline of my dress. This stupid maroon cloud prison was itching me nutso, even though Jodie kept wolf-whistling at me. I looked like an raging reality TV star in my giant blonde hair, goopy lip gloss, horrific heels, and questionable sense of propriety.

However, I had managed to sneak in my Acapulco handbag—under my enormous skirt. It was roomy enough to fit our avenging revenge tools, including a couple of bottles of fancy imported beer I'd swiped. Sorry, Mrs. Edwards.

Jodie absolutely stunned in her tuxedo, which was blue velvet and tailored to perfection. Inspired by Tiffani the Witch, she wore a long, black ponytail on top and sexy black heels on the bottom. I breathed out relief to realize that folks were telling her how gorgeous she looked instead of being horrible bigots. Huh, that was one improvement over the original production of Florida Hell Prom. Thank goodness. I had enough enemies tonight; I didn't need to pummel the volleyball team while wearing the world's most painful strapless tit sling. Nobody better tell me about sexism being a thing of the past; this underwire had for sure been forged in the fires of Mordor by every douchebag who'd ever uttered the phrase, "Well, actually…"

"Let's investigate the stage before Channing gets here," Jodie said with a tug to my arm.

My darling date had wheedled and whined on the phone when I told him I refused to get in a limo with him, and that I didn't care to eat a pre-*Carrie* steak with his gaggle of horribles.

The stage extended across one end of the room, so we slipped out a side door to go around the back. After a few trips into broom closets, we found the backstage entrance. There wasn't much here—some stairs to the stage, a bunch of suspended pipes rigged with curtains…

And a cooler.

Yes, they'd slung a sheet over it, but Jodie and I cleverly deduced that fabric can be moved. I kept a lookout while she opened the Lil Freezy.

"Well…" She dropped the lid and stood, her fingers pinching her nose. "There's good news and bad news."

The bad news' stench wafted to my angry nostrils. "Is the poop the good or bad news?"

She hurried over to me. "Bad. The good news is we were right about the blood, so we should feel smart about that."

I narrowed my eyes.

She grinned. "Polite of them to hide this in a place from which it will easily be stolen. Come on, Sir Scowls-a-Lot, help me."

At Jodie's direction, we re-covered the stinky cooler, which she then picked up. I performed lookout duty as we purloined it, her term, which she informed me was a fancy word for "stealing your shit." Literally. Still laughing at her joke, I led us out of the backstage and down the hall to one of those convenient janitor's closets we'd previously scouted.

Once inside the tiny room, the smell really singed my nostril hairs. I sank against the door. "How do you think they were going to deploy their…missiles?"

"I don't want to know. Question is, what do we do with our ill-gotten and ill-smelling bounty?"

I flipped my blonde hair straight into my ugly lip gloss. "Ugh. Let's leave it in here and await our opportunity. Perhaps when I'm chosen prom queen to Channing's king."

"Ah, of course you will be. That falls in line with the least imaginative plan possible."

We exited that room like whoa. "I am guessing," I whispered, for more and more teenagers were sweating up this hotel, "that Tracie and her goat-demons will be on stage with me as my court."

Tons more kids swarmed the ballroom now. My phone buzzed. "Channing is here." I turned and took Jodie's hand. "Wha—what do I do?" The surrealism of this whole event knotted my intestines and robbed my breath. I scratched at my tits. "Do I go on a for-real date with Channing now? For luuuuuuv? Or do we hurl cow poo at these vile demons?"

"Cow poo we hope," was Jodie's reply.

Leave it to Jodie to drill down to the real facts.

"Just…" She flapped her arms. "Just go with the flow."

I pulled a face that originated in my itchy places. "Have you met me?"

She laughed and reminded me that she was the most beautiful girl in the room, bar none. "I'll stick close. Let's get this over with so we can leave and drink beers at my house."

"Oh, no, I've turned you into a booze hound."

"Well, I'm depressed and lonely in the future, might as well downward spiral now."

I set my head on her shoulder in the glittery darkness of the room and hugged her arm close. "Not when you've got me, chickadee."

Her hand closed over mine, and I squeezed hard, pouring my every twisted emotion into her, which was probably rude. But she never let go.

A cackle opened my eyes, and I beheld le goat demon. "Channing," said the goat-demon, dressed in a purple pouf, "looks like your date doesn't even need you." Tracie's fangs dripped with venom. "She's got her..." she performed air quotes, "'best friend' here."

"Are you my 'best friend?'" I air-quoted to Jodie.

"I thought I was your best friend, but farbeit for me to argue with Grimace."

Grimace's nostrils flared; she couldn't seem to decipher the insult, only that one existed. Her friends joined her and appeared similarly put out.

I plopped my hands on my hips like friggin' Grace Kelly. "Okay, Channing, sweep me off my feet or something. Come on, let's go."

Channing scratched his head and looked to the goat-demons for instruction. They waved him in my direction, and we went to the dance floor. I craned my neck to see Jodie, and I spotted her—already by the snack table, chatting up Tiffani the Magic Blondifier. Who waved to me.

I gestured in return, but it was not a wave.

Channing's big, hot hand landed on my back, and I assumed the dancing position. He kept sweeping his eyes above my head. Ugh, his entire crew had surrounded us. Tracie with Dude #2, Nevaeh with Dude #4, and Kellseye with Dude #5. They got closer and closer, and Channing's hand, soggier and soggier. Their faces hung slack with grinning anticipation.

Cow poo, we hope.

A sticky heat, like that of a rotting Florida swamp, enveloped me, and I shoved him away. Breaths huffed from my mouth, wishing they could carry fire. The whole group laser-focused on me as I tried to shrink my existence into nothing. To let the black hole take me. Why, why, why, why, why? Why was I here, doing this?

I ran. In a friggin' ball gown, like Kate Hudson, I ran straight through the room and through the big double doors. Oh, thank Satan, it was cooler here in the hallway.

"Sophie!"

Jodie, thank my future kitty Satan.

"Honey, you okay?" She rubbed my back. "Ew! Was he that sweaty?"

I nodded and sank against a wall to the floor.

Tiffani trotted to us on stilettos so skinny, they seemed to bend and spring up again. I refused to acknowledge that she wore a dress exactly matching mine, except in pink. "Sophie, you're missing the proooooooom. You're supposed to dance like no one is watching, not *not* dance where no one is watching."

I pressed my eyes closed, if only to avoid having to take in the ugly hotel carpet—orange and pink, a winning combination. My teeth parted, the better to allow my tongue to give this silly sack of string cheese the dressing down she so richly deserved, and --

"Sophie," said Channing upon galloping to join our group.

I refused to look at him.

"You're real pretty in that dress. And I didn't know you were really blonde."

"Ugh, I'm not!"I waved my arm his direction. "What am I doing here, Tiffani? This is my true love?"

"Oh, you silly. Right now, you need patience, for good things come to those who listen to Tiffani, ha-ha!"

Kellseye joined us in order to release a screech heard mostly by dogs. "They're about to do prom king and queen!"

Every gaze landed on me, the way they expected every glob of cow poo to land on me.

"You have to go in, Sophie," Tiffani said with a wink. "I have a feeeeeeeeling you'll be delighted!"

"Me, too," added Tracie. The poison falling from her incisors melted a hole in the carpet, which improved it.

Jodie pushed through the crowd to offer her hand. "Come on, queen. It is your density." One side of her mouth twitched. "Get it? *Back to the Future*? Because you're Marty McFly. But with dating for some reason."

I laughed, the absurdity of my whole damn existence bubbling over, and took her hand. Jodie was my life raft in an ocean of bullshit."At least I'm not dating my mom."

"Ew!" declared Tiffani.

Jodie pulled me close to whisper, "Girl, this is a genuine do-over. You can go up on that stage, wield the smile of vengeance, and I will meet you in the wings with projectile poop so that you may enact your glorious mulligan! Or you can be the better person, rise above it all and --"

"Yeah, that doesn't sound like me. Let's do the glorious mulligan."

With a jump and a clap, she took off toward the broom closet. "See you soon!" When she was almost out of sight, I heard, "You're paying for my dry cleaning!"

It was the least I could do. Hey, maybe I'd steal the cash from Channing.

The pack of jackals led me into the ballroom so that Déjà Vu High School senior class could elect me prom queen. Channing twisted his hands together, anxiety rippling across his beefy features. Traciedamnnear danced, so delighted was she that I would soon meet my *Carrie*-riffic fate.

Except!

Nevaeh ran up, her face woo-woo-ing like an alarm emoji. She whispered something to Tracie, who shrieked.

I pressed my eyes closed, knowing that Nevaeh had likely delivered the devastating news that their offal (and awful) plan's most important part had gone missing. And then I opened my eyes, because I didn't want to miss this!

My nemesis shot me with a glare so hateful, my new blonde hair curled. I blinked wide, fake eyelashes at her, which foamed her mouth but good.

"I will now introduce your royal prom court, ha-ha!" said Tiffani, who had gone onto the stage to direct this retread of a play. "First up: Sophie Sweet!"

I tossed my Barbie locks and sauntered to the stage. Tracie, Nevaeh, and Kellseye soon joined me. The boy contestants were Channing, Dude #3, Dude #6, and one of the stars of the basketball team. Why couldn't that guy be my twuewuv? He was hilarious and handsome and didn't need cow poo to feel like a man. The guy was so tall I might need to climb him, but where there's a horny teenager, there's a way.

Tiffani fluttered around like a coked-up butterfly as the court assembled. She finally returned to the microphone, which she held onto for dear life as one of her shoes rebelled.

My stomach leaped to my throat with nervous delight. A grin burst onto my face, and I actually began to giggle, for there Jodie waited, in the wings to my left, crouched and ready for action. She wore gloves, and I admired her forethought.

The goat-demons clicked and hissed, not even whispering as they fought amongst themselves as to who had lost the "special ingredients" they'd brought. Apparently, some ingredient had gotten on the back seat of Kellseye's BMW, which her mom would "totally fucking kill her" about.

One goat-demon down.

Tiffani tittered on the mic. "Ha-ha! And now it's time to crown the king and queen! Who will it beeeeeeeeee?"

Me and Channing.

"Sophie Sweet and Channing Angelopoulos!"

Tiffani sank her claws into my tender forearm; she dragged me to the center of the stage to place the giant rhinestone tiara on my Sophie Dream Hair™. Channing jumped up and down, so yippee for him, I guess. Tracie flapped her arms and stamped her foot. I threw my head back to cackle, which made the crown fall off.

Exactly like I planned.

As I sank to retrieve it, I met Jodie's eye. She raised her brows in a question.

I nodded.

I nodded because screw Tiffani. She was not then, nor now, the freaking boss of me.

I nodded because screw Tracie and her whole crew, who had tormented Jodie from the moment she'd moved to this hellhole.

I nodded because screw rom-com heroines. I wasn't a heroine. I was a trailer park hoodlum, and nobody should leave low-hanging cow poo around my trailer-park-hoodlum self.

I scooped the crown off the ground and bolted to the wings. Jodie whooped and passed me a pair of gloves—they looked like the restaurant-worker kind, such a genius move.

Jodie grinned at me. I grinned at Jodie. Everyone on the stage yelled and stared as I yanked on the gloves with a *pop!*

With my gloved hand, I placed my thumb to my nose and wiggled my fingers. "After you, my darling."

A bloodcurdling scream rang out—Tracie, for she had seen the cooler at our feet. A mad scramble swept the stage, the popular kiddies clacking into one another like bocce balls.

"Don't do it, ha-ha?" Tiffani blurted into the microphone.

Jodie scooped into the bucket of hopefully cow poo, stood, and yelled, "For bullied Black lesbian queens everywhere!"

She let fly.

The world went slo-mo, like in a smelly Robert Rodriguez movie. Finally. Finally! I realized the benefit of revisiting the past—to put pieces of shit in their places. With literal shit. To put pieces of shit *on* pieces of shit in a movie I liked to call *Shitception.*

Sure, it was juvenile. Maybe even amoral. But so was I, stunted by the abuse I'd suffered from these jerk-faces. We couldn't go high every time they went low—the oxygen in the atmosphere runs out five miles up.

Blap! I hit Tracie's boobs with a blob of poop. Her scream instantaneously healed some of my open, oozing emotional wounds. Who needed therapy?

Splonk! Jodie winged Kellseye, and the castoff managed to land on Dude 3. They both melted into a puddle of sobs. Jodie and I raised our hands to high-five one another, but ew, poop.

I laughed so hard, I almost spilled the bucket of blood! Silly girl. I'd better dump that out.

Kellseye managed to stand, but could not run—the floor poop was too saturated. She collided with Dude #6, so she couldn't escape when I let the blood fly. *Splash! Scream!* Ooh, I'd gotten Tracie, too, who flailed on the stage like a dolphin on an ice rink.

As I gleefully tossed cow cookies with my best friend, I heard more cheering than condemnation. Nerds of all stripes—chess, math, theatre—stormed the stage. They ground the filth into the bullies' finery. They tossed the poo hither and yon, their faces awash in pent-up rage.

It was the most orderly melee I'd ever started, with only the truly guilty suffering. Even Mr. Peter Pubis, the geometry teacher, got in on the action. He'd taken a lot over the years.

Other teachers had begun to descend on the action, so I stripped off my gloves and yanked on Jodie's arm. "Time to make our great escape."

"No! I need to clock Nevaeh!" My BFF's face hardened with malicious glee. "She's always tagging me in posts about how gay people deserve to be thrown in prison and burn in hell. Eat shit, goat demon!" She threw and threw until *ploop!* Right on Nevaeh's forehead! "And your name is wrong!" she screamed. "It should be Elohssa!"

"Huh?" I grunted.

"Asshole backwards."

"Genius."

She snapped off her gloves. "Of course I am. And I will live on the sight of her poopy face forever."

A pain in my arm twisted me around. Tiffani, with not a speck of filth on her. She had a gift. "Come on, ladies. We need to escape, ha-ha!"

We fled with her, joining the throng of students streaming from the ballroom. In a flash, night air greeted us, and we kept going, around the building to the far corner of the lot, where Jodie had parked.

Everyone scrambled into the car, and Jodie wasted no time getting the hell outta Dodge.

Nobody spoke for a while. Heaving lungs quieted, and shoulders fell. Jodie shared a giggle with me, and then we let it all out, falling over ourselves, to the point where Jodie had to pull over she was cackling so hard, her cheeks ballooning like the world's cutest squirrel.

"Wellllll, ladies, that was a choice." Tiffani sat forward between the front seats. "What have you got to say for yourselves? Remember: Karma is the best revenge, besides having flawless skin."

Ah, yes, the old saying.

I shook my head. "Oh, nooooo. Are you upset that I chucked a bucket of blood at my true love?" With a very serious blink of my eyelashes, I asked, "Is that not what Kate Hudson would've done?"

Jodie pounded on the steering wheel. "Ha! Tell me—what happened at our real prom?"

I leaned back, elbowing Tiffani en route. She slid away with a huff. "Well, we made water balloons. And barbecue sauce balloons to take with us."

"You didn't." Tiffani gasped.

"I did. But my dad caught us as we were loading them into Jodie's car and confiscated them. I think he used them on the neighbor because the restraining order came soon after that. Anyway, we went to prom, we danced together, and got bullied as hell for it by those same people. You—" I stopped myself from telling Jodie that the night had ended in her tears, which had ripped my soul apart.

That's why I'd thrownpoo at these monsters without an ounce of remorse. Bullies only learned the hard way.

"We danced together?" Jodie pulled into the driveway of her house and turned off the car. "Darn it, that's the one thing we didn't do tonight."

I clapped. "Night's not over!" I leaped out of the car. And tripped on my 10 miles of skirt to hit the dirt. Jodie ran around and helped me to my feet. We ignored Tiffani, and the dirt marks over my knees, and shut the car door on her.

I extended my arms. "Care to dance, darling?"

Jodie yanked me in, her arm around my waist. "Sweep me off my spike heels, O poufy one."

We wound around the driveway, turning big, ridiculous circles in a polka/twist hybrid. Jodie laughed so hard she kept snorting, and my heart shook off the crust named Tiffani. Jodie showed off her Salt-N-Pepa, and then babied one more time. I dipped, she dipped, we dipped, as the classic song goes.

I started to sweat in earnest, destroying a second dress today. Jodie put her head on my shoulder anyway, her breaths coming fast as she sang "Only Girl (In the World)" by Rihanna, loudly, off key, and to the chagrin of not one, but two neighborhood dogs. I squeezed my best friend, the one person who truly understood me, accepted me.

"Thanks for being my prom date," she said, pulling back, her forehead glistening and her baby hairs sweated out. "I think we were clearly the most beautiful couple there. Especially once Channing looked like Victim #8 from *The Silence of the Lambs.*"

I picked her up clear off the ground. "I've got you anytime, anywhere."

"Anytime, you say?" murmured Tiffani. She sway on her stilettos, watching us.

"Go away, creeper." Ugh, she'd burst my blissful bubble of not remembering that she existed, and if she was going to prick my balloon of joy, I would prick her. Be a prick to her. Same diff. "So, I foiled your ingenious plan to screw my bully in a cheap motel room after a mediocre prom and probably become a teen mom. However will I find love now?"

"Yeah, leave her alone," added Jodie.

"Thank you, sweetie."

"You're welcome, queen."

The horrible psychic flipped her perfect hair. How was she not sweating? The humidity stood at 354%. "Ha-ha, yes! You foiled my plan." Her grin was as wide as the divide between us.

It...honestly, it made my stomach dip. Suddenly, I was a teenager again. For the second time. Third time? Panic swamped me like a hot flash, and I yelled, "I want to go back to my life!"

"Because it was so perfect."

"It was mine!" I let go of my life preserver, Jodie, to get in Tiffani's face. "Enough of this. I don't know if you have me roofied in your basement, or you're on a quest for the One Ring, but just...go away! I don't need your life lessons."

Jodie pointed a firm finger. "She can handle her business!"

"Of course." Tiffani flipped her hair and began walking down the driveway. "Have a fun sleepover, girls. Reminisce about old times. Or...now times, ha-ha!" She got to the street and click-clacked down the middle of it, her tiny steps barely gaining any ground. "See you later!" Where the heck was she going?

"No! No see you later!" I screamed. "See you never, go away! And maybe you should buy shoes you can actually walk in!"

Tiffani squeaked. "Excuse me, I am extremely talented at walking in hee--" She tripped. "Heels!"

"You sure you're not the heroine?" I muttered. "The heroine is always clumsy."

Jodie's front door opened, and Mrs. Edwards poked out her head. "You need to come in now, Jodie Edwards. We just got a call from the school that sent your father into a fit."

I gasped, "Shit."

But Jodie replied, "Nah. I'll defend us to the death! Although, hopefully, it won't come to that. Bring on the grounding."

The lecture was long, but so were the laughs once we told them exactly what had happened. The Edwards hadn't really ever known the scope of the bullying Jodie took in school; she couldn't bear to tell them at the time. Pride nearly broke my chest open; my Jodie was so brave. Tonight, she opened up. And had fought back!

At least I got to spend the night there still; if I had to be trapped in high school, there was no place I'd rather be. We both relaxed in different bathtubs, and then ate a fancy cheesecake Mr. Edwards had made. Tasted vaguely like celery and fish; one of his better efforts. After a while, the phone stopped ringing with the outrage of bad parents, and Jodie and I settled into a sleepover.

What an amazing night. A do-over that had been done better. But no amount of gross cheesecake stopped the panic from flooding my brain. If this were a horror movie, it would be over. The foes had been vanquished via poop by the beautiful, gawky heroines.

Yet something told me my adventure was just beginning—how the hell long would I be stuck in my old life?

CHAPTER SIX:
THE PRINCESS DIARRHEA-IES

Mmmmmm. The light woke me up. But…it wasn't bright. Kinda loose and easy, or however people describe light. I yawned and turned to talk to Jodie, but she wasn't in her bedroom. Something caught my hair and yanked it hard. "Ow." I reached and pulled off…a tiara? I'd been sleeping in a tiara?

I sat up. Where the friggidy-frig was I?

"Tiffani!" I boomed, because I knew. I just friggidy-friggin' knew. I patted my angry scalp. "Tiffani, get your Pepto Bismol ass in here! Where the --"

The giant gold double doors—gold—double—doors—flew open, a fancy chandelier lit up, and my nemesis trotted in like a frisky Miss America contestant. Today's ridiculata fashion was a pink ball gown dangling little spangly things and filmy, floppy sections; damn, it was way too tired in here for this nonsense! My shoulders tensed into my ears, which tensed into my brain.

The wretched devil yanked the covers off me. The duvet glinted gold, too, as did the side tables, the doodads on the side tables, the fireplace mantle. Even the actual floor had ribbons of gilding through the marble.

Shit, at least my shit was fancier in this reality.

"Darling Sophie," said Tiffani. She yanked the tiara from me and plopped it back onto my hair. "You must get ready for your training!"

Twenty-five people exploded into the room. Approximately. Eight women laid hands on me to help me out of bed with soft, yet claw-like demanding. The entire job of four of them appeared to be carrying trays of stuff for me to eat and drink.

Might as well make the best of it. "That coffee smells good, can I—may I have some?" The coffee lady intimidated me. She was fancier than I had ever been in a swanky sky-blue dress; it was sleeveless and sexy on top, and had a bell-kinda skirt. That's what all the buzzing bees in here wore. They had loose buns on top of their heads, rhinestones dotting the swirling hair. Coffee lady was short and had dark curly hair. "What's your name?"

She beamed. "Ling, your highness."

"My *what?*"

I pushed back to the gilded headboard. "*Ow.*" Some ugly freaking cherub had stabbed me. "Ugh. Tiffani, explain yourself. Now!"

The double doors slammed open again, but this time it was, "Jodie! Oh, thank God."

She also wore an enormous dress, hers with a gold sash going across it like a beauty contestant. The sky-blue looked gorgeous on her—it matched the ribbon tied around a big bun on top of her head. Super elegant in a way I could only dream of being.

"Oh, Sophie!" She hurried to my side. "Only two days 'til your wedding!" she exclaimed with a little clap.

My eyes grew three sizes, and my heart grew three fangs. Well. Three *more* fangs. I almost had a full set now.

I took a deep beath. "My fucking *wedding?*"

Tiffani clucked, "Language, Princess!"

"Yeah, I hate the 'w' word, too." Oh, boy. I went dizzy, my chest heaving, the room spinning, the bed opening up into my usual void. Black hole, table for one.

"Girl, you're hyperventilating." Jodie climbed onto the bed and sat beside me. "Ow! I hate these pokey angels. Anyway," she squeezed my hand. "It's gonna be okay. Princess Regina is going to adore you, and Tiffani and I will be right there for the press conference."

Princess Regina? *Princess* Regina? Princess *Regina*?! Oh, God. Oh, no. Oh, ew, my hands were gushing like Niagara Falls.

Tiffani slithered to my other side. "We must get you dressed, breakfasted, and ready to train to become a proper princess to the people of Ugh."

I reared back. "The who?"

"The Ughians."

I sank into Jodie. That word sounded like how I felt. "The who *who*?" I gripped Jodie's arm, and she yelped. "She didn't actually say," I whispered, "Regina," end whisper, "did she?"

Jodie blinked her big, brown eyes. "Ughians are your people here in the land of Ugh. Drink more coffee, you're really useless without it. Like you don't even know where you are. Or who Princess Regina is!" Giggling, she scooted off the bed and began ordering the blue ladies around.

They offered me fruits I'd never heard of, a robe made of spun sunshine, and enormous pastries. I reached for one of those, but Tiffani rushed in for the block.

"Nope, you must fit into your wedding dress." Tiffani sent the pastry lady away and, with her, my hopes. "Up, up! Out of bed. You know what they say, early to bed, early to rise, makes a woman's eyes less puffy."

The horrible bon-bon yanked on my forearm and dragged me damn dear off the bed! She was still stronger than she looked, which was to say, she was strong at all.

I slapped her hand and retreated to the middle of the mattress, approximately one-quarter mile away. Six of my childhood trailers could fit in here, FFS. "Stop. Stop! Next person who touches me…off with her head!"

The blue ladies gasped.

Tiffani pressed her lips together, her eyes, for once, clear of subterfuge. "The princess and I must have a chat. Wedding jitters, you know. Off you go, ladies."

"Jodie, please stay," the princess begged.

"Jodie, please go."

I stood in my golden bed, with swags of sky-blue velvet flopping all over it, stifling me, as if they wound around me, closing in like a boa constrictor. "Tiffani, hear me. Jodie stays, or else I will take a literal pissin every room in this…castle?" Her jaw dropped. "You know I will. I don't care. This isn't real life, and dignity is a luxury I have never been able to afford."

Jodie kicked off her high heels and climbed onto the bed to stand next to me. "Um…" she leaned close to my ear. "What is going on?"

"Tiffani is about to tell us." I leaned away and gave her a once-over. "Did you win second prize in a beauty contest, collect 10 dollars?"

"Second?" She gave a friendly huff and added, "This is what I always wear as your lady-in-waiting. Mostly because your father, the king, would not agree to let you put us in skin-tight leopard."

I shook my head. "That guy ruins everything."

"Ha-ha!" said Tiffani, adding much to the conversation.

With a mighty point—holy moly, look at the huge bling rock on my finger!—I said, "Explain yourself, Tiffani the Psychic-Guidance Counselor-Goodwill Manager."

"I am the Princess' Private Secretary."

I waited for more.

She blinked. Today, her eyelashes glinted with rhinestones.

I waited for more.

I stomped my foot. Or, I tried to, and then I fell over because this mattress seemed to be made of clouds. I ground out, "What have you done to me now? And if you play ignorant one more time, I will set fire to this room. Get me my lighter!" I screamed.

Ling peeked in. "Right away, Princess."

My smile's smugness could not be contained.

"Oh, Sophie. So violent, ha-ha!" Tiffani pranced to the bed, spread out her gargantu-gown, and perched on the edge. "You are Her Highness, the Princess of Ugh, a principality in Europe."

"Where in Europe?"

"Don't worry about it." Tiffani fanned her hands as she thickened the plot. "You are engaged to Princess Regina of the realm MacGuffin, and you marry her tomorrow! Isn't that romantic?"

It couldn't be my Regina, right? The stunning goddess who'd made me turn back flips for her approval? Which I had done gleefully because I'm a sucker for beautiful women who treat me like shit? One time, Jodie had asked me why I take no guff from dudes, but let ladies grind me to dust.

What a rude question.

"Realm MacGuffin," I said to Tiffani, pointedly, as if my tongue were a dagger. "Now, I wasn't the best in English class, but that sounds like bullshit to me."

Jodie said, "Oh, Princess Regina is real. This marriage has been arranged since the two of you were toddlers." She shot me a wide, expectant gaze. "Of course, if you don't want to go through with it, you don't --"

"Yes, she does." countered Tiffani. "After all, love and marriage go together like a matching lip and cheek stain."

I drained a second coffee, yet it did not reassure me the way it ought to have. My stomach still stabbed me with worry-jabs. My gaze darted around, as if Regina would pop out of the curtains or from under the bed at any moment. "What year is it?"

"Don't worry about it." Tiffani stood and fluffed up her costume. "You are Princess Sophie, you're 26 years old, and the entire castle is at your disposal."

"Great, then I can leave."

"Not like that, ha-ha!"

A new wondrous lady in a blue dress refilled my coffee, which I drained again. If only it had bourbon in it. I wiped my mouth with the back of my hand and said, "Jodie, you are going to have a difficult time believing this, but none of this is happening in real life."

Jodie squeaked and sat up on her knees. "Does it feel like a dream to you because you're so happy?" Her voice dipped. "Or a nightmare because you don't want to marry that woman? People say she's striking, but I never saw it, really. She's not gorgeous like you." She waggled her eyebrows and got a giggle out of me.

I shook my head. "Oh, boy. Tiffani, tell her. I can't bear to disappoint that perfect face."

"Ha-ha!"

My jaw set alllll the way to one side. Clearly, my threats needed to get more creative. "Tell her. If you don't, the first time I meet my future bride, I will embarrass the country of Argurgh, or wherever we are. I'll—I'll confess my everlasting devotion to Lord Fartula, the constipated Dracula I am in love with, and who will be the third in my marriage with PrincessCharm School."

"Princess Regina."

"Sure." I picked at my fingernails until one started bleeding. They'd been buffed very nicely, to be honest, until I got to them.

Tiffani sighed and bunched her mouth together into a butthole of disapproval. But she knew I would do it; I was already imagining how I would give an exclusive interview to the local paper, *Imaginary News Today*. I'd tell them about the ongoing sexy adventures of Lord Fartula, who, despite his digestive problems, possessed two of something, and they weren't in his mouth.

And so, Tiffani the Psychic-Guidance Counselor-Goodwill Manager-Private Secretary explained to Jodie why we were trapped in a rom-com. She corroborated that Ugh did not exist. In her telling of my tale of woe, she was some kind of love heroine who personally pulled me from a cesspool of, well, cesspool; cleaned me up; and saved my very existence from pathetic waste. Honestly, I perked to be described in such a badass way. Everyone knew that sullen people were the coolest.

My bestie blinked. "Um…what? But we live in Ugh! In the palace. We grew up here." She extended her arms wide. "Swimming in the sacred Spurious Springs. Picking wildflowers on Phony Hill. Galloping—wait, I'm starting to hear it."

"Yup. In reality, we went to high school in Gator Riviera, Florida."

She reared back, which was the proper response. "That place sounds fake, too."

A trickle of sweat meandered down my spine; I needed Jodie so badly to believe me. How would I convince her? I took her hand. "Tiffani, show Jodie where Ugh is on a map."

For once, the psychic sputtered. Her squirming made me horny, I reveled in it so thoroughly. Her reply was, "Uuuuummmmmm…"

"She can't!" I turned to my bestie. "Jodie, what other countries is Ugh next to?"

Her dark eyebrows came together as she counted them off. "We're on the Southern border of Pretendia, East of Shamistan, and West of Tiffani-Upon-Gucci." Her head whipped Tiffani's direction. "Hey!"

I put my thumb to my nose and wiggled my fingers. "I need you to believe me. Best-friend style. Ride or die."

She didn't hesitate for one second. "I got you." Our wiggling fingers intertwined and squeezed. "Yup, I got you. Wow. Shamistan?" She took a few deep breaths. "So…this is an elaborate fantasy orchestrated by this hot lady?"

"Awwwww." Tiffani brushed hair out of her eye. "Thank you, sweetie."

"You're welcome, hot, hot, *hot*."

My stomach churned. "*Okay*."

Jodie, her mouth wide open with rapture, clasped her hands to her bosom. Really, she would make such a better princess. A friggin' blue bird would land on her shoulder any minute now. "Wait, does that mean, Tiffani, that Princess Regina really is Sophie's carefully selected true love?"

"No!" I huffed. How could someone who kicked me out of a car, on the highway, at night, while it was raining, because I didn't "respect her choice to lie about her other girlfriend" be my true love? I pressed my eyes shut. Hadn't even dumped her after that.

Tiffani lifted one shoulder. "Of course she's Sophie's true love! It's in the plot and everything."

"Ugh," said Jodie and I in tandem. Leave it to me to be the princess of a place named after a disappointed groan.

Jodie sighed and passed me a muffin. Even in make-believe land, she looked out for me. "So, in real life, what…what's happening with me?"

"Well…" I scratched my head and ran into the tiara. Crumbs exploded everywhere—crap, the muffin was in that hand. I picked a gloop of blueberries off my chest and ate it. "You're a high school physics teacher, and your AP kids do exceptionally well on the SATs and ACTs."

She lit up. "I'm awesome!"

"Hell yes, you are. You're always awesome, in every iteration of existence."

She gave a half-bow. "Well, so are you."

Tiffani emitted the kind of scoffing noise designed to make me add a new chapter to my upcoming saga, *Lord Fartula and His Extremely Unroyal Journey to the Emergency Room Via My Nether Regions.*

"Do I have a girlfriend. Or… wife?"

I hesitated, because…argghhh. My guts churned so hard they tried to make butter. *Romance cannot happen without butter!* Tiffani had said. Somehow, I don't think she meant this disgusting feeling. Then again, she was Tiffani, the human answer to the question, "What if sugar somehow tasted like vomit?"

Jodie deserved every happiness she could carry, and more besides. However, I already despised her eventual wife. "No, but I have no doubt that princessy true wuv is right around the corner for you."

Tiffani put on her Smug Face #3. "I guarantee it."

"As long as you guarantee it." Jodie picked a piece of muffin off my lap and popped it into her mouth.

Horrible Tiffani leaned on the bed. "You must behave yourself this time, Sophie. Like I always say, 'Those who live by the sarcasm, die by the psychic.'"

"The last 'one true love' you saddled me with bullied me through high school."

"Well, Princess Regina is a wonderful woman full of darling MacGuffin courtship rituals."

Huh; the word "wonderful" apparently meant something different in Ugh. The bed seemed to fall away, so sinking was my sinkish feeling of stomach sinking. At least it replaced the gut pain. "What. Courtship. Rituals?"

"The kind you start training for now." She pointed at me from the side of the bed. "Play nice, Sophie. This will not end until you understand the value of true love. Of compromise. Of appreciating --"

"Yeah, yeah, embroider it onto a throw pillow. I gotta take a leak."

One of the side doors to the room opened. "I have the Royal Chamber Pot, Princess!" offered a courageous young woman.

My head fell off and rolled to Tiffani's feet. "Bitch, you have got to be kidding."

My torturer giggled. "Ha-ha! The water closet is that way."

I pressed my tired-ass eyes closed. "You go away now."

"I'm leaving to get your training ready." Her hot pink mouth grinned. "Ciao!"

Tiffani swept out of the room so that I could use the "water closet," because I couldn't guarantee the year wasn't 1742?

After the only relief I'd probably get all day, I asked Jodie, "Do we have smart phones in this hell?"

"What's a smart phone? Are other phones...stupid?"

I shrieked. For the second time, Tiffani's evil made me scream. No, no, why? I was a modern chick. Modern. I required a bra without an underwire (or no bra at all), Doritos, and glorious technology through which to avoid people. My fingers started to twitch, I'd gone on so long without scrolling something. No wonder my rage burned out of control—it had been days since I murdered a zombie robot with help from my band of killer racoons in a video game.

However, the number of people who exploded into the room after my scream, some of them armed, gratified me somewhat. I told one of the fellas with the giant machine gun to go arrest Tiffani. He saluted, shouted, "Yes, Princess!" and ran from the room, so one could only hope.

"Do it on video!" I called after him.

My spine sweat shifted to the front, my poor boobs going soggy with angst. I squeezed my eyes closed, trying to catch my breath. That vile Tiffani creature picked at the seams of me. Threads dangled, and my armor gaped.

And I couldn't even begin to think about seeing Regina again.

Then Jodie scooted to me and squeezed tight. I sank into her clean, sweet scent and pushed my panic down, down. I asked, "I am terrified to ask, but what kind of training am I expected to endure?"

Jodie gently pulled the tiara off me, and then petted my head. "Do it for me?"

I pried one eye open. It throbbed. "You're evil."

"I'm delightful, and you know it." She pursed her lips. "It seems to me that if Tiffani is the author of this rom-com, the only way out is through. Besides, I promise you, if Princess Regina is a rat, which she probably will be…"

"She is," I squeaked.

"Then we will blow this pop stand and set fire to everything."

Because of her infernal promise, I allowed her to drag me off the bed. I stripped and stood there shivering. I really needed that arson right about now. "Have… have you actually met Regina?"

Her one shoulder looked embarrassed as she shrugged it. "I just arrived up in this magical fantasy, and everything in my memory is a lie—from my childhood at Jurassic Archipelago to our vacations on Klingon. Gimme a break." She scrambled off the bed and clapped in a very official way. "Now, it's time to train to be a princess."

"If I'm already a princess, why do I need to train to be one?"

She settled onto one hip. "I will bean you with a tiara."

Fine! Although, if I wanted anyone to commit tiaracide against me, it would be her.

My gaggle of hot chick helpers, *I could get used to this*, ran in like a dance team to deliver me my very own sky-blue dress. The fanciest sky-blue monstrosity of them all. The top was tight and strapless, the bottom, layers and layers of netting stuff. And the underwear underneath! Pinchy and uncomfortable. I looked like a toilet paper cozy knitted by the kind of grandma I never had. Naturally, someone drilled a 10-inch-tall tiara into my hair. Then…

"Daaaaaaamn," I said.

"Yup," yupped Jodie.

Even a demon like me could appreciate the sheer volume of diamondriffic carats now dangling from my ears. They weren't my style, being giant and reminiscent of Elizabeth Taylor, but selling one would surely fund my escape to Klingon, a place where I'd always felt like I could really thrive.

Jodie, a handful of servants, and a legion of armed soldiers trailed behind me as I tripped through the halls of Ugh Castle. I fell more in these high heels than Tiffani did. Jodie somehow managed to skip in five-inch platforms, which should be an Olympic event.

After I bounced off the walls of no less than seven long, gilded corridors, my servants pushed me into a huge room. It had so many columns, it was the Sunday *Times*.

I turned to run, but my heel slid from under me, and I took out two guards on the way to the floor. From the bottom of the pile, I spied, with my little eye, someone…red-faced.

"Gezzzifhsgshuzick!" said the man, approximately. In a chartreuse track suit, he kinda complimented all the blue. *Kinda*.

"You don't order me around," I said, pushing my crown back up to vertical with one hand. "I'm a fucking princess."

Tiffani came running at that moment while emitting the kind of, "Eeeeeeeee!" a famous soprano might envy. "Sophie, this is Bartolomeo Flim-Flam, the world-famous beauty expert."

I nodded from the floor. "Sure. That all sounds very real."

Bartolomeo Flim-Flam said many harsh words in a flurry of what might be Italian. As he cursed me, I was pulled to my feet, dragged to a salon chair in the middle of the room, and deposited thereon. To my utter horror, Tiffani kneeled and buckled a chain around the chair, and then my waist. Damn. Good thing Tracie and her crew of horribles hadn't thought of this during their makeover.

And why did everyone feel the need to make me over?!

My torturer began lifting pieces of my hair with two fingers and clucking at them. Which made me grit my teeth, because the mirror told me my giant, amazing blackhair had returned! It curled over my shoulders in a super hot way, aw yeah.

He said something like, "Gjwfhueiwfhuhuihiefheuhfuhfuahu!" and slid a pair of scissors out of his chartreuse fanny pack.

"Nope." I stood. I tried to stand. I flopped to one side and gave myself the Heimlich. "My hair is perfect!" I croaked. "It's the only good thing about my appearance, you will not --"

Snip.

My vision went pure red, and I flailed my arms to grab the scissors.

Jodie came a running. "Stop! You almost sliced your wrist open!" She caught my hands and kneeled in front of me. "And there are many good things about your appearance, Princess. Great, even. Gorgeous. All of the G's! Trust Signor Flim-Flam." Her face screwed up. "I hear it, and I don't care. Besides, Tiffani padlocked the chain around your waist and took the key, you're stuck."

Bartolomeo swiveled the chair away from the mirror right as I was strategizing a way to break it with a swift kick, then hold the shards in my mouth with which to murder everyone. Except for Jodie. And my helper ladies, they were just doing their jobs.

Next was a montage of *snip, snip, Italian curses, snip, Italian jabbers, snippity snip snip,* and Tiffani *ha-ha!s.* Finally, Bartolomeo finished by using a brush to sweep away enormous chunks of my beautiful long hair from my sagging shoulders to the floor. Bartolomeo's Italian sounded self-praising as he re-deposited the tiara to my head using what felt like a nail gun.

I craned my neck to see the results of this drive-by-grooming, but Bartolomeo turned my head front and center. Also, I couldn't see anything anyway. *"Fjafjiafiojfrfiajf po hsfoijeafijsgyudyhd,"* he said, and I just nodded. He would *iafiojfrfiajf po hsfoijeafij* me no matter what I said, anyway.

To my left, a new shape emerged from behind a column; had they been there the whole time? This chartreuse shape sauntered over, carrying a large black thingie.

Tiffani flapped forward, but I couldn't escape. "Sophie! Next step in your makeover will be makeup!" She plopped a claw on my shoulder. "You super-duper need this. And perhaps a beautymask or two first? Please meet Cristofano Flim-Flam, Bartolomeo's twin brother."

I thrust out my hand and connected with something soft that made him yelp in pain. Heh heh. "Hi, Cristofano."

Cristofano walked a slow circle around my chair. Then again. "Bartolomeo, her hair is magnifico!"

"Ksgdhihiefaheufhiuf uh!" replied Bartolomeo. I still couldn't understand a damn word he said and didn't at all understand why his twin spoke amazing English, but not Bartolomeo.

And really, none of these bastards were treating me like a fucking princess! How was it that Tiffani had created a scenario where I was literally royalty—with *no* upside?

I sighed. From here on out, I would insert my own dialogue for the snarky Bartolomeo.

Cristofano tut-tutted like he was Tiffani's twin. "This one's face is a mess. We need moisture, we need radiance, we need a chisel."

"Screw you, brother," said Bartolomeo. "She is a goddess, with a butt like that of a great Kardashian."

What? Those chicks are bleeping hot. Also, I liked Bartolomeo a lot better now.

I jumped as something cold and wet slapped onto my face.

"This is a moisturizing, wettifying, fixifying mask," announced Cristofano. "Once I treated my wife with this, she was good enough to bring home to Bartolomeo."

Did they…share the wife?

Bartolomeo said, "Ah, yes—the woman-swapping sex dungeon we have going on is much improved by cold, wet mud."

The mud had warmed up, which was more pleasant, but began to…sting. My cheek twitched. "Um, by the way, my face is burning."

Tiffani spoke-sang, "No, it isn't."

"Yes, it is!" I screamed-sang. "Get it off! I'm melting likeanything I try to bake!" Burning, itching, stab, stab, stab! "Aggghhhhh, off!"

Jodie ran forward to help. Cristofano protested, but some swift movement later, he flailed on the floor while Jodie wiped the burning off my face with a wash cloth.

When I could finally breathe again, I said, "Thanks."

"You're welcome," Cristofano replied.

Jodie-shape tilted her head. "Your skin does look radiant."

Tiffani marched her away so Cristofano could work on the horrible nightmare that, apparently, was my face. I mean…I'd never considered myself a supermodel, but I didn't attract angry hornets or anything, damn.

Finally, finally, my chair turned around so I could survey the damage. "What? How?"

My hair was blonde again! Noooooooooooooooooooooohowwwwww? They hadn't even wet it!

I laugh-whimpered, for I'd been turned into Princess Diana circa 1981. Blonde hair swooped and bangs fluffed, and it was genuinely hideous. My whimpers turned into chokes as I remembered that things had…not gone well for her.

Wait—I leaned forward as far as my chains would allow. Huh. This was probably the best my skin had ever looked. I'd never known what people meant when they said "dewy," but I was damnspankin' dewy. Hey, at least the horrible hair cut 'n' color took me down a few notches, so my self-esteem failed to rise. Thank goodness.

Cristofano declared, "I'm a genius!"

Bartolomeo declared, "I should be shot!"

I agreed with both.

"Great," I agreed while pressing my throbbing eyes closed. "May I please die now?"

"Ha-ha!" Tiffani replied, which probably meant the sweet release of the grave would not save me. "Now for the rest of your hair."

Something in her tone made me sit straighter and yank against my bindings. "What hair?"

A woman, in yet another chartreuse track suit, emerged from behind yet another pillar. How many of them were there, lurking in the shadows? And what language would this one speak?

"This is my Italian wife, Niccolosa," said Cristofano.

"Howdy, y'all!" she drawled. Sure, okay. Maybe she was from Southern Italy. "I'm the waxer. Lift up them skirts, and let's get a-goin'."

I slammed my hands on the arm rests of my prison. "No!" The day I allowed myself to be assaulted with hot wax was a day I'd go to jail. Nothing wrong with a nice trim, but pain in the name of gendered "beauty" could suck my entire butt.

Quick as lightning, Jodie snatched Tiffani's keys away from her. They were on a giant ring, as if she was the evil matron of a mildew-smelling orphanage. While Jodie fumbled to find the key to my lock, Cristofano yelled, and Niccolosawaved a popsicle stick dripping with hot wax at my nethers. I kicked at them both like a lawn mower blade made of legs.

Cristofanoscreamed when hot wax landed on his arm. And chest. And face.

Niccolosa hollered, "My stars and garters!" Like, for real.

But victory! Jodie grinned and held up a shiny silver key.

In a flash, I was unlocked and wriggling out of the chain. No sense in leaving a perfectly lethal chain behind, so I backed away from the melee while whipping it in a circle, Jodie behind me.

Tiffani plopped her hands on her hips. OooOOooOOoooh, I was in trouble now.

"You must get waxed!" she trilled.

My chain still twirling, I said, "I can do what I want. And Regina can do what she wants with her body. Who are we, 20-year-old frat bros shaped by porn who can't find the clit if it doesn't have a day-glo arrow next to it?"

Behind me, Jodie cracked up. "I concur. You shouldn't even let that woman touch you if she won't respect your autonomy. And…maybe for any other reason. Who needs a wife, anyway?"

Oh, how Tiffani dramatically sighed, and squeezed her eyes shut, and siiiiiighed again. "Fine, Sophie. You win. May we please move on to the next thing?"

Victory! "Yes, O horrifying Pepto-witch."

Niccolosa, Cristofano, and Bartolomeo took themselves, and their confusing array of accents, away as Tiffani led Jodie and me to another room.

"Good. We shall now attend the ballet."

Oh, wonderful. Something snapped in me; it was far past time I started acting like a spoiled rich bitch. I clapped my hands. "Fine. Let's just get through this. Ladies in waitness, hello?"

My buddy Ling trotted forward and curtseyed.

"You seem cool. Do you want to be the princess, by any chance?" I asked her.

Her mouth fell into a shocked "O." Guess not.

"Anyway, hi. I'm going to need some rubber snakes. A lot of them. And a real one would be cool, too. Venomous." I said. Tiff began to tut, tut, and also one extra tut, so I screamed, "I'm the pretty, pretty princess!" And after that, I laughed, because I saw the value of this now. "And Tiffani—if I have to go to a ballet, we will eat Doritos Surprise there."

She gasped.

I pointed a finger full of malice. "You will eat it, too, or off with your head!" I stomped outta the room, my entourage trotting behind.

I figured there was some kinda opera house in the castle, tucked between the bowling alley and the peasant storehouse, but my posse led me outside to some grandstands. Where a ton of people began standing and cheering. Okay. I craned my neck as we went, wondering where the ballerinas were.

Jodie wound her arm through mine and whispered, "They're cheering for you, Princess Sophie."

Well, I knew this was fiction now. I laughed but, after a withering look from Tiffani, lifted my hand to wave. I did it fingers-together, like they do in pageants. And in a scooping motion, like I do when I eat Cool Whip straight from the tub.

My chest warmed to be cheered on like this. Usually, groups of people did not end up being fans of mine. I proceeded into a fancy box built in the middle of one side of the stands.

I asked Jodie, still snuggled into me, yay, "Where are the ballerinas gonna dance? The grass?"

Jodie snorted. "No, silly. It's not a human ballet. It's --" she gasped. "Oh, *no*."

CHAPTER SEVEN:
IT HOPPENED ONE NIGHT

turned to see what caused Jodie's groaning. Hooray—the Doritos Surprise had arrived! And I owned an actual throne to sit my ass in. Things were super looking up. Suck it, Mom!

I mean…suck it, Tiffani!

"Eat it, Tiffani," I ordered, for Doritos Surprise Women offered us each a golden bowl of the marvelous concoction. I employed actual Doritos Surprise Women! Maybe I had died and gone to…hmmmm. Really not sure about the answer to that. But if that place featured Doritos Surprise Women, it couldn't be too horrible.

I sank regally (mostly)and straight-backed onto my throne. Boom! Princessed. Then, Jodie and Tiffani sat on either side of me. The servants moved a long table over our three sets of knees and placed the food on top, along with golden forks and such.

Tiffani's nostrils flared. "I am not eating this, ew!"

"But it's yellowish-greige, not white."

Her bottom lip trembled.

"Oh, sweeeeetie," I said. She perked. "I order you, as Princess Sophie of Ugh, to eat it."

Jodie shook her head. "Just give in, Tiffani. It's not too bad going down. It's the going out you have to worry about. But that's later."

The look Tiffani shot us then told me that perhaps Tiffani had magicked herself out of the need to number two.

Ah, they had gotten the recipe exactly right. It was almost a lasagna, except where those long noodles would be, Doritos hung out instead. The cheese was still cheese, but spaghetti with meat sauce also layered in there. Naturally, Nerds candy dotted both the top and filled a thick middle layer. A proper recipe required 12 boxes of candy. And on the side: hot sauce!

Tiffani tried to snatch my gourmet dish away. "You have an enormous dress to put on for the courtship rituals later on," she said. "You cannot—"

"Enough!" I said, interrupting her rudely, which I was pretty sure gave my skin some additional glow. "Jodie, what is a not-human ballet?"

"A jackalope ballet." She jabbed at the Surprise with a spoon. The spoon did not puncture the candycrust. "It's a longstanding tradition."

"A…jackalope?"

"A jackrabbit with the horns of an antelope. See?"

In the direction of her point, the, er, "ballerinas" hopped onto the grass. The crowd went wild! They were so cute, hippity-hopping along, willy-nilly. There didn't seem to be any artistry to it—just adorable animals being adorable. Except for the giant horns on their heads, which felt ominous and awesome, though the blue bows around their necks balanced out the murderousness.

"Mmmmmmm!" Oh, yeah. The first bite of Doritos Surprise was always the best. Mostly because the heartburn hadn't yet begun, as well as the fact that when the whole thing cooled, it became a gluey, soggy mess of rainbow-speckled brown.

Jodie was such a bra; she ate mostly without complaint. Of course, she understood that hot was the best way to go with this stuff.

"Jodie," I said, "where do jackalopes come from?" I hadn't been the best student, but something told me jackalopes came from the same place as unicorns or dragons.

"They roam the Fraudulent Forest in packs."

Of course. "Then they don't actually exist."

"They do, of --" Her shoulders fell. "Damn it."

"Still…" I took a drink of soda, a necessary step when eating the Surprise. Helped you burp instead of explode. "They're the best dancers I've ever seen." My heart thrilled to see so many adorable cuties! "I love you, sweetie-weetie widdle jackalopes! Yay!"I gave them the applause they so richly deserved for daring to exist in a hostile world. "Oh, look— something is happening on the other side."

A group had entered the grandstands opposite us—a lady in a huge dress with a gaggle of smaller dresses.

I gasped to see her. And *yes*, it was her.

Jodie pulled on my arm. "That's your fiancée. The *other* princess, Princess Regina."

"And the other team," added Tiffani.

I closed my eyesto block out that *other* woman's gorgeousness. I'd never actually been to a ballet, but I kinda knew they didn't have teams. Right?

My team of jackalopes hopped and leaped toward the other end of the green. Awwwwww! As much as I hated people, I loved animals. They were fluffy and lovey and never made fun of my orphan-like childhood.

A shadow fell across the entire ballet, uh, field. As one, we looked up. As one, we screamed.

I pointed, like in a monster movie. Not that anyone needed me to draw attention to the hulking shapes circling overhead and blocking out the sun, but it seemed the thing to do. "What the hell are those?"

Tiffani clutched her pink chest. "Those are the Realm MacGuffinunidragons."

I didn't have to ask the next silly question, for a unidragon was obviously a fire-spitting dragon with a three-foot pointy horn on its head. The horn was rainbow, and the dragons, bright cherry red. They would look majestic and adorable both when goring me with flames…which was exactly how my relationship with Regina had ended the first time. Three of them landed on the MacGuffin end of the ballet, uh, field—the entire grandstand shaking as they did.

Munching on the Surprise kept my heart rate down, mostly because the saturated fats and salt clogged the whole works. I shoved in bite after bite as the surreal scene unfolded before me. The cute lil jackalopes hopped toward the unidragons, who squared off at the 50-yard line. Or where it would have been if this were a normal game and not why everyone in the world hated the rich.

The jackalopes made a gobble-gobble sound, which…sure. The sound made us laugh in its adorableness, and our collective shoulders fell. I'd been holding my breath for some reason, but it wasn't like my engagement was going to begin with her, uh, pets eating the shit out of mine, right?

Hmm, the Doritos Surprise was getting cold.

Jodie dropped her spoon, and I looked up from fetching it to see a stream of fire blow through the field. Jackalopes gobble-screamed and tried to hop away, but the unidragonslazily extended a few talons and SQUISH. I stood, Jodie stood, Tiffani swept a hand, and her Doritos Surprise hit the floor.

"Whoops," she said as half my jackalope corps de ballet got chomped in one fiery bite.

"Stop!" I screamed, dribbling a soggy Dorito on my boobs. "Why is this ballet so full of murder?" Jodie picked the chip off me. "Is *all* ballet full of murder?" My voice dipped to a whisper."Is that why people go? Is it just WWE with extra rhinestones?"

Tiffani shook her head. "Not this much murder. It's too bad we're losing." One of the jackalopes managed to stab the foot of a dragon with their antlers, yetits victory was short-lived. SQUISH.

"Stop. Stop!" I climbed over my throne and scurried down the steps to the railing. "Stop the murder ballet!"

The field went silent, save for my and Jodie's running footfalls. Even the unidragons stopped their attack, although one still sat on my team goalie/soloist. Rude.

I got to the grass, kicked off my pointless high heels, and carried what remained of my jackalopes away from the unidragons. There were referees, human, but they cowered behind the row of water dishes on the side. The only other person with any ovaries around here was Jodie, who snatched up jackalopes right alongside me.

The jackalope in my arms shook like a vibrator from fright, and I petted her(?) between the antlers. Which I kept having to dodge, lest I join the bloodletting. Poor thing couldn't help it.

"Regina!" I screamed to the other side. "What the hell?"

My "fiancée" stood, a goddess on Earth—tall, Black, and dripping in red finery. A cheerful laugh wafted to my ears, and then they all flooded my memory. She'd giggled the time she'd sold my comic book collection out from under me "because you need to grow up." Comic books had been my only friends for a long, long time, and I hadn't even seen a penny from the sale. She'd laughed when we spent Christmas with my dad, and they reminisced about my every failure, plus a few they made up for funsies. Being short isn't a fucking "failure"! *Why are you so upset, Sophie?* she'd asked. *I would have thought your dad loving one of us would make you happy.*

She laughed and laughed, and the unidragons attacked, and she laughed. And then she and her whole group turned to leave. Nice. Just wonderful.

With numb, shaking fingers, I petted my jackalope, who released a gobble of alarm when a shadow engulfed us. Suddenly, I shook as hard as my furry buddy, and I backed away to my side of things without peeking to see how close the burn-eyend of the unidragon was to me. The grass below me glommed with…let's just call it "mud"…so I turned and ran through the bloody muck as quickly as possible.

Yes. That's why I fled.

Heat swamped my senses, and I peeked up in time to see the biggest unidragon rear back, smoke at its nostrils. Its eyes beat down on Jodie, who trotted in circles trying to catch the last jackalope.

"Nooooo!" I screamed, sprinting between her and the monster. Terror injected my muscles with power. "Jodie, run!"

"Ack!" she yelped. The evil beast was almost on her! She shoved the jackalope under her armpit and tugged on me with her other hand. "You have to run! You're the princess!"

"I'm rescuing you!"

"*I'm* rescuing *you*!" she insisted.

We held hands, and jackalopes, and rescued one another from Reginaand the Dragon-Monsters, the worst band I've ever heard. Finally, we put distance between us and the charming behemoths of the ex-girlfriend I was obligated to marry. Frankly, the fact that Reginaimmediately murdered a bunch of my sacred pets was super on-brand.

The unidragons took to the air and flew off, probably to terrorize a snack bar, commonly known as a petting zoo. I set my jackalope down and snatched Jodie into my arms, holding her so fiercely that both she and her jackalope sounded an alarm-gobble.

I held her perfect face. "I saw that thing coming toward you, and I got so fucking—I was-- "

She managed a small smile. "Scared?"

"Can we call it something more metal?" My hands still shook.

"Aghast?"

My stomach flipped. "Use a real word!"

After a rather pointed pause full of judgmental eyebrows, she said, "How about…Predator-ed. You felt very Predator-ed."

I nodded, my hands falling. They'd turned into spaghetti. Wow, this queen knew me. "Very Predator-ed. I love you so much."

My amazing Jodie tucked her bottom lip under her top, set her jackalope on the grass, and took me in her arms. I sank into her—my soft, warm, wonderful oasis in hell.

Tiffani"ahem-ed" right next to our ears. Loudly. "Well, wonderful job, Sophie the Charming. You ruined the ballet."

My jackalope lunged for her. Good girl!

I pulled away from the person I liked to address the one I didn't. "Why would you do this?"

She shrugged. "It's tradition. And you know what they say—mildew grows on the vine of tradition."

I thought about that for a second. Hmmmmm.

"Look, just because some batshit fellas in 1462 dreamed up this nightmare in their scurvy-plague-brains doesn't mean we have to keep doing it." I snuggled my jackalope, who I'd already named Jodie Jr. in my head, and whispered, again, the question of the hour: "What the hell is wrong with rich people?"

Her lips pursed, Tiffani said, "Well, we must get to the courtship rituals now, anyway. Princess Regina is eager to see you."

"By 'eager to see me' do you mean 'eager to have her unidragonsburn me into barbecue in order to steal my royal throne for my own good?'"Regina had loved doing things for that reason.

Tiffani's pursed lips did not answer my perfectly intelligent question. She huffed, turned, and started back toward the castle, her usual graceless, wobbling walk made worse by the grass and "mud."

Good.

Jodie hooked her arm through mine and led me and the remaining jackalopes back to my princess suite, where we had a bathroom break through no fault of the Doritos Surprise. Several of my servants washed my and Jodie's jackalopes, even blow-drying them to ensure maximum cuddliness. We wanted to take a nap after, which is a normal reaction to terror and Surprise.

Jodie, Jodie Jr., Anne Listerfluff (Jodie's jackalope), and I flopped on my golden bed. Everything was so soft, so snuggly, that I relaxed for the first time in what seemed like a month.

Jodie and I faced one another, the terrorized jackalopes softly purring in their sleep between us. My eyelids drooped, but I kept fighting them because Jodie looked so pretty. Her fancy bun had loosened, and several beautiful black curls escaped to fall over her neck. I went warm all over, and I put my hand over hers. She sighed, her eyes closed, and snuggled closer. Finally, being a princess wasn't the worst.

I didn't see how I was the princess, yet everyone else ordered me around. No wonder I looked like Lady Di, who experienced something similar. Although, I hoped nobody had ever hurt her jackalope.

Much too soon, our amazing snuggle sesh was obliterated byguess who? The double doors crashed as Tiffani flung them open. "You must get ready for the press conference," she announced. "I have the official gown you must wear for the first MacGuffin courtship ritual, ha ha!"

I peeled one eye open to find her clapping above me. What was worse, the "ha ha!"'s or this new clapping habit? Jodie Jr. growl-gobbled, and I petted her for being such a good girl.

No more of this meek crap. Was I not the woman who'd harassed seven little brats until they stomped gum into my hair? Was I not the woman who'd so terrorized her gym teacher with fake cockroaches that the woman road-raged a pest control van and got arrested?

My chin lifted. I had once been a justifiably annoying asshole, and I could be one again!

"Tiffani," I began, pushing myself up to sitting.But, like, in an authoritative way."I am the royal here. I order you to leave me to my nap. And Jodie. And our jackalopes, who I'm getting super fond of. Gonna need you to build them mini-palaces for inside the main palace. Also, I'm not wearing any more official gowns, I'm not sucking up to *that woman and her murder pets*, and you can go…go…"

Jodie peeled open one eye. "Go play with a rabid unidragon?"

"That is perfect, thank you."

"You're welcome."

"Ha-ha!" Tiffani said while clapping.

The answer was both. They both made my vision go red at the edges.

Twenty-five people exploded into the room.

Here we go again.

Eight women laid hands on me to helpfully drag me out of bed, and several more sagged under their offerings—huge, impractical piles of the kind of fabric you'd see on *RuPaul's Drag Race*. But at least there were still food and drink minions, yay!

I munched on a bon-bon and whispered to Jodie, "How ludicrous is the dress I'm supposed to wear?"

She rubbed her eyes all cute-like and sat up. "It's a replica of the one worn by Queen Artificiaupon her engagement in 1734, and features a ton of skirts, whaleboning, and a cage."

There were so many horrific words in that sentence, I fell across the bed, nearly squishing Jodie Jr. I think it gave her ballet PTSD; she leaped off the bed with as snarky a look as a jackalope could manage. Pretty snarky. *Good girl.*

Of course my dress came with a cage. *Features* one.

Tiffani clapped her hands more, and a dozen blue ladies trotted in to surgically stitch the BDSM dress onto my person. I liberated another bon-bon from the nearest snack lady, even though Doritos Surprise wasn't done with my intestines.

I tried to run away, but my army of servants surrounded me, like a posh mosh pit. Apparently, my new outfit would have no underpants, since old-fashioned ladies didn't wear them? I guess babies needed to be made somehow in the time of no deodorant and weekly baths.

A nightgowny thing got thrown over my head while cool air blew up my bits.

Next, they put white stockings on me, held in place with a ribbon tied over the knee—the snobby version of tall 70s gym socks. The shoes were pointed in front and open in back. Short heels, so at least that was something. They were almost modern; except they were gold and lined with what looked and felt like hay.

My skirt was next, a giant bell thing. Pretty, honestly, although so not me, and I refused to compliment any of this crap. Jodie ooh-ed and aah-ed for me. It was cream-colored, with floral patterns stitched on in golds and blues. And heavy. No wonder women in the past frowned in all their paintings.

I sagged under the weight of three-hundred-year-old oppression.

Jodie pressed a corset thing to my stomach. I closed my eyes and thought *do it for Jodie, do it for Jodie.* Then, one of the blue ladies stuck a long piece of wood down the front. Wood! I weebled like a wobble. "What the hell, I can't bend."

Tiffani helpfully explained, "Ladies don't bend. They float, they giggle, and," she batted the bon-bon out of my clutches, "they decline dessert."

My poor bon-bon! It had been caramel, RIP. "Is that a pithy saying?"

Her chin tilted. "Benjamin Franklin, I think."

The laces down my spine yanked me backward, powered by a masochistic maid, and it took four pairs of hands to keep me upright. "I can't breathe!" I gasped. "I'll never mock a fainting woman in an old-timey book again," I gasped some more.

Jodie knocked on my tit-plank. "Maybe they passed out to get away from Princess Regina."

"They certainly couldn't run. And hey—I thought you were supposed to be encouraging me."

Her eyes went devilish. "Encouraging you to what?"

I considered that. "You're right; let's keep it open to whatever madness inspires us."

Oh, no. A dark shadow fell over me. I grasped at my corset. "Isn't this the cage?"

"Unfortunately…" Jodie trailed off, grinning.

I tried to sag, but my clothes wouldn't let me anymore. "You're enjoying this, you witch."

"I'm enjoying that I'm wearing a bra made this century." Her eyebrows puckered. "Whatever century it is."

The thing loomed closer. The giant, wooden thing that looked like the skirt version of a dog kennel. It stuck out two feet on either side of me, and suddenly, I was cosplaying as a couch. A maid I would soon throw in a dungeon belted it around my waist to a hole three sizes smaller than my physical dimensions. Tears sprang to my vision. "How did women not be constant serial killers back then?"

"No HBO to inspire them." Jodie set her cool forehead against mine. "It's only for the press conference. Then, I'll get you mac and cheese and the snuggliest flannel I can find."

"But Lady Jodie," protested the corset asshole. "There are four outfits for the four events scheduled for today. None of them are made of peasant flannel." Her eyes went wide. "They do get progressively tighter, if that helps."

"No, it doesn't help!" Jodie shoved her out of the way, ran into my left-side cage, bounced, and made her long way around me. "Not much more, girl. Just your inner pockets, second petticoat, fichu neckerchief, gown, and then we'll sew the ruffles onto your sleeves."

I glared at her, my face as pinched as my body, which had already gone numb. "Please tell me I have a booze maid."

A hand raised over the crowd.

I waved her over and looked down. "Would a flask of whiskey fit into my inner pocket? Wait—'inner pocket' isn't code for 'vagina,' right?"

Jodie grinned. "I have a feeling today's gonna go very, very well."

* * * * *

I requested a crane to drop me into the press conference, rather than me having to waddle there, but Tiffani threatened to push me onto my back. She fully knew I would flail like a turtle if that happened.

After I bounced off the walls of literally every corridor, my gaggle of servants pushed me into a huge ballroom. A hundred chairs filled the center; even they were gold-colored. At the close end of the room sat two thrones.

Not gonna lie, I did perk at the thought of my own *throne*. Of course, no one saw me perk, since my spine had been immobilized. My fancy ass-perch was all red velvet and scrolling doodads. I would have preferred a sword-chair, like in *Game of Thrones*, but in a pinch.

I bee-lined straight to the throne without the arm rests, for I stood as wide as I was tall. Ahhhhhh, I sank into it, my breaths coming deeper at last. Just the walk from the bedroom, down the stairs, down the other stairs, and into this column room had winded me because the patriarchy decided thar air going into my lungs would make me uppity.

"No, no! Get up, Princess." Tiffani flapped her hands at me. "Those are not for you."

I did not get up. "Who the hell are they for?"

"They --"

"Am I not a princess? A pretty, pretty princess? Why does no one worship royal people in this delusion?" I fluttered my eyelashes. "Am I not wearing 80 pounds of pain and deserve to rest on my exalted ass?"

Trumpets blared, and I jumped near out of my cage. An imposing door to my right slowly crept open, and I forgot about the non-groveling happening to me. Regina. I would soon see Regina. Who had dumped me by moving to San Diego without actually telling me until I discovered half my furniture was gone.

Tiffani yanked me to my feet, and, because of my oxygen-deprived brain death, I couldn't seem to fight her. I lurched forward until Jodie caught me.

Jodie propped me to the left of the thrones. A bunch of manly servant men streamed through the side door. In a screaming shade of red, like a river of blood, they circled behind the thrones, and then stood at attention, giant golden guns at the ready.

Awesome. My stomach fluttered like I'd eaten Surprise again. I usually wanted to play with any giant gun I saw (Florida girl, what can I say?), but these fellas just made me feel...trapped. Or maybe that was my many cages.

Next, the double doors at the end of the room opened, and a throng of people poured through to sit in the audience chairs. A flash went off.

Tiffani put a stop to that. "No photos yet!"

Yet.

I turned to Jodie. She cleared her throat.

"Jodie," I began in a tone like that of a mighty lioness growling at another ridiculous psychic lioness' shenanigans.

My bestie licked her lips and avoided my gaze. "This was orchestrated without my knowledge. It's…tradition."

"*What's* tradition?" I whispered, my voice shooting into "only dogs can hear it"range. My BFF danced on her feet and admired the ceiling. "How do you know it's tradition if you have no knowledge?"

Her eyes went wide and wild. "But she's so persuasive! She guarantees your true love, or I get $20." She leaned closer. "I figure we'll ditch the dragon princess, steal the $20, and go to the movies."

I nodded. "Good plan."

"You do the stealing," she said.

"Naturally. It's the least the white friend can do."

The journalists (I'm guessing) filled the audience quickly. None of them held smart phones but took out pen and paper and cameras. Actual film cameras. Freaking TV cameras filled the space behind the chairs.

My heart went positively vomitous at the possibility of meeting my unidragon-wielding ex slash current fiancée. Somehow, every moment of my life's loneliness gave me more satisfaction than this bullshit parade. It wasn't real. None of this was real.

So why couldn't I catch my breath?

More trumpets! Blaring! Blare, blare, blare! Where were they coming from, though?

I was still searching for the invisible orchestra, and clutching my thumping heart, when a red carpet rolled from the side door all the way to the front of the thrones. Pompous people streamed onto the carpet, an entourage that matched in both hue of red and angle of upturned noses. They spaced themselves behind me, between the thrones and the machine gun men.

My entourage consisted of a woman who'd commandeered one of the photographers to perform a very special episode of *America's Next Top Psychic*.

The room began to go…gray at the corners. Oh, good. A rage stroke. I shut my eyes to make all the freaking people go away. They were giving me the sweats. Not that anyone would know; I wore more layers than an onion. Jodie started talking to me from far away, like the mystery trumpets.

"Sophie!" She stood right next to me now. "You're hyperventilating. Let me… let me loosen your laces. Tiffani, come here please!" she added, practically in song.

My lungs expanded a quarter of an inch, a cool wave splashing over me. Tiffani took one of my hands in hers and proceeded to *slap, slap, slap*it, as if it had fainted like a woman in a gothic novel. Jodie threw her arms around me from behind, keeping me upright. I leaned into her, gratefully, blinking to clear my vision.

Wish I hadn't.

Ten dancing women, er, danced, from the side door, down the red carpet. They wore the red, too. Sort of. The bikinis didn't cover much, but the waist sashes were 90% see-through, so all in good taste. They twirled and tossed red rose petals upon the carpet, upon the enraptured journalists, and at my face.

No, no, *this* was the rage stroke.

I slid sideways as far as my rib cage could go—well short of the side of my skirt. "Jodie, why does my eternal love snookums need a harem of dancing women in order to walk into a room? Am I marrying the lead in a vaguely gay 1930s movie musical?"

She snorted.

Tiffani groaned. At least she stopped assaulting my hand.

I jumped when the trumpets gave their mightiest blat yet.

"Here she comes!" squeaked Tiffani. She could not resist adding a joyous, "Ha-ha!"

Wonder Woman sauntered through the door. Tall, gorgeous, and maybe one of her unidragons qualified as an invisible jet. Regina. She never didn't take my breath away, which may have actually been panic. I had to give it to Tiffani—Reginawas hot. The kind of hot that unknotted my shoulders, for they were the most shallow part of me. Well, maybe not the *most* shallow. But those bits were hidden under so much clothing, they may not actually exist anymore.

She had copper-brown skin and a smile that shone with straight-toothed perfection every time a camera flashed. The dancing ladies sighed, together, right on cue, and kneeled on either side of the red carpet. Yet my beautiful ex did not deign to gaze upon them, for her eyes locked with mine. I couldn't break away, they bored into me so.

Unlike me, in my dress the size of Ohio, she wore a super modern militaristic red suit, black high heels, and a black button down done all the way up. Box braids encircled her head, creating their own crown. She also wore a fancy gold crown that super complimented her skin.

"She's not that great," Jodie whispered. Her nails dug into me. "And remember all the jackalope murder?"

"I like jackalopes," I murmured. I almost said, "Remember when she would never just let me be in the bathroom by myself, because I was 'probably hiding something' from her?"Regina would burst in at random moments and then just stand there, watching, no matter what I was doing. She'd taken the lock off my bathroom door, and I had no idea when it even happened.

"I don't mind the dancing girls, though." Jodie shot me a leer, and I broke out my first smile of the day. "Is it empowering if they're dancing for a lesbian?"

"Who cares?"

Behind the beautiful lady came trotting an equally beautiful dog. An enormous shaggy beastie, like the kind who deliver booze to tired mountain hikers. He bounded onto the smaller of the thrones.

I set my hands on my hips and spluttered. I didn't get a throne to rest my forty-pound dress on…because of Regina's dog? The furry asshole didn't even offer me one ounce of rum!

Suddenly, Regina stood before me. And over me. Wow, I'd forgotten she stood so tall! I suddenly fought the urge to anxiety-burp and anxiety-pee, like the fine anxiety lady I was. Ugh, I dug into my itching side as she bowed.

"Princess Sophie," she said in her marvelous Disney heroine voice.

My eyes could not seem to settle on her but skidded across her marvelous cheekbones like a beam of adoring light. "Um," I replied. And scratched. "Hi there." I nodded. So far, so good. "Hello, Regina."

Tiffani whisper/screamed, "*Princess* Regina!"

Nope.

She laughed. "It's easier when one speaks MacGuffin. But you never were much one for good grammar, huh Sophie?"

"Woof!" said the dog on his throne.

Sure.

Regina chuckled some more, and it was so good-natured, my mouth tilted upward on its slutty own. We stood there, two giggling, star-crossed lovers; her entourage; the press; and the partridges and palm trees on my dress, the theme of which confused me.

"I'm so glad to see you, Sophie," she murmured, extending her hand for me to take. "I have no idea why you ghosted me."

I ghosted *her*? She'd stolen half my life when she disappeared! And all of my bank account. I'd gotten evicted and had to live in my car for six months. Oh, God, this dress was strangling me. My breaths came too, too fast. Okay, five months; eventually Jodie had figured it out and moved me in until I got back on my feet.

I gave Regina a once-over. "How is it you look like a modern military layout for *Vogue*, and I'm dressed like some character from *Dangerous Liaisons* who dies of VD?"

"Ha ha!" screamed Tiffani.

Regina smirked. "I'm dressed for the official mating dance, of course."

My gaze leaped up 10 feet to meet hers. "What dan-- "

Regina stepped back and bowed again. The press shot to their feet in unison. Trumpetey-classical music wound up, *from freaking where?* I tried to find Jodie, but Tiffani the Jerkface hustled her off to the side.

And nobody had taught me any damn stupid damn damn crap dance!

While I sweated brand new onion sweat, all the things I hated to do in public flashed before my eyes:

- Singing

- Dancing

- Talking

- Mating

- Whatever the hell this was.

But Regina had been born to do whatever the hell this was. While I stood there, my arms flapping in panicked spasms, she stepped to the right. She clapped. She stepped to the left. She clapped. "That evil cow," as Jodie dubbed her, circled until she arrived beside me and my open mouth. With a sexy grin, she turned again to arrive behind me. I craned my neck to see what came next... hopefully not a hungry unidragon, but with Regina, you never knew.

Her next move was amazing. As in, it amazed me that she reached one long arm way up, yelled, "MacGuffin!" and spanked my ass to the beat of the camera flashes.

They really definitely should have taught me the dance. Because I was pretty sure I wasn't supposed to turn around and kick the shit out of her.

I liked my version better.

CHAPTER EIGHT:
1613 GOING ON 1630

The room sucked in such a collective gasp, I swayed from the air current. Everything went silent, with one lone trumpet *blaaaaat*-ing to a pathetic end.

Clickity-clackish echoed Tiffani's furious heels on the marble. "This is the official mating dance of MacGuffin!" she informed me, her nails digging into my elbow flounce.

"Then you should have taught it to me," I replied through clenched jaws. "Or at least supplied me with some kind of butt shield." See, I was *so* trying—this was my best version of a smile, a baring of teeth reserved for catcallers and ass-slappers. "And dearest Regina," I hisspered to my true love, who'd barely swayed from my assault by foot, "if you ever hit me again, I'll stab you in the face in your sleep after our blessed nuptials."

She clapped, and I reared back, expecting my very own "guards, seize her!" moment.

But…she grinned and bowed again. "Princess Sophie is right!"

This new gasp sent me careening sideways. Jodie caught my cage and righted me.

"This courtship dance has been a tradition in my royal family for centuries, and it belongs back there, centuries ago. She is *right* to object. And her *right foot* isn't bad, either."

Everyone clapped.

"I --"No. I balled my fists. I refused to play Regina's fucked up games anymore. Or Tiffani's fucked up games. No more fucking or upping!

I waddled over to the throne, snaked my finger through the dog's ruby-studded collar, and gently led him in the direction of the other seat. "Come on, fluffy sweetie-boy." With minimal droolage, he leaped over the arm rest to land on the taller throne. "Aaaaaaah," I moaned as I fell on the furry chair he'd almost offered. "Thank you, wonderful doggo baby." While digging in my uber-pained side with my thumb, I searched amongst the extreme floof to see if he wore a name tag.

Regina, still smiling with that fabulous, damn her, face, said, "This is the Archduke Bogus. He is a MacGuffin Shepherd."

I sank into the cushy velvet, not even bothering to address that nonsense, which was frustratingly adorable. "Good thing you haven't fed him to a unidragon."

The press stood, visibly enraptured, and followed the princess' every step with pure worship. Regina always affected people this way, which is why no one but Jodie had ever believed the stories I told about her. Gah, she was majestic AF, and I was pretty sure I wore the same stupid look on my face I'd plastered on the entire year of our so-called relationship. Damn it. Damnher! Damn Tiffani most of all.

I buried my burning, sweating face into the doggo's luxurious fur. Ostrich-style hiding was my only option. I'd only just shoved Regina into the dark recesses of my black hole. I'd even found someone nice after her—Earl! Whom I'd run away from because he was too good for me.

In conclusion: I was amazing at dating. Clearly.

"I want to thank Princess Sophie," said *Princess* Regina. "For teaching us a valuable lesson about traditions, which are, well, basically guilt trips from dead relatives, right?"

I burst into laughter, and my hand shot up to cover my mouth. Oh, hell, I'd forgotten she was witty.

Regina had heard my laugh anyway, damn her doubly, and bent onto one knee before me. She put on her angelic face—the one she wore when I got too close to "I've had enough of your shit.""Some traditions deserve to die. That dress must be heavy, my dearest Sophie."

The press went wild for this basic human noticing of my discomfort. Wasn't society grand? I was forced to wear a torture device for the entertainment of the masses, and Regina could magnanimously wave it away and be lauded as a heroine…when she was the reason I'd been caged in the first place.

Still, she performed her role so sexily. Well. I meant so *well*. I twisted my hands in my lap.

One of the reporters in front stood. "Princess Sophie!" he called.

"Yo."

Tiffani uttered an incoherent squeaking sound. It made my mouth twitch in a suspiciously happy motion.

"Do you intend to take a stand for women's rights once you are Co-Queen of MacGuffin?"

So many of these sentences today were ominous in their ridiculata. "Is - -"I scratched at my sore spot more. Was…was I bleeding? The pain loosened my tongue, which didn't take much, let's be honest. "Is that some sort of *stand* I must take? 'Women are humans, *claimed* one of the woman queens controversially.' What the hell is wrong with --"

"What she means to say is --" Tiffani began.

I didn't bother to listen. What the hell kinda princess would I ever make? This kind of attention and adoration from the masses—it just wasn't me. I didn't deserve it, anyway. Look at these people! I sank my fingers into Archduke Bogus' magnificent body of fur and amazed at the glam surrounding me; even the reporters were gilded. Sooner or later, the, um, Ugh-ians would figure out I was nothing but a hoodlum from Gator Riviera, Florida, whose mother and father played a masterful game of emotional "not it."Regina's words. Said to me on my birthday.

Nobody had ever wanted me, really. Except for video games and Jodie.

Tiffani screamed, "Let us proceed to the next courtship event!"

My, er, *intended*, added, charmingly, "A costume change is in order."

"That was the whole dance? A few circles, followed by a little woman-spanking?" I asked. "Sure, okay. Well, I have to go do more female things now, anyway, like clothes and bleeding."

Everyone laughed.

Note to self: Speak the truth, and no one will take me seriously. I was merely a woman, after all.

I rocked forward, my arms flapping, and slid off the throne. My side spasmed, and then I kept falling. Jodie caught me by one armpit while I tried to get my feet under me. My guts were so squished, my regular center of balance had twisted into my center of flail.

She's beauty! She's grace! She hates your fucking face! Princess Sophieeeeee.

Tiffani saw me drifting aft, and she couldn't have that. "Can't have that," she declared, pushing me forward. She plopped my hand on top of Princess Regina's—mine stuck straight out to starboard to escape the diameter of my dress.

Do not notice how soft Regina's hand is, do not notice how soft *Regina's hand is.*

"Bye, Archduke, my sweetie snugglekins," I said to my favorite citizen of MacGuffin. "You're much better than her other pets, you gorgeous fur angel. Stay strong, dude!"

He made a groaney sort of noise and laid down. Same, perfect pupper. Same.

And so, we began a stately walk down the red carpet, toward the next courtship ritual. Perhaps my teeth would be examined, like a mare for sale. Or the princess would haggle with Tiffani over how many goats I was worth. Or some other, third thing, involving misogynistic animal comparisons.

Once we arrived, er, backstage, in yet another amazing room—this one with fat, painted babies frolicking around the ceiling panels—approximately 800 minions in red flocked to us.

Regina lifted my hand to kiss it, which gave me a weird shiver full of a dozen conflicting feelings. Felt far too intimate, since my hand was one of my only parts not covered in excessive clothing. Being a lady, I grunted and snatched it away.

"So what fresh hell is next?" I asked. Had to get through this. Had to get away from Regina.

She laughed that music-laden chuckle of hers. "Well, perhaps your private secretary can explain. I must..." Regina faltered for the first time, licking her lips and blinking in a manner that made my pits sweat. "It's for your own good!" she added brightly.

I shrank from her, pure terror oozing down my spine. That's what she had said the time she abandoned me at her other girlfriend's house to babysit that asshole's six cats for two weeks while they vacationed in Italy. And I'd done it. I dug into my side with numb fingers. It wasn't the cats' faults.

"Do I at least get to take off this cursed dress?" I muttered.

"Yes!" She blurted it waaaay too loudly, then beelined for the exit at the other end of the fat babies. "No historical dress for the next part. You're the best, Sophie!" Oh, yes, I was always the best.

And then she was gone.

"Good," I said. "Um, how do I get to a place where I can rip this thing off? Follow-up question: Is it the same place where we will set it on fire?"

Tiffani came flapping by. "Oh, Sophie. As I keep insisting, you're sooooooo funny." She began leading me somewhere. Jodie ran to the other side of me. "Now, for our next ceremony, remember the old saying: Purity makes the heart grow fonder."

There it was. My sinking gut again. How did my stomach keep falling? It was already located a mile beneath the castle, getting chummy with the bones of other wayward women burned to death by their toxic ex-girlfriends' unidragons.

We made it back to my mansion-like bedroom, and blue minions went to work on my laces right away. As they loosened, bit by bit, my lungs found their purpose again. The cool air rushed to my brain, which fired with grateful glee.

My head shot up, because my brain had finally understood the words being thrown in my direction. "*Purity* makes the what*what?*"

Oh, thank goodness, my horrible corset came off. Felt like an hour later when the dozen ladies in blue stripped the rest of the gown away, down to the nightgown thing next to my skin.

Jodie hurried into the room, snatched the corset, and said, "Light the fireplace."

"I love you," I told her.

"You're bleeding!" she replied.

Yup. That's what love was, at least with Regina.

I snatched up the nightgown to view an angry wound in my side: red, oozing, stinging. A nurse blue lady leaped into action, pressing alcohol to the seeping place, and I hissed.

Jodie sat on the bed and turned the corset thing inside-out. "Oh, my God," she whispered. "The boning in this is as sharp as a knife! It stuck straight into your skin." She swooped in for a fierce hug. When she pressed my overheated face into her cool neck, it was the singular best part of this courtship dance so far. She rubbed my back and told me she would take care of everything. I knew she would. Of all the people here constantly assuring me I was happy and content, hers was the only word I believed. Felt like a sleepover. Just the two of us, nothing but snuggled warmth and acceptance.

The nurse applied a big bandage and pressed my hand to it. Meanwhile, I yanked the under-dress over my bits.

"All pain, all gain," advised Tiffani the Torturer. "Now take off your shift, lie back, and think: Ugh."

I blinked. I sat. Taking off my "shift" would leave me only in stockings. I narrowed my eyes. "Why?"

"I told you, ha-ha!" Tiffani clapped again, and several men stormed into the room. They wore long, red robes with giant gold tassels and enormous beards .I swear, the invisible orchestra started playing The Imperial March.

I clutched my remaining clothes and scrambled to my knees behind Jodie. "Is this something new? Am I in the wonderful wizarding country of Whoops?"

"Princess Sophie of Ugh," boomed the wizard man with the most tassels. His beard was so straggly, he'd be the king of Coachella. "The next courtship ritual is the Confirming of Purity. We shall check for virginity, reproductive health, and make sure you have good, solid teeth for smiling—a very important job for a queen."

Everyone nodded. Tiffani clapped.

"You will lay down for examination now," continued the man from 1630.

"Wait, wait, wait." I waved my arms, thought better of it, and settled my hands over my bits. "Why do I need to be, um, 'checked' for virginity? To marry a woman?"

"Yeah," Jodie said. "No need to enforce patriarchal ideas about the hymen when there will be no penis involved. Or, you know, even when there is one."

"What she said," I agreed.

Oh, but the wizard men clucked and shook their disapproving beards. "It is the law."

"It is the *stupid*," I said.

"What she said," Jodie agreed.

I clutched her and blurted. "I have to take a piss!"

Jodie slid sideways off the bed, pulling me with her. She backed up, slowly, shielding me behind. We knocked the bedside table, but kept going. "Yes…" she said, the growl in her voice the only thing between me and a very ladylike hysteria. "The princess needs to…take a giant piss. You wouldn't want her to do that in the middle of her not-misogynistic-at-all examination, right?"

The red wizards' beards curled in dismay.

"Right," Jodie agreed with herself. We were almost at the side door now. "So we'll just go freshen up…and return really soon."

"Use the chamber pot," ordered wizard number two, whose beard was a horrible shade of orange that did not enhance the red of his outfit.

"No!" I screamed. "It's—number two. Like you. And I'm so very shy." I reached behind me, turned the knob of the door, and pull—pull— "Holy crap, this thing is heavy. That's why I have servants, right?"

"Yes, Princess!" Ling the Wonderful rushed to heave the door open. "By the way, Princess," she whispered. "I put the items you requested in the bathtub. That seemed like a good place." With no further explanation, she closed the door behind Jodie and myself.

We heaved a sigh of relief.

Wow. I could marvel at this bathroom all day. It was legit bigger than the trailer I'd grown up in. And pink. Pink fucking tub, pink fucking sinks, pink fucking vision as I sank to my knees, and…

Pink fucking frolicking jackalope wallpaper. Woulda been cute in black.

"No, no despair." Jodie joined me on the floor and took me by the shoulders, her perfect brown eyes boring into mine. "I was a little worried this whole thing would go south."

"What tipped you off? The Anne Boleyn Memorial Beheading Ceremony at 3p.m.?"

She snorted. "I love you. Maybe when they showed me the dress. And the ass-slap dance. Also, I saw the wizards loitering around the hall."

"They're creepy as hell," I gasped.

"Hell, yes." She wiped a tear from my cheek.

"And…Regina," I whispered.

Jodie cleared her throat. "And Regina," she said in an altogether darker tone. "Don't let her do her—she's basically your mother. You don't deserve her emotional abuse, and you never did."

I sat straighter. "You remember her?"

Her eyes went far away. "I remember the feeling she gave me, which is pure, unbridled hatred, like what happens when I receive an unsolicited dick pic."

Yup, that was Regina.

Crap. I didn't cry. I never cried. But for some reason, being kidnapped, threatened by a unidragon, stabbed by a corset, sexually harassed by an ex I still wanted to please, why???, and threatened with assault by a bunch of gross old men made me go mushy. I blinked, and another tear fell. Dammit. I turned my face toward the pink fucking floor.

Jodie crawled over to a cabinet and slid something out of it. A bag. She hefted it up and grinned. "Wanna jet?"

CHAPTER NINE:
MY BEST FRIEND'S ESCAPE PLAN

Jet, space shuttle, whatever you got," I begged Jodie. I managed to smile and breathe. "What the hell is wrong with Tiffani? How the hell am I supposed to love some terrible ex who sends creeps to creep on my vagina and sets jackalopes on fire? Why the hell in hell hell?" I ended my intelligent rant by stomping around the pink bathroom.

And then I saw the items I'd requested! Oh, wow, a boatload of rubber snakes lined the bottom of the bathtub!

"Hooray!" I ran toward my fakey snakies and fell to my knees. "It's been so long since I used rubber snakes for evil." I scooped a whole load of them in my arms to hug them close. They came in different colors! Black and blue and yellow and…I fell backwards onto my ass. "Oh, my God, that red one is moving!"

Jodie hurried over and let out a squeak. "Yikes! Well, you did ask for a real one. A venomous one."

"Ling is good! Maybe I should have requested a cage, too."

We nodded at each other.

Jodie backed away from the tub and returned to her bag. She tossed some things in my direction. "Back to our previous discussion, I have no idea why the hell in hell hell." She handed me something—my battered white tee shirt with the Heart band logo. *Yesssss.* "But I agree." Jeans! "This whole thing is bullshit." And a red leather jacket.

I traded the rubber snakes for the jacket and cradled it to my less-than-maidenly bosom. "What do we do now? We're stuck in a bathroom." I leaned over to peek in her bag. "Did you bring my brass knuckles?"

She passed them over, and I finally stopped flop-sweating and stomp-stomping. I threw off my shift-thing and stood, the cold of the bathroom goose-bumping my everything.

Jodie blinked, stared, started to say something, stopped, giggled, and stared at the floor. "Um, here, uh, here are your jeans."

I tore off the gross stockings and shoes and grabbed the jeans. The wonderful jeans! I guess underpants were not to be found anywhere in this reality. Fine with me. And yay—no bra. "I wonder how we get out of here?"

"Here are your Vans." She gave me a brand-new pair of the black-and-white checked slip-ons.

"Where did you get this stuff? I mean—this is my real Heart tee. Its holes are in the right places."

"A real-i-*tee*," she punned. Brilliantly. I applauded her.

Jodie chewed on her lip. "Well, "she sagged against the pink fucking cabinets. "When we returned from the first disaster just now…"

"You mean the jackalope slaughter?"

"Yes, the jackalope slaughter. I figured I had to rescue you. And that we'd need clothes." She stood to begin changing herself. "Somehow, I sorta…*knew* exactly where that stuff would be. In the bathroom. Everything I wanted, including the brass knuckles."

She removed her silly Ugh outfit and stood there in an adorable blue matching bra and panties. This woman took my breath away. Loveliest thing in this whole horrible fancy place. I could barely swallow. She stepped into a jumpsuit—it was rust and white mud cloth and buttoned in the front.

My own outfit assembled, including the knuckles plus several snakes stuffed into my jeans, I faced her. "So, you imagined what you wanted, and it just appeared?"

Her eyebrows came together. "Uh-huh."

I nodded. "Maybe we can imagine ourselves a way out of this bathroom. And maybe a hook for that snake."

Bam bambam! Someone banged on the door. We jumped in unison like the kindred spirits we were. "Do you require assistance, Princess?" Sounded like one of the wizards.

"Nope!" I yelled. "I'm pooping! And peeing! And maybe getting a period!" Why was I constantly lying to assholes about poop problems?

"Extreme lady stuff, piss off!" added my lady-in-waiting.

There was a grunt, a thump, and no more sounds. Heh-heh.

Jodie pulled me to the opposite side of the room. "Where would we like a door to be?"

My shoulders loosened; I actually, finally, started to have fun. I surveyed the bathroom, even though the fucking pink made my eyes bleed. "Not that way, because on the other side of that wall is my dressing room, right? Which connects to the bedroom."

"Correct. Bedroom equals bad."

"Yes. So, maybe this wall…" I proceeded that direction, "which leads to…"

Jodie shook her head. "That's Tiffani's suite."

"Of course it is. The better to kidnap me." I flapped my arms and invoked the name of my mighty country. "Ugh! The only other wall is the outside of the castle. Shit, we're stuck." My urge to adultly stomp began to rise.

"No, we're not." She hurried that direction—the bathroom was huge—and eventually arrived at the outside wall. "Because there is no window this direction. Therefore, I imagine there's a secret passageway between the outside wall and the castle's rooms. One that will take us downstairs, around the castle, to the back garden. It's what I would do if I'd built this place."

My feet danced with happy instead of stomp. "I pick up what you're putting down. Yeah, I also imagine your imaginings." I surveyed my toilet-ey dominion. "I think when I put this pink fucking candle in this pink fucking sconce," hope lifted my arm, "the secret passage will be revealed. *Put ze candle back!*" With that invocation to Mel Brooks, I put the candle --

The wall slid sideways!

"Holy shit!" Jodie jumped with glee.

Bam bambam! "Princess Sophie!" sang Tiffani. "We have a schedule, ha-ha!"

"Didn't you hear me?" Jodie replied. "She's taking a holy shit!"

I dropped to my knees and searched under the sink—there was my snake hook! I slid it out and approached the tub. Carefully, I rescued a bunch of rubber snakes to take with us in the bag. Then, I scattered rubber snakes across the floor while Jodie giggled in the open doorway to the passage.

"Be careful," she urged me as I went for the real snake.

"It's okay," I whispered. "I imagine that this snake will not bite either one of us, for he loves us."

The red fella slithered to the top of the heap and…smiled?

Awwww…back at ya, snakey.

With my hook, because safety first, even in pretend-nonsense-land, I placed him right in front of the door to the bedroom. "Guard our escape well, snake friend."

He replied, "You got it, Princessssss!"

OMG. "Let's take him with us!"

"No!" Jodie shook her head and yanked me into the passage. She grabbed her magic bag of wonders and followed behind me. As we crossed into the narrow hallway, the wall behind us slid closed.

"By the way, I very much approve of your filthy fucking mouth," I whispered to her in the dark. The hall was chilly, so I instinctively scooted closer to her warmth.

She set her head on my shoulder. "I do as my princess commands," she said elegantly. "Bitch."

I snorted. She snorted. And, for the briefest of moments, the whole bizarre, fake world went away. It was us at the movies. Or on the beach in the wee hours. The darkness blocked out the unnecessary, the unwanted. Funny how I usually, well, *willed* myself to feel safe. Because only losers run around weeping like a coward when life is a pile of rancid garbage. But here, with nowhere to hide, I knew that Jodie was my safe space, even when she wasn't around. Merely the thought of her made my heart hurt less.

I took my Jodie's hand. Probably too hard. We just stood there, and I struggled to draw in a raggedy breath.

"What's wrong?" she asked, softly, rubbing my fingers with her thumb.

What's wrong was everything. What's wrong was that I was actually trying not to cry, like some kind of friggin' victim. I pressed against my stomach, and I swore I felt that ulcer growing—a hungry acid mouth swallowing all my hurt and rage and humanity. The later in the day it got, the more I burned from the inside-out.

I swallowed down the sneaky emotion crap and cleared my throat. "Nothing's wrong. Shall we run away?"

"In the style of Monty Python, yes."

Heh. "I do have killer jackalopes." I rooted around in the bag she'd brought, hoping to find a flashlight. Felt like, "A lighter, but no flashli -- wait..." I held it up to behold an actual torch. Fire. Fire!

I nearly jumped outta my Vans, and Jodie laughed at me, of course.

A huge *bang!* sounded behind us. *Bang, thump, crash!*, followed by, "Aaaaaaaah! Snakes!"

Ha! Jodie and I put thumbs to nose and wiggled our fingers in joyous victory. But not for long, because it was definitely time to run. I lit one of the torches, a rag wrapped around the top of a carved wooden handle. It roared to life, showing us the way out, if not home.

Screams and nervous, "Ha-ha!"'s sounded from the bathroom, and Jodie took off, me behind her.

"I am wishing magically that they will not find our secret passage!" I whispered.

Jodie, not even breathing heavy from running, the witch, said, "I am wishing magically that the killer jackalopes don't eat us."

"Nah, they won't eat us. I am their princess." Princess of Ridiculous Fake Animals and Also Snakes seemed about right.

We shuddered as one and paid attention to our flee-dom. The passage was sufficiently secret and cool, wrapped in stone and an acceptable level of dank—as in, it created atmosphere, but didn't actually drip on us. The path curved around the edge of the castle, and I wished we could explore the random doorways we passed on the left. But I'd probably just see Regina cheating on my princessy ass, so.

Jodie stopped short, and I damn near fell on my ass trying not to sether hair on fire. "Oh, boy," she said. "There are stairs. A ton of stairs."

"Let's go," I urged, shining the torch generally downward. "Before the guards come, and we have to skewer a few like Errol Flynn."

"Not gonna lie, I've always wanted to swashbuckle." Jodie trotted down, fast, and I barely kept up. "That's definitely a lesbian thing."

"Just like setting things on fire is a bi thing," I added.

Down, down, down. "These are the kinds of stereotypes I can embrace. The world needs more sexy Black lesbian pirates."

I missed a step thinking about sexy Black lesbian pirates. They all looked like Jodie, except for when they weren't lesbians and resembled Mahershala Ali. I'd get kidnapped by that crew any day.

"Arrgh there, dread pirate Bonny Jodie," I said."I don't suppose there's a bit o' rot gut in yar bag on yar shoulder. Yar."

We came to one of the landings, and Jodie stopped with a grin. "I like Bonny Jodie," she said, rooting around in her bag booty. "Alas, I'm a nerd, not a pirate."

"Why not both?"

She wiggled her eyebrows, and then pulled a small bottle of rum from her bag. Even the liquor was pirate-themed. "Then I want to be Bonny Jo Curie! We plunder, but give the money to poor, inner-city science dorks."

I grabbed the offered bottle and took a fine swig, yo-ho-ho. "Perfect. I can be your sidekick, Mean So the Fire Starter."

She screwed up her mouth. "Ain't nobody letting a fire bug onto a wooden ship. I'm the captain, I have to look out."

We started down again. "Yeah, fine, you're the cap'n."

"How about, 'Mean So the Rom-Com Hater'?"

"Long, but accurate."

Yar! We arrived at the end of the stairs!

If we were average-height persons, we'd be bent over in the tiny alcove, the ceiling was so low. Jodie pulled on the tiny wooden door. "Damn," she said. "Locked."

I handed the torch to her and shimmied past her to examine it. The hinges on this thing went 1/3 of the way across the dark, smooth, old wood. They had a pin! I fiddled with it, but that thing wasn't moving. "Is there a hammer or anything in the bag?"

"No." She rooted around, her huffs growing by the moment. "Dammit, I do not want to haul my butt up those stairs again."

With all my might, I pushed on the bottom of the pin. No matter how much I sweated and grunted, the centuries of gloop and muck in there refused to budge. The room was becoming too close. The smoke from the torch had successfully plundered the oxygen in here. I coughed and ground out, "We can't stay here."

"We can't go up."

My Vans twitched with the urge to stomp again. "Why… why the hell do we have a magic bag, and killer jackalopes, only to be stopped *here*?"

Jodie jogged a few steps up and yanked a cold torch off the wall. She replaced it with the fiery one to send the smoke away. "I don't understand any of this. Tiffani wants you to marry the hot, maybe violent, princess, yet we have been provided a means of escape?"

"Valid points, Dread Jo. I know what's going on even less than usual." I fell against the cold stone wall. "I'm probably dying in a hospital bed of a coma right now, and this whole thing is justthe last firings of my diseased brains. Maybe one of the Karens I shut down at Target finally retaliated."

"You're incredibly talented at tearing apart the assholic amongst us."

"Mean So thanks you."I slid to the ground, also cold.

Jodie plopped next to me. "But it almost seems like Tiffani doesn't actually want you to be with Princess Evil."

I pushed my Diana hair behind my ear, from which it immediately escaped. "I'm not jumping on her one way or the other. I've mostly learned my lesson from Regina. Her way of flirting is murdering our national pets. How would she celebrate our wedding anniversary, by bombing the neighboring country of Fakeatopia?"

She giggle-snorted, and the sheer cuteness made me wind my arm through hers in the dark. Warmer now.

"Look at it this way," said my bestie. "If this existence is a fantasy, then jackalopes aren't real."

"Jackalopes *aren't* real."

"That's the spirit! And if they aren't real, they cannot actually be stomped by unidragons. Therefore, by the scientific principle of silly psychics, the jackalopes didn't feel pain."

I nodded. "You're the science person. And that genuinely makes me feel better."

"Damn right." She shivered and scooted closer.

The floor chilled like ice, and even my juicy ass couldn't battle the cold forever; I began to shiver. With a sigh, I said, "We'll probably be caught the moment we set foot outside this door, and Regina will make a big show of putting me in an iron maiden."

"The lesbian-esttorture device."

I snickered, and she squeezed my knee.

She assured me, "I'm not letting anyone iron maiden you. Unless it's me. Or the band. Wait! Oh, wait, wait!" She jumped to her feet, and I waited, as instructed, with added bated breath.

My bestie rooted around in her boobs, and I probably should have looked away sooner. But she…just…well, she had such better boobs than I did. They were too amazing to ignore.

Pure jealousy on my part, of course.

Soon enough, she pulled out a long chain, with a huge, old key on the end. I gasped. The thing was as sufficiently dirty and twisted as the door.

Her face took on wonder when she gazed on the ancient thing. "I forgot I put this on this morning; it was next to the rest of my uniform. Hoping it opened a fancy wine cellar or something."

"Try it!" I scrambled to my feet, brushed the dirt from my booty, and set my chin on her shoulder from behind as she tried the (hopefully magic) key.

It turned.

It turned!

We whooped as the door creaked open, and then we whoop-whispered, for we were soon outside. I scouted right, she scouted left. The coast was clear, whew.

A quick survey of the grounds told me we might actually pull this off. One sprint through the garden, a climb over the wall, a lucky visit with a witch in the forest, and I would be home with my sweet kitty who bit everyone but me and Jodie.

My BFF wiggled her fingers at me, and I swept her into a hug. Which was not the proper response; seeing that she squeezed me back, it seemed to be okay.

"Thank you," I whispered to her, those pesky emotions choking my stupid throat. Horrible Tiffani and her roving band of nincompoops had destroyed my chill. I just wanted to be cold and evil again. Was that so much to ask?

"Hey, hey," she gently held my face in her soft hands. "It's gonna be okay. I'm not letting any fool psychic and her roving band of sexist weirdos touch you."

We locked eyes. In my whole life, nobody ever looked at me that way. Like I was made of golden candy or something.

So, naturally, I ruined it. I stepped back and cleared my throat. "I would also save you from the Vagina Wizards."

Jodie shook her head. "I don't like that name. It implies they are good at vaginas, which I believe in less than the Loch Ness Monster." She lifted one, playful shoulder. "*I'm* a Vagina Wizard. I own one, I've operated them, and I've got references."

I laughed and bowed to the vagina queen!

She started toward the entrance to the garden and turned right through the arch of the walled garden. And screamed.

The bottom fell out of my soul, and I sprinted to save her from --

Reporters.

A hundred reporters!

"Princess!" they screamed at once, launching toward us, poly-blend suits flapping in the breeze.

I pulled Jodie behind me and bolted straight through them—we had to get across the garden to climb the wall. But I stopped short, Jodie crashing into me, to see Tiffani directly blocking our path.

Regina stood next to her, a wide grin plastered on. "Was it something I said? You always were overdramatic, Sophie."

The cameras click-clacked around us.

I stood straighter. "Well, you sent old men to force me to strip and check my 'virginity,' which is gross, offensive, sexist, and also a useless social construct. Tell me, darling, exactly where do I check your mileage? Are you still cheating on me with three other people?"

The onlookers sucked in a collective breath, and more than a few were released in the form of chuckles. Feminine chuckles.

I pressed my advantage, because we might be in a hell world of nightmares, but I'd be damned if I or any other woman in my kingdom would be treated this way. Especially by other women!

Besides, I *really* needed someone to unload my stew of fee-fees all over.

"It's disgusting to treat women like fuck toys. I banish such things in Ugh!" I paused for applause. Jodie obliged me. "Thanks, girl. So, what's next in our 'courtship rituals,' Regina? Something vile, no doubt."

The cameras swiveled to my opponent. Her nostrils flared as she replied, quietly, "The, er, dowry ceremony."

My jaw tightened. Any minute now my skull would split open and my 17 rows of alien teeth would bite off her head, like a praying mant --

Jodie elbowed me, and my gaze followed hers to see my lady-in-waitness Ling lead a tethered line of goats into the garden.

Goats.

Goats?

G O A T S.

They wore pretty blue bows around their necks.

Tiffani teetered that direction, her arms waving, her heels sinking into the grass so that she bobbled up, down, left, right, up, down. "Stop! Not yet!"

I ground my teeth. And my organs. And my hair! My rage boiled over at such a fevered pitch that I shook with it.

"Oh, shit," whispered Jodie. "I haven't seen her this pressed since—since…"

I looked at her, my vision red; it was dripping with the blood of my enemies.

Her eyes went wide as saucers. "Don't hurt the goats. They're innocent."

"Oh, I'll save the goats. I'll feed my future wife to them!"

I leaped forward. Jodie caught me around the waist, but my momentum pulled us both to the grass. I struggled, dirt in my face. I couldn't—wha?—"Get off me!"

"No!" Jodie continued to sit on me. "So, Princess Charming, how many goats is a woman worth?"

A man in a long, fancy red coat stepped forward. "Well, for the Princess of Ugh, we think at least a hundred, which is pretty goo --"

And then, we were saved. A tall reporter in a fancy hijab stepped through the throng. "Princess Regina, are you literally saying that women are worth a certain number of goats?" Her eyebrow rose. "How many goats is the average woman worth? How many goats are you, yourself, worth?"

I took a deep breath. Jodie slid off my back onto the turf.

Regina put on a grin. "It's a heritage ceremony, you see. Symbolic of a simpler time."

I pushed up to my knees. "Would anyone like to hear about the simpler time I had earlier? When old dudes in long robes tried to check me for virginity?"

Tiffani stepped forward. "I'm sure we're aaaaaall grateful to Princess Sophie for reminding us that sexism is super-duper bad. You know what they say: What's sauce for the goose offends the gander."

The reporter cocked her head. "I beg your pardon?"

So say we all.

Things teetered toward haywire. Other journalists stepped forward, as my "virginity check" line smelled like controversy—an aroma delicious, yet rank, like French fries cooked in nuclear waste. Tiffani dealt with three reporters in her face, and several glommed onto Regina. Ling danced away as one of the goats tried to nibble on her blue dress.

"Now's our chance!" Jodie clutched my arm, and we fled toward the vine-covered garden wall. Several minions milled there, until their mouths fell open when they realized we were about to bulldoze them like short, angry linebackers.

They got the hell out of the way.

Regina yelled my name, a plaintive call that fell on screw-you ears. At one time, I woulda stopped dead in my tracks. But my chest constricted to hear Jodie's voice from that time ring in my ears: You don't deserve her shit.

At the wall, I fell to my knees. "Climb up!" The wall stood about eight feet or so.

Then, a white jackalope hopped toward me from under…a shrubbery!

"Attack them!" I ordered the murder jackalope.

Unfortunately, the jackalope just stared at me. So…*not* a murder varietal then. Jodie Jr. would have risen to the occasion.

"Good try." Jodie planted a foot on my back and climbed. When her weight came off me, I looked up to see her straddled over the top like a floppy stuffed animal. She extended her hand, and I took it to haul myself up. Except, I went nowhere, because I was a weakling computer nerd. The leather jackets were deflection; what I lacked in strength, I made up in meanness.

My bestie shook her head. "You have arms made of spaghetti."

"Hey! They're not useless. They have tattoos."

"Princess?"

Ling! She got on all-fours, her dark curls falling over her shoulders. "It is my honor to help the princess escape. Because I'm pretty sure the amount of goats I'm worth is an offensive number."

"They all are," I said.

She nodded. "That's how I know."

"Thanks, girl. Tell Tiffani to throw you a spare family jewel," Jodie said. "And hurry, Regina's people are almost here."

A wall of red soldiers trotted toward us. I climbed, Jodie pulled, and we both leaped down the other side of the wall. Yes! Victory! We stopped to wiggle nose-fingers at one another, then ran for our lives. Shouts wafted on the air behind us, propelling our feet forward.

Jodie pointed. "There! Toward that copse of trees!"

Ugh, all this running was bad for my health. "What tree corpse? Why don't we run into that group of alive trees?"

My best friend stopped. "You're unreal."

"Thanks!" I yelled over my shoulder.

We made it into the live trees and squatted behind a giant one to catch our breaths. Jodie groaned. "A copse of trees is a group of trees. Copse, not corpse."

"I'm sorry, guvnah. I'm not a 14th century lady who wuttalks fancy. I'm a modern princess running away to an uncertain fate."

"Addle pate."

"And a merry ass paste to you, too."

She snorted. "Okay, Princess. We need to keep going. There's a proper forest thattaway." In a flash, she hauled me up. "I hope we find a free store full of food and liquor."

"According to fairy tales, we should be able to rob seven dwarves soon enough."

"Or maybe a witch."

Perhaps it was our flippant joking about burgling innocents, or maybe Tiffani's revenge, but at that moment, the sky decided to growl. Then grumble. Then weep on our desperate heads.

"Aw, crap, my hair!" Jodie gasped.

I yanked off my jacket and held it over her head. "Here, use this. Run!"

We sprinted, I panted. We got pissed on, I got pissed off. A few squishy minutes later, we'd passed into the forest, and the canopy prevented at least some rain from drowning us. We kept going, slower now, me leading Jodie in as fast a walk as we could manage through the trees and mud and forest things underfoot.

Jodie's teeth chattered. Seemed like they shook her whole body. Or maybe that was me, because my skin had frozen to ice. I wrapped my arm around her waist and kept tugging her deeper into the woods, hoping to find…friggin' *something*. The leather jacket had almost soaked through, and I couldn't ruin Jodie's hair like that. Also, pneumonia is bad and shit.

"There!" From my brain to Tiffani's psychotic fantasy, there was a cottage. With smoke in the chimney! "I don't care who's in there, we're joining them right now."

With one last, splashy sprint, we arrived at the fairy-tale looking place. The door was dark wood, decorated with lighter wood forming an X, like something out of Shakespeare. Straw lined the roof, and even the windows were a rainbow of stained glass.

Jodie knocked.

I walked right in. It was pouring, and hopefully whoever was in there would forgive my intrusion—after all, I wore a white tee, no bra. If we were in a spring break bar, someone would have offered me their motorcycle by now.

We rushed in, breaths panting, hearts racing, to find…

"Nobody." Jodie hurried to the fire, threw the soggy leather on the brick step, dropped her bag, and thrust her hands at the warmth. "Thank you, ancestors. Come on, Princess So; my fire-bringing ancestors think you're all right."

I obeyed because my ice-skin gave me the soggy-titty shimmies. "Thank you, ancestors. I hope white supremacists don't get to share your glorious afterlife."

Jodie gave me a teeth-clacking chuckle.

The whole place was one big, deserted room. A tiny kitchen tucked into the corner—it had what appeared to be a wood-burning stove. The living room featured a single loveseat, a two-person dining table, and a pile of furs on the floor before the fireplace. Dominating the room was a huge bed covered in more furs. And laid across them…

"Bathrobes!" I shook my way over there to hug the fluffiest, snuggliest robe I'd ever seen. It was Ugh blue. "Come here, come here! You're freezing, ditch those wet clothes."

She shivered her way to me. "I saw a porn that started like this once." With a snort, she added. "It featured two wet ladies, too!"

I giggled and felt my face go hot, and my mouth go dry. Jodie out here talking about porn, made me…made me— I giggled and stared at the floor.

Robe. Now. I slid my splashy tee off and threw it in the general direction of the fire. The jeans didn't come off nearly so easy. After I hurked and groaned them over my frozen ass, I got on the floor to try to pull them off from the ankles. Ooh, those furs (hopefully fake?) were soft and cozy on my bottom.

Jodie stopped laughing at her porn joke and started guffawing at me flopping from side to side. "You are a mess." She kneeled at my feet and pulled at the jeans, which she also flung toward the fire. But not in it, which was good. Didn't need a headline reading "Princess Caught Bare-Assed in Sapphic Scandal."

Although, that would be metal.

"What you smiling about?" Jodie asked me, matching chuckle for chuckle.

"Uh…" My imaginings caught in my throat.

"Are you blushing? Oh, my God. I've seen you naked a thousand times!" She leaned forward and pinched my cheek like annoying grandmas the world over. "Very cute, by the way."

One arm across my boobs, one over my bits, I managed to stand despite my goosebumps doing their best golf ball impressions. "Okay, okay." My breaths heaved, but—but I didn't know why. Ack, this day. My heart wouldn't stop thumping. This week! This eon! Which is what might have legit passed while I flailed in Tiffani hell.

Jodie put one of the robes over my shoulders from behind and wrapped herself around me. "You get the first one," she said, squeezing me hard, her head on my shoulder. "For the jacket. Thanks to you, an expensive hair-do paid for by the citizens of Ugh has been saved." She shoved her bun back up to the center of her head.

"Hey, priorities." I resisted the urge to sink into her warmth and managed to pull myself away. My skin needled as it returned to life. "Let's get you changed. You must be freezing."

She managed to drop her jumpsuit fast; it collapsed on the rustic wood floor in heavy defeat, and I tossed it away while she removed her soggy unmentionables. I returned the favor and wrapped her in a robe-n-hug. I squeezed her, with all my might, and she relaxed into me, her shaking easing.

I don't know how long we stayed there, but the peace and belonging of the moment; if I stayed there forever, nothing bad would ever happen. That's how it had always been with Jodie. No amount of cruelty from my parents, or the world, couldn't be washed away by her comfort. If you looked up the word "safe" on the internet, a gif of Jodie smiling, big and goofy, would appear. An algorithm I'd get behind.

One time, very early in our friendship, my dad left town for a church retreat, a.k.a. Let's Roll Up to the HQ for a Woman Senate Candidate and Scream That She's Going to Hell for Unspecified Reasons. Except I didn't know that was happening until after he returned, 11 days later. I came home from school to a padlocked trailer, but I wouldn't be alone, oh no! Before he left, he'd told the violent alligator-collecting lady in our trailer park that I would be her "gator wrangler" for a few days.

For some reason, I ran.

I found an unlocked car to sleep in the first night, and I showed up for school the next day in repeat clothes. Jodie noticed, browbeat me when I lied about the circumstances, and forcibly shoved me in her car after school while matching me curse-for-curse. That's when I met the Edwards fam. It was the first time they wouldn't let me be homeless, but not the last. I'd cried that night, and I hadn't even known way.

A wave of… something… washed over me. I had to swallow it or stop breathing. Some kind of tears? Some lump, maybe. Some warm shiver. A series of feelings whose names escaped me because they all escaped me.

But it was nice. A wonderful emotion that wasn't food or gaming or flipping a middle finger, who knew?

Jodie and I sat before the fire and began the process of turning back into humans. The cold melted away like snow sliding off my skin. For a long time, we didn't speak. We didn't need to. I rubbed her shoulders and hoped that maybe this one time I might give her one percent of the comfort she offered to me over and over and over again.

I swallowed again.

Jodie finally broke the silence. "So, Princess. What do we do next?"

I shook my head. "I don't know. I have no business being a princess, so this rom-com scenario is a bust."

"I think you'd make an amazing princess."

"For whom, a cell block?" *Scoff*, I scoffed, with extra -*off*. "In this reality, I kicked another country's leader, shocked the masses by revealing royal secrets about gross wizard-men, and then fled. I'll soon be locked in an attic somewhere, screeching my head off while Princess Regina settles in with a rich, proper princess not from Ass Crack, Florida."

Jodie faced me with a determined set to her jaw. "What I saw was a princess who refused to be the tool of the patriarchy. Who shone a light on modern internalized misogyny disguised as cutesy medieval ceremony. Remember Ling? You inspired her to reconsider some of the stuff she'd been taught, especially about goats as a method of barter." She tipped my chin. "I'm proud to have you as my princess."

All I could do was stare at my chilly feet. My chin tingled. My whole face tingled. "Well. Anyway." I flexed my frozen baby toes. "Princess Jackalope Murderer ain't gonna marry me now. What a shock! I can't imagine the kind of rom-com hero or heroine who would."

"What do you mean?"

"Ummm…" I leaned sideways on one arm and bit the nails on my other hand. Ick, blue nail polish. I ate it anyway in order to not speak.

Jodie yanked my finger outta my mouth. In short, clipped bites, she repeated, "What do you mean?"

"I mean who the hell would love me?" I shrugged and sagged and was my ulcer for real coming back? Shit. "I'm a disaster in every possible way. The only thing I'm good at is video games, and that's because they're violent and solitary. Some dudes get really upset when you beat them."

She cocked her head. "Then it's a good thing you like girls, too."

I snickered. "True."

"I might be biased."Jodie's gaze darted to the fire. "What I can't understand is why you only ever date your mother."

The wind fled my lungs like a skittish hummingbird. I managed to grind out, "Earl was not my mother."

She heaved an elaborate sigh. "I mean the women you date." Her mouth formed a pressed line. "Women like *Regina.*"

"Regina was not my mother!" I continued gnawing on my fingers. "They… they both were tough, but…fair. Mostly. Not. Um. Both tried to turn me into something they could be proud of. Both failed, I guess. Or so they said." Wow, look, there was my black hole. Yawning toward me like a giant space creature ready to swallow me into blood and dust. Could I actually see it? Or was my vision going dim? "I mean my mom was probably a narcissist—you told me that—but Regina just demanded attention at all times, or she would punish me psychologically with no care to how I felt and yes, my ulcer is super-duper coming back."

I pressed my hand to my screaming stomach and reeled. The only thing saving me from falling into the fire was Jodie's strong embrace.

Manisha had used me to get a job at my gaming company, and then tore me down to every manager even tangentially above me. We'd still gone out three weeks after she got me fired. She had cheated on me with my boss. They came together to the Christmas party where I was also her date. She explained that was my mistake, and why was I embarrassing her with my insecurities?

Jodie turned my head, but I looked right through her. "Your eyes are very big," she said. "This is the look you get at CES. You're scaring me, Sophie."

My mouth was so dry I couldn't—ugh, couldn't. After Manisha, there was Sophia. Sophia and Sophie, ain't that cute? Or at least, it was until the night I interrupted her usual monologue about how she would surely win the Pulitzer Prize in journalism, and it was a crime she hadn't already, but the committee had emailed her to say she was too good, and it intimidated them, and she screamed, "Enough about your ovarian cyst! If it's so damn bad, go to the hospital, you whiny bitch, but don't expect me to be here when you get back!"

I'd called her for weeks post-surgery. She'd stolen my TV after the ambulance came.

"I. Date. My…my…"

"Mother." Jodie turned me to face her. "You date your horrible mother over and over again! Even the men are sometimes your mother."

Yeah. Alex had been an engineer. He'd delighted in jokes about how me writing code was not really STEM. Not like *engineering*. And my game wasn't even a real game. Not like he played. And wouldn't it be better if I got a boob job?

"Earl was nice!" I nearly screamed it.

Jodie's jaw snapped shut. "He…well, I guess he didn't really treat you like the rest."

Why had I dumped Earl? Oh, yeah, he'd wanted to love me and live with me, couldn't have that. No, apparently the only people I got hung up on were those who would stomp on my chest on their way out the door. If my mother had stayed, would I be living in Suburbatopia in a McMansion with 2.7 kids and 19.7 TVs?

My burning stomach and flailing brain told me I would need therapy until I was 102. Point seven. Ha-ha-ha, no, therapy was for chuds who can't manage their pain with violent video games.

I flopped backward to land on the cold, hard floor. "One thing all my people can agree on is that I'm a freak. I'm gonna die alone with only my cat to eat me. Kinda metal, honestly. Emotions lead to ulcers, obviously, and *true wuv* is for advertising slogans and Tiffanis."

She pushed her hair bun upward. "Oh, Sophie."

I sat up on my knees. "True love is the lie people tell themselves when they're upset that they will die alone with only their pet to eat them. I've embraced it! I've already told Satan to eat my face first for maximum horror impact. So, you see, I'm well-adjusted and have no need for," I waved my arms to indicated all this crap, "fairy tales."

"Ridiculous." She stopped short and blinked at me. "That's just ridiculous talk, and a little horrifying. Just because you don't believe in love doesn't mean it doesn't exist."

"Huh?"

"Love exists! I love you."

"That's…" I shrugged, my breath catching. "Different."

She sighed, long and longer. "Sophie, if the people of Ugh could see you the way I see you, you'd be as beloved as the inspiration for your hairdo." And just when I was eye-rolling her, she took my hand and added, in a whisper, "Sophie, if *you* could see you the way I see you, you'd believe in all the love in the world. Because you deserve it. And you don't have to be wrapped in sugar and spice and everything nice *in order to* deserve it."

I sucked in a ragged breath and ran out of acidic words. I just stared at her. My best friend. The person who believed in me more than anyone had ever believed in me. More than I believed in me. Jodie was the anti-Regina. Gah, she made me want to be a better person through her example. Kind. Loving. Honest. Less likely to set fires. And so beautiful…

She was so friggin' amazing, I…I cleared my throat and managed to say, "Well, that proves you've been swashbuckling on the high seas for too long."

"And you can't take a compliment."

"None of my mother-dates ever gave me one."

Too many feelings. They screamed in my head like a cop siren.

"Hell, your eyes are jangling around like pinball machines. There, there, I won't emotion you anymore. Come on," Jodie squeezed my forearm and pulled me up as she stood.

This close, she didn't even have pores. Magazines told me that no pores were a good thing on a lady person. They were very good on Jodie.

I pulled back, tugging my robe belt closed with enough force to chop my soggy ass in half. Heat swamped me as the last of the rain chill fled, and I pushed my wet hair behind my ears. "Maybe we'll find Doritos Surprise hidden in the cupboard." That would settle my ulcer for sure.

"Twice in one day? I believe that kind of torture was outlawed by the Geneva Convention."

And then my stomach fell clear into the mud below the cabin. "Wait! Jodie. Earlier, you knew what Doritos Surprise was. You remembered eating it before. And you remembered all my evil exes. That's from real life. It doesn't belong in Ugh!"

Her jaw dropped. "You're right!" She jumped and gave a dorky little clap. "I… I don't remember much from Ugh except for the palace, and the royal family, really. But I do remember the gross glop of Doritos Surprise and the gross glop of Regina!" Her eyes positively danced, like they were starring in a --

Rom-com.

Jodie ought to be the heroine. Of every story. I raked a hand through my hair. *She* was the gorgeous, girly, floaty, inspiring one! And she was the one who deserved to have a happily-ever-after kind of twuewuv.

The bandage on my ribs give way from all the rain. The robe's sash kept it on me until I got to the bed to see the damage.

Gingerly, I sat and pulled the center of the robe apart as best I could without flashing Jodie. "I'm still bleeding." The stupid bandage was sopping with blood and rain, and it slid down me in a very sexy way to splat on the floor.

"I'll search for a fresh bandage." Jodie turned around in a circle. "There's no bathroom here."

"Of course not. Well-behaved women don't need one." I pressed one of the furs to my oozing self. "Look in one of the bedside tables? Maybe if I say it, a band-aid will magically appear."

"Ah, the old Tiffani flim-flam. Let's test it."

With a grin, Jodie danced her way to the adorable painted table, which probably came out of a German folk museum. The kind of adorable thing I'd always hated. She whipped the door open, and --

I got up on my knees. "Yes—magic bandages!"

"She's a witch!" Jodie held up a first aid kit.

"She's a nurse," I said.

"Only for you. Get off your knees, you're a princess. Scoot back to the headboard."

I did as ordered, arranging my robe so that it split at my navel. I had to show her the corset stab wound. And she had to lean over me to tape a new wad of cotton there. She traced the lines of the tape with her finger, pressing it into place. I shivered from her light touch.

Jodie looked up at me from my waist. "How does that --"

I swallowed and met her gaze. She smelled like the rain. Such a pretty, pretty rain, with eyes so big and deep and soft.

Slowly, she rose, and pushed my hair off my forehead. My chest thumped, and I throbbed. My side throbbed, I mean. I hadn't felt this way in—how did I feel? Like a heart attack?

Jodie pushed her bottom lip below her teeth, drawing it out again. It glistened. She took my chin in her tiny hand and came closer. "Is that better?"

I nodded because I couldn't seem to speak. Everything I ever was was better. What was happening to me?

She smiled. I closed my eyes, it was too much, the, the rain and stuff, and she traced my jaw with her finger. Why couldn't I breathe? I was shivering again, and God, the urge to—

Crash!

We screamed as the door flew back, thrown to the wall. And Tiffani the FuckingWorstPersononEarth clackity-wobbled her way right over to us. "Here they are. Silly girls!"

I yanked my robe together up to my chin, and Jodie moved to the edge of the bed to stand.

Regina sauntered in after Tiffani. "Look, a romantic shack for us, my darling!"

She rushed forward and tried to take my hands, but mine clutched my fluffy-ass robe and refused to participate any further in this parade of bullshit.

My evil ex continued, "Let us sit by the fire, and, "she waggled her eyebrows, "see what happens."

"I'm not dating my mother anymore, you evil troll."

Her beautiful lip curled to hurl an insult. Screw that. "Enough of this, Tiffani!" I scooted myself off the bed, like a pissed off dog with a butt itch. A butt itch of justice. "I am not marrying this person." Pain made me wince, but frowning was kinda my thing, so. "And lots of people think my boobs are perfect, Regina!"

My ex-mommy-princess threw back her head and laughed. "Sure, pointitties."

I clutched my robe tighter. Jodie started…growling?

Tiffani inched toward me, her arms extended like I was a rabid dog. Good. "Sophie, you muuuust learn to embrace love. To live in love instead of fear."

We circled one another, and I inched toward the door. "Maybe if you gave me an option who wasn't a total nightmare, I'd give them a chance. But for some reason, my childhood bully and my adult bully here don't turn me on."

Poor, misunderstood Regina clutched her chest in dismay and ranted about how I never learned to embrace tradition because I'd grown up trash, I'd learn to love the vagina wizards if I weren't so narrow-minded, and that she was the best catch in the world so I could never do better. Hard to believe that one, since neither Ugh nor MacGuffin actually existed, and Chris Evans did.

Mmm. Chris Evans.

Jodie backed up toward me. "Mean So, you want to lead the charge, or shall I?"

"I will swashbuckle all these motherfuckers, Bonny Jo." I raised my fists and screamed the least ladylike noise I could manage. A dying donkey ain't got nothin' on me.

Jodie joined my warrior's cry, and we charged to the door, but Tiffani rushed to physically block us.

Good.

Blam! I burst right through her, and she went down, hard, into a mud puddle just outside the door. For a brief moment, the mud overtook her pink, and her shocked face lit up my tender places with joy. Or maybe that was the cold breeze under my robe. Jodie sailed past me with a quick leap over Tiffani the Flailing Psychic-Guidance Counselor-Goodwill Manager-Private Secretary-Vagine Examiner.

"The horse!" Jodie veered right, and I followed. It had stopped raining—score!

With one motion, Jodie leaped atop the giant beast, and I skidded to a stop out of sheer awe. She'd had horses growing up. I'd had roaches. Her pets were more useful.

"Careful of your wound!" She hauled me up by the elbow to sit behind her.

Careful of my vadge, more like. I still had no underpants on.

Regina ran out just as we galloped away through a gaggle of press. They pushed and shoved, feet squelching in the mud, to get the best shot of us fleeing.

I raised my fist and shouted a war-cry of victory!

An ominous, "Ha-ha!" sounded on the heels of our galloping steed.

I buried my face in Jodie's back, her warmth once again saving me from the demons, figurative and literal. The wind whipped around us, cold and glorious and made of sweet freedom. I didn't care at all where we went, only...

CHAPTER TEN:
BRIDGET WHATSHERNAME'S FIANCÉE

Stop screaming!" Jodie shook my shoulder. "It's okay! You had a dream."

I sat up and flailed. "She's right behind us! She --"

No. My bedroom. My apartment!

I wore my Heart tee. It was dry. I was dry, Jodie was dry, the window outside was dry. "Where the hell are we?" I tried to stand, got tangled in my sheets, and fell off the other side of the bed. "Dammit!" Ow, my side still hurt. I lifted my tee…no more corset wound. Maybe I throbbed because I hit the nightstand corner on the way down.

Jodie ran around to help while tut-tutting about my clumsiness.

"What day is it?" I asked. Ooh, my hair was long again. And black!

"November first. Are you okay? You must be hung over from the carnival last night."

I pawed beside the bed for my phone. There it was! Latest model, with blessed, blessed internet!

"Real life." I jumped. "It's my real life! The Ghost of Halloween Pink has returned me to my life!" I leaped and screamed and twirled Jodie around, who was all too happy to be the Ginger to my Fred.

"I don't know what we're talking about," she said, laughing, "but this is fun!"

"I don't either, which is why I'm glad I'm here!"

We jumped, hugged, giggled, and such a rush of pure joy engulfed me, I swear, it made me dizzy. I fell back onto the bed and sprawled. Ha! Suck it, Tiffani. I wasn't ever gonna marry whatever shithead excuse for a human person she paraded in front of me. "Let's eat Doritos Surprise."

"What's one of my rules?"

I sighed. "Never before noon."

"Or after 8 p.m. You know the doctor said my intestines can't handle it." A song rang out, and Jodie ran over to her bag. Wow, she looked spectacular, her hair in a medium-large Afro that really suited her. She must have been up for a while—she was out of her wrap and everything. "Hold that thought—Bridget's on the line. I probably won't get to talk to her again until I see her at the altar!"

Jodie gave a cute shrug while I wondered who Bridget was, and to whom or what she worshipped at her altar?

My mouth tasted like cheesy death, so I downed a few handfuls of water in the bathroom.

Snippets of Jodie's convo came to me. "Of course we'll be tame tonight," "You'd better behave yourself, too, baby," and then, "Love you, too. I can't wait to be married to you!"

I dropped a glop of water on mypoin titty.

"What?" I peeked around the corner, inch by inch, as if a monster awaited me. "What? Who? Married?"

Jodie laughed. "Very funny. I gotta jet. I'll see you tonight, 8p.m., the drag show. I expect to be wined and dined and drag-queened to gay heaven!" She threw her bag over her shoulder. "But not overly wined—no hangovers for my big day tomorrow, got it? Aw, look. Bridget sent me a selfie." She gave a fluttery little sigh. "Can't believe my future wife is so damn beautiful."

She flashed the phone at me; a stunning—*stunning*—woman smiled up into the camera at the perfect angle, with perfect lighting, and perfect blonde hair cascading behind her perfect face.

I blinked.

I dripped.

Jodie grinned, stuck her thumb to her nose, and wiggled her fingers. And then sailed out the front door.

What the fuck what the fuck what the fuck what the fuck what the fuck what the fuck what the fuck what the fUck what the fuCkiTyFuckING*fuck*FUCK?

Earth's gravity suddenly doubled, and I collapsed to the bathroom floor. My face went numb, and my heart double-parked in my lungs. Jodie was getting married?

Tomorrow?

I screamed. I just... screamed. I couldn't stop. I heaved, and I screamed. No, no, no, Tiffani had gone too far this time!

"Stop that noise!" squeaked Tiffani.

Oh, God. She was entirely inside my brain now, redecorating my frontal lobe in pink. I was a pod person. A pretty pink pod person! Aaaaaaaaaah!

Click-clacks of doom sounded from the bedroom. "My goodness, Sophie, this is not Best Woman behavior. It is wonderful to know that you scream like a girl, though. Ha-ha!"

No. Not in my house. I peeked upward through gloppy lashes to behold the demon, the witch, the monster *in my house*!

I swung a fist, but she danced away on her red-and-pink polka dotted high heels with another, "Ha-ha!" She threw her hair over her shoulder, where it convulsed in slow-mo. Or maybe that was my chest. With another giggle, she left the bathroom. "Come on, now," she called, "let's go through the big day one more time."

As if pulled by the Stockholm Syndrome Express, I crawled out of my bathroom, through the bedroom, and into my living room. Tiffani perched on my sofa—gingerly, like she might catch something from it.

Fair.

I still breathed so hard, I couldn't talk, but at least I wasn't screaming anymore, I guess. Why had I done that? I fell against the wall and wiped my eyes on my tee.

"Hi! I'm Tiffani the Wedding Planner. I have the venue, flowers, cake, decorations, etc. aaaaaalllllllready for tomorrow." She posed with a grin that appeared distinctly shit-eating.

This wasn't happening.

"Who the hell is Bridget?" I growled through a raw throat.

"Isn't she gooooorgeous? Jodie met her a year ago at the farmer's market. They tried to grab the same eggplant, then they joked about how lesbians aren't really into eggplants, and then they fell madly in loooove!" The horrible beast actually clasped her hands together like a discount cartoon character.

Cartoon beast kept babbling. "Now, be sure to get to the club early tonight, because you'll have the tickets." She slid a pink envelope out of her bag and waved it. "I will put these on your kitchen counter. If I can find a place free of stickiness caused by a mystery substance, I don't want to know the name of."

Because she failed to wither into a pile of ash no matter how I glared, Tiffani teeter-tottered over to me and stuck a finger in my face. "Show Jodie a good time tonight, okay? But not tooooooo good, ha ha! Then meet her at the hotel at 11am tomorrow so everyone can get ready together." She stood. "I emailed you a copy of the whole itinerary."

I pushed up against the wall and managed to stand. "And where is my prince charming or lady love this time?"

She wobbled with self-satisfaction. "I can't just tell you that, silly!"

"You shoved my evil ex at me last time and just told me it was her."

Shrugging, she said, "I guess it wasn't. We'll keep trying scenarios until Bitchylocks finds someone who's juuuust right, ha ha!" She cocked her head. "LOL, 'Bitchylocks' was Happizzez's joke. She's hilarious, for an angel." Her voice dipped to a whisper. "They are remarkably unfunny."

Huh. My brass knuckles were in my ratty sleep shorts' pocket. I slid them over my fingers while looking her dead in the eye.

Tiffani narrowed her gaze at me. "I'll see you tonight at the bachelorette. Wear the dress in the garment bag I put in your closet. Yeeeeeeesssss—wear it! And don't bring these knuckle things, they're unseemly."

She stomped on my toes. I screamed and collapsed, and she stole my brass knuckles while I cradled my foot with its new stiletto hole.

At my front door, Tiffani the Psychic-Guidance Counselor-Goodwill Manager-Private Secretary-Vagine Examiner-Wedding Planner said, "You know what they say, Sophie Sweet: Among the paths leading to a woman's heart, cocktails are the shortest one. Ha-ha! And ta-ta! Ha-ha, it rhyyyyyyymed!"

Mercifully, she left, and I fell all the way down again, my foot in my hand, my face on the cold, fake wood floor. The room spun. My brain spun. I'd been dropped into three different rom-coms in less than a week, and I could die of tired. Emotions kept punching me in my burning gut and, God, I missed my life before and --

Fine. Fine. FINE FINEFINE. "I give up," I groaned to Satan, who'd wandered over to lick my forehead.

If getting with whatever horror show "love" Tiffani picked for me was the only way out of this nightmare, I would surrender. *Lick.* I didn't have to bang them. *Lick lick.* I didn't even have to be polite to them, clearly. *Liiiick.* I scooped Satan into a hug. Plus, divorce was a thing.

So was shoving someone off a cliff.

* * * * *

Since I decided to give up and let Tiffani win (perhaps later to burn her psychic tent to ash?), I wore the stupid dress she left for me. Actually…it was kinda hot. I'd been afraid of a pastel pouf, but she'd gotten me a black leather minidress, sleeveless, with a square neckline. Together with my favorite pair of over-the-knee black leather boots, I got a lot of compliments at the club—and everyone knows that compliments from women are the best.

Actually, the most cherished were Jodie's, who stopped, whistled, and slapped my ass, heh. She looked bonkers amazing in a short dress, flared skirt, with a green and blue pattern; Kente, she called it.

The group was us and a couple of her teacher friends, Britney and Lanelle, and the table we got hugged the front of the stage. When we sat, a waiter bustled over to deposit a bottle of champagne on the table, as well as a small white box with Jodie's name on it.

Jodie was about to open the box when Tiffani echo located the table via vowels. "Haaaaaappybaaaaaachelorette, Jodie!" She bobbed and weaved over to us, yanked a chair from the next table, and sat across from me. Wonderful. "Thank you sooooooo much for inviting me. Ohemgeeeeeee, what's in the box?"

"Yes, what's in the box?"

We all turned to see a supermodel.

"Bridget!" Jodie leaped to her high heels, reached up to take Bridget's face in her hands, and kissed her.

The table applauded.

Except for me. I was unable to move because every muscle in my body seized. I twitched my fingers, like a seal's flippers, but that's as far as I got.

Oh, this Bridget person was perfect. A head taller than Jodie, with golden curls and a cupid's bow mouth. Huge eyes, like a doll, and a body that I was not ogling, thank you very much. She, too, wore a little black dress. I gritted my teeth so hard it hurt my jaw. Her black dress wasn't better than mine. No. Not sexier or better filled out or taller or --

With a giggle, Jodie opened the box and grabbed an envelope. "It's a note. From *you*." She tittered at Bridget. "You want me to have an amazing night, so you sent the champagne!"

I examined the chilled bottle in its ice bucket: Dom Perignon. My mouth barely managed to obey me into a smile.

"There's more." Jodie pulled another item from the box; it was wrapped in white floaty fabric and a red ribbon. "Holy crap!" It was a giant wad of cash, from ones to tens. "Money to tip the queens with."

The whole table clapped for Bridget the Wonder Bride. I slapped the table three whole times and didn't even flip it over. Jodie and Bridget sure weren't paying attention—they were making out. I temporarily went blind for some reason.

Jodie finally tore her mouth away from her blonde succubus and clutched the note to her chest. "I cannot believe how lucky I am!"

Oh, how the table giggled. I yelled for a Scotch from a random waiter. And then another, better safe than sober.

"I'm not trying to crash your party," said Bridget through her catalogue rows of expensive porcelain teeth. "I simply wanted to make sure your night was perfect, and that you have everything you might want."

Jodie pulled her in for a hug and set her head on Bridget's chest. "I will by this time tomorrow."

Everyone at our table aww'ed them. I tossed back one of my drinks, which hit my throat like a fireball.

"Hey, that was mine," Lanelle said.

Britney, a zaftig white brunette who wasn't exactly pretty, but sexy AF with a sneaky grin and curves to inspire poets, poured the champagne for the group. Lanelle, a striking Black woman who shaved herself bald and sported even more awesome tattoos than I did, ordered appetizers for us while still side-eyeing me.

Everyone chattered and teased Jodie and Bridget about the impending nuptials, so I sat back and wondered at the surreality of this scenario. Who was my twuewuv? The twink waiter, or the married queen hosting the event? I bet none of them were as amazing as Briiiiiidget, who annoyed me so much, I was cogitating in Tiffani.

The first Scotch chased Lanelle's cocktail down my throat in rapid succession, and just made my burning stomach and misfiring nerves worse. I pressed against my eyes to make them stop hurting.

"You okay there?" Lanelle patted me between the shoulders. "I think that's sipping Scotch."

"I think it's mind-your-own-business Scotch."

Jodie and Bridget pulled apart to stare at me.

"You must be Sophie!" chirped Bridget. "I can't believe we haven't met before this."

I glared at Tiffani. "Lots of things are hard to believe tonight."

"What's wrong with you?" Jodie asked. "You okay?"

I stood so fast, my chair skidded into the table behind me. "Sorry! Sorry. Yeah, I… I gotta bathroom. Toilet. Whiz."

What the hell was wrong with me? Jodie was obviously happy! Except it wasn't real? I didn't know this imaginary blonde.

The bathroom toilet whiz line snaked out the door, so I sailed right past that mess to an exit. My hand slipped sweaty on the knob, but I shoulder-checked it, and the outside air greeted me like a warm, wet towel. Ugh, Florida.

Wait, not Ugh!

I stalked by a couple of smoking queens to the back of the alley. It reeked at the same frequency as the inside of my brain.

"Are you okay?"

I whipped around to see Jodie. Shit.

"That wasn't a friendly face." She stared at her feet. As did I. "So…why are you full of drama? Aren't I supposed to be the star of the evening?"

Shiiiiiiit. Just keep examining Jodie's beautiful feet. "I thought Latrice Royale was the headlining queen tonight?"

"Of course." She stepped closer. "What gives, Sophie? Come on. It's gross out here, and I don't want to smell like this all night; this dress is dry-clean only. You look super-hot, by the way. You should wear leather every day of your life."

My heart shot into my throat and set off every molecule of my blood. "It's nothing, okay? I have a headache."

Jodie nodded. "Sure. Which is why we're standing next to a rat king and his court."

I met her gaze and blurted, "This isn't real!"

"I know. It feels like a dream to me, too." She sank into herself and hugged around her waist with a soft, blissful smile.

My teeth ground into one another. "It *is* a dream, Jodie. Or…a spell. Or something, don't you remember Tiffani from last night at the carnival?"

"Are you drunk already?"

I held her by the shoulders. "She was the psychic from last night's carnival. She cursed me into a rom-com. A… a series of rom-coms, to teach me about love and accepting love and giving *love*." I said "love" like a four-letter curse. "My last rom-com was a royal princess one where they tried to make me marry *Regina*, and you were my lady-in-waiting. Before that, we were in high school again."

The expression on her face. "Have you cracked your skull?" She stalked away from me a few paces and flapped her arms. "Tiffani is my wedding planner. Last night, we saw Gwendolyn the Fantabulous, like always."

I shook my head, *no, no, no*. "No. That didn't happen. Why—why is Tiffani doing this? Am I supposed to meet my true love in your wedding party or something?" She just gaped at me. "I mean it, Jodie!" I stuck my thumb on my nose and wiggled my fingers in the sacred gesture of *you have to believe me*.

"Stop that!"

What? I felt my cheeks go hot and abandoned the gesture.

Jodie smacked her hands on her hips, and I recoiled so hard I hit the alley wall. I was in for it now. "Sophie, I get that I'm your one friend, okay?

You will always be my closest friend, but I have a wife now! I love her, she's the one. You're just gonna have to share me. And Bridget is amazing, if you would give her a chance."

I pressed my eyes closed. If I couldn't see it, it wasn't true, right?

Yet I still heard.

"You're stubborn beyond all measure," my best friend, my only friend, went on. "You're cantankerous. But usually, you treat *me* well at least!"

My head snapped up. "Hey, I take offense to that. I'm not a shitty person to everyone. I'm perfectly nice to people who deserve it." I pushed off the wall. "However,I refuse to take shit and eat it." Except when dating, apparently. Fuuuuck. "Um, I refuse to let misogyny slide. To let homophobia slide, or racism, or whatever the world has in store for people they call inferior. You know this. I refuse to let you eat shit, either, and I guess that makes me cant—cakan—rude."

"Did Bridget deserve that?"

"I just met her. How can you marry some bitch I never met before?"

"Bitch?" Jodie's face hardened to stone, and I lost my breath.

"I didn't—you know what I --"

"Yes, I know exactly what you mean." She stuck her finger in my chest. "Everyone who doesn't bow down to freight train Sophie is a bitch, or an asshole, and they deserve it, right? Because if you lash out first, you'll never be a victim again."

My jaw dropped. "Again—? I'm never a victim in the first place!"

"Of course not. You don't hop from bad relationship to bad relationship, so you never have to take anyone seriously. You *never*stew in a mire of your own fear and isolation to the point where I'm your only friend. Nope! You're just *strong*, is all."

The spin she put on the word "strong" corkscrewed straight into my sternum, and I choked on my own spit.

"You listen to me, Sophie." Jodie sucked in a deep breath and smoothed her skirts. "Go home. I don't want you here tonight. I will not have you ruin this for me because of your incessant need to despise everyone I'm with. Go home. Get your shit together! And don't show up at the wedding tomorrow if you can't be genuinely happy for me!" She spun on her heel and walked away.

A few paces out, she said. "After all, you say that you're my best friend. Prove it."

She left me.

She left me four times smaller.

She left me sliding down a filthy alley wall.

One of the smoking queens hurried over to me. "Yikes, honey, you okay?"

"Fuck off!"

"Yeesh, fine. Your friend is right about you."

Finally, I was alone. Gloriously alone. I stopped holding in the bullshit tears drowning my head. My nose burned from cigarette smoke. My heart hurt so much that I welcomed the death that seemed imminent.

And then I threw up pure Scotch all over the rat king.

When I was on my knees, coughing, aching, too horrified to even scream, things got worse. How could things get worse?

Tiffani.

I knew it was her by now without visual confirmation. Like how pets can sense the demonic spirit in the cold part of the room. Plus, her perfume was clearly named "Sinus Headache."

"Oh, Sophie. Sophie, Sophie, Sophie." Tiffani shoved a hand under my armpit and hauled me up. "Come on. Let's get a drink."

CHAPTER ELEVEN:
10 THINGS I HATE ABOUT MYSELF

I met Tiffani's gaze, and…there was no smirk. No abuse of vowels. No squeaky tone. My chest still ached like a heart attack, and I had no fight left. In a daze, I let her lead me out of the alley and down the street.

My body didn't feel real except for pain. How had any of this started? Why was I fighting Jodie? Why was I here at all? Dressed in a costume given me by someone else, playing a part in a script I wasn't allowed to read.

Our walk went by in a blur. Tiffani pulled me into a corner bar full of neon, drag queens, and drag-queen hangers-on, crowded even this early on a Friday night. I did love drag, that's why we came to South Beach, despite the tourists. Somehow, the queens being themselves, no matter how hostile the world, gave me a rare sense of hope as a queer gal. Usually.

My captor found us a free corner table, which was weird, since the crowd packed in like the organs crowding my throat. The wretched woman took my lack of speechifying as permission to order us drinks (Cosmos? friggin' ick) and interrogate me.

"Sophie," she began in the kind of voice you address a growling dog with, "why don't you want your best friend to be happy?"

My forehead thunked onto the table.

"Aw, sweeeeeeeetie! It's going to be okay. Once you --"

"Ooooh, I know!" I sat up. "Live in love, and never fear anything! Because life is sunshiiiiiine! And raaaainbows!"

She shook her head. "I never said to not fear anything. That's not possible, ha-ha! But the only thing you have to fear is fear of love itself."

A marvelous person delivered liquor, and I drank it despite its level of pink. It oozed down my gullet on wings of acrid sugar. Heh, maybe ingesting pink would help me ingest Tiffani better.

Tiffani placed her hand on my forearm. "Why do you believe you're not worthy of love?"

"Gaaah!" I shook her off me. "Stop your psychobabble! I see the benefit of having a…partner, okay?" Dammit, these tears kept welling up. Tiffani was a communicable disease. "I am not immune to the…gentle, er, feelings for, uh, humans. I just don't intend to abandon who I am for someone."

"You don't have to."

"Of course I do!" The crowd pivoted to stare at me, so I swiped at my eyes and forced myself to not scream at her. I took a shuddering breath. "Of course I do. Men don't want a partner, they want a mommy bang maid. Women don't want…" I ran out of my usual set of excuses.

She merely stared at me with a small smile.

I pressed my lids together hard enough to burst my own eyeballs. "Nobody wants someone fucked up like me. I'm not good at mushy. At words. At big, wet, sloppy discussions about relaaaationshiiiips." God, I really was turning into Tiffani, so I glared at her. "I just want to be me, but I'm broken. Who wants to hug barbed wire? Your experiment was doomed to fail, so let me go home!" My voice broke. "Pick a worthier candidate for your reign of terror next time."

Our drag queen waitress, a tall South Asian looker with a toothy grin and the sparkliest headscarf I'd ever seen, dropped another Cosmo in front of me with a, "You need this, Gloomy. You're officially the first weeper of the night."

Lookit me, accomplishing things. I saluted her with my gross drink.

Tiffani sipped delicately at her Cosmo and pursed her lips. "You don't have a very good opinion of women or men."

"Or anyone else." That's what Jodie had said, too. I held fast. "That about sums it up."

"Why?"

I downed Cosmo number two and involuntarily shook, which helped it go down, this $15 cough medicine. "I've been bullied my whole damn life. As a kid, I was too skinny, because my dad barely fed me. I legitimately think he forgot I was there." My shoulders fell a bit. "I was dirty, and my clothes were old and too small. Who doesn't love the smelly girl who steals her classmates' lunch money so she could eat one meal that day? My dad couldn't be bothered to buy peanut butter, not when the horses were running at Hialeah!"

"Oh, God," declared our waitress. She sat and slid another Cosmo over.

I swallowed this one a little easier and burped my appreciation. "Thanks, girl."

"My dad was shit, too," she told us. "First time he caught me in drag, he threw me out. I was 14, and my heinous sin was singing the Carpenters while wearing an old hijab of my mom's."

I shook my head. "That sucks. Let's go burn both their houses down."

She shot a half-smile. "If only. I'm Pamazon the Glamazon, by the way. Your leather dress is hot."

"I'm Sophie the Rom-Com Heroine. I like your sequined tits."

Pamazon raised one of her also-sequined eyebrows. "Rom-com?"

"My blonde hair is in my other purse."

"Ha!" She slapped the table and stood. "Let me get another round. I'll be back."

Tiffani tut-tutted all over me. "You're not that kid anymore, Sophie. You have a successful career, a vibrant side-hustle that will equal big bucks in the future, a --"

I scooted away. "Big bucks?"

She wagged a finger. "I can't give too much away!" Relaxing into her chair, she continued. "But your future will be bright if you abandon this 'not like other girls' nonsense."

I shot to my feet. "What? I… I am not like…not like other girls!"

Pamazon skidded to a halt next to me. "Come again?"

I swiped a Cosmo off her tray and swigged half. "I resent that. 'Not like other girls' is some self-hating misogynistic bullshit, and --"

Oh.

Shit.

I collapsed back into my chair.

"This was why I brought a bunch," said my new queenly friend, scooting four more drinks onto the table.

I could only stare, my eyes so wide they went dry. I wasn't a "not like other girls" girl. Was I? I hated women. I hated men. I hated everyone who was both or neither. Equally. Right? I told myself I was above it all.

Yup. There it was.

I slumped into myself. I was just as garbage as everyone said. My worthless dad. My asshole mom. My bullies. My teachers. I was the kind of garbage who treated the shining light in her life like trash, too.

And then I did a horrible, vile thing, in front of everyone. I burst into tears and collapsed over the table. I sobbed. Just sobbed. Every frustration from the last week. Every gut punch of my life. My armor had been cracked by sword after sword, until it finally shattered. I was the pathetic, drunk chick in the bar, and I couldn't stop crying, heaving, wailing. Oh, God, it went on forever.

"I give up!" I screamed, swaying to my feet. "Tiffani the Psychic has broken me!"

A guy next to me yelled, "Sounds hot!"

"Is she any good?" asked his friend.

"No, she's a menace. I demand a citizen's arrest! I -- *acck!*" I spun too fast, fell over my chair, and crashed to the floor. "Ew." It was sticky down here. Secretions of animal, vegetable, or patron?

Pamazon said, "At least the public embarrassment part of your rom-com is proceeding apace."

Through the dizzy fog in my brain, gentle hands rubbed my back—Pamazon on one side, Tiffani on the other. They lifted me into my seat.

"See?" said Tiffani. "You suffer from soul-shattering self-doubt and feelings of inadequacy as a byproduct of your abusive childhood. And you turn these negative self-images into outward aggression because nobody taught you how to cope."

I blinked at her. "And you got that from me falling on the floor?" I muttered, wiping my sticky hand on the tablecloth.

"I did," said Pamazon.

Tiffani played with a piece of her hair. "I should be a therapist."

"Yes!" agreed Pamazon.

"Except that I'm also a genius psychic with mysterious, yet potent powers."

Our glamazon's eyes went enormous. "I actually believe her."

"Hey, whose side are you on?" I slurred.

"Sophie, do you know why I'm so confident?" Tiffani asked.

I didn't answer. I hiccupped and cried. She would tell me anyway.

"I'll tell you." She paused. Dramatically! And leaned in like we were sharing secrets at a sleepover. "It's because I *decided* to be."

Wut. I lifted my head enough to shoot her a soggy glare. "That will solve all of my problems, thank you."

"Miss, you should listen to this lady," Pamazon said with more back pats. "Her hair is the shiniest hair I have ever seen, and I have wigs made of latex."

Tiffani nodded. "That is accurate. It might seem simplistic, but the gist of it is, if you believe you're garbage, everyone else will, too." She turned my head. Her eyes reflected blue neon, giving them an angelic glow. "You're not garbage, Sophie. You're not. If you told yourself all the great things about you, instead of replaying this toxic monologue to yourself, you might begin to believe it. Maybe not today. Maybe not tomorrow. Sooner or later, the positive messages you send your own way will start to shout over the nasty ones. When that happens, everything in the whole world is going to look brighter. I mean—doesn't it feel refreshing when you stop hitting yourself?"

My lip curled into a habitual snarl, but I pressed my twitching lips together because—I couldn't seem to argue.

"Now, loving yourself doesn't mean you have to suffer fools. Or bigots. It doesn't mean you have to stop dressing in black or telling sexist gamer jerks to shut up." With a soft hand, she swept the hair out of my eyelashes. "It just means your chest will stop hurting all the time. Wouldn't that be amaaaazing?"

"Yes!" Pamazon dabbed at her eyes with a napkin. "Do you have a book?"

My whole body shook uncontrollably. Pamazon wound a long arm around my waist and I sagged into her. I reached for the rest of my Cosmo, which wasn't so bad actually, but Tiffani slid it away from me.

"No more booze." She yanked some napkins from the holder and pressed them under my eyes, then wiped the snot from my nose. "You have to decide if you're going to stand up for your best friend tomorrow. If you're going to support her the way she's supported you."

I nodded, and more tears fell. "She deserves that," I whispered through snot.

"Yes, she does."

My head bobbled, empty and overflowing all at once. How could it be that simple? Or complicated? Telling myself I was great—*for real*. Great just for being…a human? Not because I wore awesome shirts or dominated at Warcraft? Seemed like I was being asked to climb a cliff with oven mitts on.

"Ugh, my boss is having a fit," Pamazon groaned.

I swerved the balloon containing my brain enough to see a tiny queen dressed like a green alien gesturing from the bar.

"Ladies," my favorite waitress ever began, "I've seen a lotta crying chicks in this place, and I'll tell you what I told them."

"What?" I asked.

"Be sure to give me a good tip."

I busted out laughing. "Of course." I reached into my not-sequin tits. "I swiped some of Bridget's cash."

Tiffani giggled, loud and bright, and I accidentally joined her. Growth?

Pamazon stood. "Also, go shake your ass on the dance floor, it'll make you feel better."

I handed the whole wad of money over. "Tiffani will pay the bar bill."

"Ha, ha!" she replied.

That had better mean yes.

She yanked on my arm. "Come on, Sophie Sweet. We're going to dance like everyone's watching and laugh like hyenas are our cousins!"

"Sure, who am I to disobey a classic quote?"

The pink freight train choo-chooed me to the center of the dance floor.

"I'm not much of a dancer!" I yelled above the pounding music. Ow, my eyes ached like my soul.

Tiffani popped me upside the head.

"Hey!" I hollered, jumping away, colliding with a man behind me. "Sorry, dude."

"Enough with the negative self-messages!" Tiffani screamed. "Who cares if you're not Rihanna? Just have fun! Say it—say, 'I am wonderful, and I deserve to have fun.'"

Nooooowhyyyyyyy? I sagged.

She popped me again.

I slapped at her, but she danced away, ha-ha-ing, of course.

"I am wonderful, and I deserve to have fun!" Tiffani yelled.

Some folks around us repeated it: "I am wonderful, and I deserve to have fun!"

She started toward me once again, her shimmy full of intention. I rubbed the back of my head and grumbled, "I am wonderful. I deserve. To have fun."

"Not good enough!"

"Come on, say it!" said a dancer next to me, his face red and bright.

My face screwed up to tell his face to screw off, but he grinned at me, nodding, encouraging.

I bounced on my boots, once, and breathed into my drunken state. Fine. I said, "I'm wonderful and deserve to have fun."

"Again!" demanded my tormentor.

I planted my feet, threw my head back, and screamed at the top of my lungs: "Aaaaaaah! I'm fucking amazing, and I deserve to have whatever the fuck I want!"

The crowd joined in our chant, people inserting their own adjectives and needs—whatever they, themselves needed to hear. It was either that, or nobody knew the words to this song. A big, drunken, grinding crazytime unfolded in which everyone improved their self-esteem and dance moves alike.

Thing was…with every jump, every jostle, every silly affirmation, I started to have fun for the first time in what seemed like forever. Maybe it was the booze. Or the damn crying. Or just me giving up. But I stopped commentating on the fun in my head and just let it happen.

Tiffani nodded to the beat and swayed in place delicately—like one of those bobble-heads you put on your dashboard, and it was the funniest thing I'd ever seen. Yet, the incessant need to mock her failed to rise from my gut. I laughed with her. And joined hands to jump around. We screamed our heads off to the music, even when the words got confuzzled, and we didn't know them from Eve. I didn't know the wordy words to any of this, but who cared? My body disappeared into a blur of drunk joy for hours and hours and…

Outside the club blurred into the cab blurred into the diner with the best pancakes I'd ever eaten. Tiffani did not eat the pancakes because they were white and made of fattening, and it went against her morals or something. She blurred on the sidewalk when we cackled at a guy who tripped after creepily trying to follow some innocent lady, and then Tiffani gave me my brass knuckles back so I could threaten him, which was awesome and funny lol. My apartment blurred, too. Everything blurrrrrr. Satan meowed, and I decided that *he* was my Prince Charming. Prince Charmoewing. I laughed and Tiffani laughed, and then I tried to hug Satan and fell down bye.

CHAPTER TWELVE:
IT ISN'T ROMANTIC

Perhaps it was another example of Tiffani's magic, but she and I awaited Jodie in the lobby of the hotel the next morning at 10:45am. We had not exchanged a word. Yets he'd handed me a coffee bigger than Satan when I pried one eye open in my apartment earlier. Maybe Tiffani's true talent was B&E.

I wouldn't say I liked her, curse her rom-com shenanigans to hell. However, my murderous urges had diminished along with my Cosmo-soaked brain cells. My head…well, which hurt more, the physical or emotional hangover?

Yet somehow my heart ached a little less. Sure, my stomach fluttered because Jodie might despise me this morning, but some of my baggage seemed lighter. Because I was good at dancing even when I wasn't, and I deserved to have fun. I deserved other positive things, too. Apparently. These words echoed weirdly in my brain, yet they were there. Hanging on by their tippy fingertips.

Hopefully, Jodie would allow me to maid-of-honor in sunglasses. Thanks to Tiffani, they were designer and enormous. Glam bug was a hot look for me. See? Positive affirmation crap.

I could not, however, overlook Tiffani's outfit today. On her head sat a pink and orange sculpture attached to a headband, and the sculpture appeared to be a physical representation of screaming. She wore a giant pink cupcake as a skirt, with a corset kind of thing on top. The ball of skirt had orange ostrich feathers sticking out of it.

I shook my head; that poor orange ostrich had died for nothing.

My heart leaped into my jugular the moment the automatic doors split, and my dearest person walked in the hotel. Mrs. Edwards and other family flanked her, and they all stopped short when their heads turned my direction.

Yeah. Why, oh why won't a floor open upto swallow you when you need it? Didn't I deserve *that*? Sunshine state, give me a sinkhole already!

Tiffani chirped into action. "It's the bride! Yay!" She jumped and clapped, and I almost broke into the club dance, like Pavlov's drunk. "The suite is ready for your amazing selves. Come along." She waved a hand, and the group moved forward.

"Jodie," I said. It came out a croaky squeak. Wow, too much screaming Flo Rida half the night. Welcome to my house of pain. "Jodie, can I talk to you for a moment?"

Mrs. Edwards shot me such a frown, I withered.

"It's an apology!" I croak-blurted. "I swear, I only have groveling to do. Happy to get on my knees, I --" My hand flailed toward the nearest faux-Grecian pillar for ballast, and I made it halfway to the floor.

Jodie stepped forward. "Stop, it looks like you won't get up again if you hit the carpet."

"Aaaaaaacurate," said Tiffani. She took Jodie's elbow and cocked her head. "We had a great session last night, and she's very sincere this morning."

"Oh, is she acknowledging that my fiancée is real today? And not a plot to some stupid movie?"

Thank you, bug glasses. Because that word—fiancée—pierced my soul.

I nodded. "Yes. Of course. I'm so sorry, Jodie. You deserve better than all of that yesterday. I --" My face screwed up without permission, and I started damn crying. Mrs. Edwards literally gasped. "I'm sorry. I love you, I only want your happiness." I sucked in a long, wailing breath that sounded like an air-raid siren made of cats. "Whatever you need from me today, you'll get it with a smile."

And then I smiled. It came out like a clown's in a horror movie, but I did it.

Deep breaths, Sophie. "Even the annoying jobs," I continued. "I'll sit next to mean old MawMaw Odessa and deflect the blows when she hits people. I'll punch anyone who asks, 'Where are the grooms?' because you know --"

"Some fool will say it," Jodie finished.

"Yup. I'll yell at people so they obey you during the photo session." I took a pull of coffee. A Tiffani pull—a loooooong pull. "And if any guest walks into the church wearing white, I will 'accidentally' spill sacramental wine all over them."

Made Mrs. Edwards giggle with that one. "Jodie, you've got a maid of honor and a bouncer in one. I say you should consider forgiving her. This girl is actually crying, which may be a sign of the apocalypse."

"No! I can't allow the apocalypse on Jodie's wedding day." I wailed, because the friggin' tears were happening again. Gah, Tiffani had broken me! The floodgates had opened, and I kept weeping like a human person why why why?

Jodie threw an arm around my shoulders. "Damn, Sophie. You're having the kind of emotions you only hint at late at night in the dark during sleepovers."

"Um, isn't everyone supposed to cry at weddings?"

The Edwards ladies agreed with that one, so they allowed me on the elevator and into the getting-ready suite. Jodie hadn't thawed, not completely, but she didn't appear to want to bludgeon me anymore. I could breathe again.

Her happiness really did matter to me more than any fucking thing in this universe. More than my game. More than my misguided pride. I pressed a hand to my chest and sank into a fluffy white couch. I had to do right by her today. No matter what.

"Thank goodness we got a makeup artist," Tiffani said. To me. And only me.

Moooore coffee. "I thought we were trying to build my self-esteem?"

"Of course, silly!" She flipped her hair. "Because you'll look soooooo pretty once we fix last night."

I nodded. "Yes, fine. I will be a pretty maid of honor, she said affirmation-ly."

"Eeeeeeee!" she screamed straight through my ear canal and into whatever now-shattered equipment lay beyond. "That's the spirit, Sophie!"

My ear ringing as loud as my hangover, I fled to Jodie's side. She sat at the elaborate triple mirror desk setup, a queen amongst commoners. I flipped through the wad of papers Tiffani had shoved at me first thing to get my marching orders. "Um, so I am going to call the restaurant downstairs and have them bring the brunch and mimosas now, is that okay with you, Madam Bride?"

She shot me a halfway smile, and it bolstered me enough to take off my sunglasses. Our eyes met, and she smiled all the way. So did I. I did *not* cry. Me and my best friend, my person, shared a moment of total understanding. She'd seen my bad, my ugly, and my occasional good. I'd have to get more good in this life if I expected someone this awesome to stick around.

I was gonna have to grow as a person. Dammit. Life lessons, who needed them?

"Mimosas, my queen?" I repeated.

"Yes, I shall allow you to fête me with champagne, maid of dishonor."

Panic shot up my spine, and I searched through the menu. "Oh, um, I don't think that kind of cheese is coming, but I'll jump on the phone and order it. We have brie, does that help?"

My best friend snorted at me. "I missed you."

I rushed forward and squeezed the hell outta her. "I'm so sorry."

She returned my iron hug. "I forgive you."

I pulled back. "Did—did you have fun last night? I hope you did."

"Yes! Relax, baby. Call for the champagne. We're good. You missing Queen of Queens, Latrice Royale, was punishment enough."

My shoulders sagged. "It's what I deserve." I adored Latrice. She'd been through hard, terrifying times and emerged through them to be a joyful drag queen in a weary world. I admired the crap outta her. She made a more womanly woman than I did, but somehow, I didn't mind sequins and sparkles when they were attached to her.

I fetched Jodie champagne. I gave her a hand massage, and a foot massage, I touched up her nail polish—neatly even!—and I sat like a good girl and endured a Picasso's worth of paint glopped onto my face. My smile never wavered as a sadist gouged my scalp with hair pins and singed it with a curling iron. Why the hairdresser had to straighten my curly hair, just to curl it again, just to pin it up, I didn't know. Being a woman was the literal worst.

The look Jodie gave me when the make-pretty people had made me pretty, though...it was worth any amount of torture. I hadn't been this glamorous in, um...

"Wow," Jodie breathed. "You are stunning. Watch out, single everybody!"

I swallowed the lump in my throat and tried to say *not as stunning as you*, but I'd been struck speechless.

She'd changed into her wedding outfit. My favorite bride wore a white, short-sleeved jumpsuit with a long cape in the back, trailing across the unworthy floor. Wow, the inside of the cape was sparkly, clear sequins or beads or something, so it shimmered like a cool stream with every move she made. The jumpsuit was high necked and hugged her in every right way. In every elegant way. The pants could be mistaken for a skirt, they were so wide and swingy. The deep, rich brown of her skin glowed against the white like a rare, dark jewel. She belonged at the Oscars!

Her hair had been teased and pinned into an Afro-kind-of-mohawk. Badass! I don't know what hairstyles are called; they should name this one

"The Jodie." She wore a long, chunky silver necklace, like a flapper might, with a giant aquamarine sphere dangling, shining right under her…

I closed my eyes and swayed on my feet, for I was overcome with a wave of… hangover. Probably. "Jodie, you're the most gorgeous thing I've ever seen," I whispered. "All other brides should give up. Um…except for Bridget. Who will also be gorgeous, I'm sure. How could she help it?"

Her arms closed around me, and I willed every ounce of love in the universe through mine to hug her back. Time seemed to stop, and all I thought was no matter how great this Bridget was, nobody deserved Jodie. Not even me.

Especially not me.

We broke apart, and her family crowded around her, offering her every bit of praise she earned every day of her life. Not by being perfect, but by being true.

I changed into my maid of honor tuxedo, and I looked pretty snazzy, honestly. Made my waist cinched and my butt bubbled. The silky aqua blouse underneath needed more opening, though, so I slid one last button free.

Jodie wolf-whistled at me, which I would live on forever.

After that, time blew by like a blur, although not a drunken one. Tiffani barked orders in her giggling way, Mrs. Edwards shot me wary glances, and I tried to be helpful. Quiet. Not stepping one toe out of line. I knew Mrs. Edwards loved me, but the truth was, I was Jodie's hoodlum friend and sometimes, I proved it.

"*No!*" I heard Tiffani's voice between my ears. "*You are her close and loyal friend. Even when you're an idiot, ha-ha!*"

I laughed, short and small. Oh, no. Tiffani was starting to make sense to me. I was clearly in the throes of Stockholm Syndrome! Soon, my knives would be scented, and my Sabbath, Pink.

Jodie and I waited in a small room off the back of the church while folks were being seated. I would walk down the aisle with Bridget's brother—hope he was as hot as his sister. Maybe he'd be my prince. I could use the distraction.

As time ticked closer to zero hour, Jodie babbled a lot of excited words, and I joked around with her as if on autopilot. But my face was still numb with nervous. Magic or no, this seemed extremely real. The smell of the sacramental wine tanged in my nostrils. The murmurs of the crowd ebbed and flowed.

Magic or no, this seemed extremely final. Something I would never come back from.

She would never, I mean.

Tiffani peeked into the room. "It's time!"

My breath fled entirely.

Jodie stood and smoothed the front of her fancy jumpsuit. "How do I look?"

Impossibly beautiful. "The woman who wouldn't marry you is a fool," I managed to say.

She swept me into another hug, but my arms wouldn't cooperate. Maybe they knew if they squeezed back, they'd never stop. It would get awkward. She might call security on me. Did they have security at a church? Would a priest leap through the door in his awesome long dress thingie and sweep the leg? Why was I thinking about this nonsense? Anything not to consider what was about to happen in this reality!

I tore myself away and crashed into the open door. *Ow.* "Jodie, you deserve every happiness in the world, and I hope you get that every day of your life with her."

"Oh, Sophie."

"No! No crying!" I busted out in a laugh and fetched a tissue for her from the desk. "We can't mess up your face. Let me. The makeup artist said to dab, not wipe."

She giggled, and I dabbed. "You listened to a makeup artist?"

"Only for you."

Tiffani waved me out of the room, and I couldn't speak anymore around the boulder in my throat, anyway. I squeezed Jodie's hand and damn near bolted from that suffocating room.

Just smile. Obey instructions. Smile. Obey. And maybe ogle a priest in a dress.

Do it for Jodie.

I walked to the organ music. I grinned while Jodie glided down the aisle like an angel. I gazed beyond and around her, the way you would at the sun. Everything went dim, and I squinted, and I kept on smiling. *Do it for Jodie.* Held her bouquet. *Do it for Jodie.* Listened to the preacher woman as she joined Jodie Edwards with Bridget—

Jones?

BRIDGET JONES?

My fog fled, and, from my perch beside Jodie, I shot eyeball daggers at Tiffani in the front pew. Much less satisfying than actual daggers, but my imaginary hot priest probably frowned on that kind of thing. The witch pursed her lips into a sneaky smirk. Ha. And also: Ha.

I smiled, I smiled, I smiled so hard my teeth hurt, because the joke was on me, right?

Do it for Jodie.

<h1 style="text-align:center">CHAPTER THIRTEEN:
BRAINWRECK</h1>

And so, they got married. *So.*

So.

SOSOSOSOSOS

CHAPTER FOURTEEN:
THE WEDDING PITY PARTY

At the reception, the Edwards family gave me the sacred and dangerous responsibility of hanging with MawMaw Odessa, Jodie's Great-Grandmother. She'd turned 100 this year, upon which she declared herself to be immortal and infallible. In truth, she'd always considered herself that way, but the birthday meant she felt even freer to belt people with her cane, run over them with her wheelchair, and throw groceries at them. Or knick-knacks. Apparently, half of Mrs. Edwards' ceramic kittens collection had taken flight during the engagement party.

I loved MawMaw for that. She inspired me, for I had often dreamed of trashing those kitties with their smug, judgmental faces. When you're 100, nobody puts you in jail for mayhem.

"MawMaw," I said, circling her chair at a safe distance. "It's me, Soph --"

"I know who you are, Jodie's white hoodlum friend."

"Aw, it's nice to be notorious! Don't you agree?" I caught her cane on the downswing. "Now, do you want some food?"

Her well-preserved face went sideways. "I don't want any sushi shit!" Honestly, she didn't look a day over 80.

"Yeah, me neither. Which is why I ordered a pizza." I waved the waiting delivery guy over to us and wheeled her to a table. "Double pepperoni with onions, right?"

Her eyebrows rose. Her razor-gaze glinted. "I guess that'll do."

One point for Sophie.

People glared at us, huddled at the side of the room, sucking down pizza at a table alone. MawMaw burped like a champion, and she did it louder every time someone looked shocked.

I caught Mrs. Edwards' eye as she made her rounds, and she nodded at me. Heh. Two points for Sophie.

"Sophie!" Tiffani click-clacked over to us. "Pizza? Ick, that does nooooooot go with our theme of a Coastal California Wellness Retreat and Collegial Kale Harvest."

MawMaw slurped pizza into her mouth and gnawed at it with uncertain dentures. "What the hell is Coastal California Wellness Retreat? Sounds like a hippie sex cult."

"It is," I assured her. "Although what they do with the kale, I don't want to know."

"Sophie!" Tiffani pursed her pink lips. "I have a list a mile long for you."

"I've been assigned to MawMaw."

Warning grumbles rumbled out of MawMaw's mouth.

"I mean, I enjoyspending time with MawMaw."

The grumbles turned into growls.

Damn, I couldn't tell what this lady wanted. She was so friggin' awesome.

Tiffani cocked her pretty head. "MawMaw --"

"You don't get to call me that," said MawMaw. "I don't know you."

I gave MawMaw a shoulder squeeze. I didn't catch the cane that time.

While I rubbed my freshly bashed arm, Tiffani said, "The point is, Ms. Edwards has a bounty of wonderful relatives, all of whom I'm certain are delighted to see *ouch!*" Tiffani hadn't caught the cane either, and earned herself an ass smash. Ha-ha!

Bam! MawMaw's cane slapped across Tiffani's backside again.

"Owwwwwwww!" wailed Tiffani.

I was definitely not laughing my friggin' ass off. "Good shot, MawMaw."

"Don't patronize me!"

Sigh. I adored her, especially since she made Tiffani run away like a squeaky giraffe.

I scooted my chair away from her a few inches. "Are you available as protection whenever Tiffani kidnaps me?"

MawMaw shook her head, slowly, her coke-bottle glasses glinting, her beehive trailing behind. "That chick ain't right."

"That's what I've been telling everyone!"

"Mm-hmm. Demons. I seen it before."

I looked her dead in the eye. "Can you exorcize her?"

"I need another pizza, a Bible, and a calendar of Denzel."

"What's the calendar for?"

Plop! She slapped me right upside the noggin. Owwww! Damn, she had a swing. "The calendar is to look at! I ain't dead yet! But also, he's known for demon-hunting. You don't know that 'cause you're white."

I grinned and waggled my eyebrows. "Oh, so it's *Black* magic."

"Don't sass me!" *Blam!*

I leaped out of swinging distance, cradled my stinging shin, and nodded. Dammit, I believed her. If Tiffani could be magic and ruin my life, why couldn't MawMaw suck the demons from her with a calendar of Denzel Washington? Maybe she'd return me to my reality using a cookbook and an action figure of Billy Dee Williams.

"It better be a nude calendar," said MawMaw, low, and with warning.

Um…

A few taps on my phone, and I ordered her another pizza. I requested a nude Denzel calendar in the comments section of the order, along with a huge tip, but I held little faith that Larry's Budget Pizza Explosion would come through.

Mrs. Edwards bustled over to us. "Sophie, uh, the speeches are about to start. You, uh, you have a speech?" Her voice went squeaky there at the end, like a synthesizer on the fritz.

My stomach dropped; I figured out what she was asking. People give speeches at weddings. The maid of honor did, too? Fuck, shit, fuck.

Probably shouldn't say "Fuck, shit, fuck," in my speech.

I placed my smile back on. "Yes.Of course," I ground out. "I have…a speech." I picked at my stubby fingernails. "It is a…speech that exists."

"I doubt that," said MawMaw.

"Don't sass me," I shot back.

Mrs. Edwards just blinked. "I'm…sure it is…a speech. That exists." I tried not to notice the panic filling her eyes."Come to the front. There's a seat at the head table for you. I'll have someone watch MawMaw."

"I'm not a damn kindergartener!"

I fled just as her cane deployed.

The DJ put on a soft track, and people began the speeches. Fuck, shit, fuck. Mr. Edwards. Mrs. Jones. Voices droned while my face went numb. To my right, Jodie giggled and grinned and sipped champagne, and I told myself not to stare. My stomach, as an organ, was just plain gone by now, replaced by the black hole void again. Hello, void-ness, my old friend.

Jodie nudged me.

"Hi!" I said.

"Hi," she replied. "It's your turn."

The void encompassed the earth and swallowed me whole. It probably would have been smart to listen to the other speeches because I had no idea what to say. This was why nobody should dress me up like an adult, okay?

Davy Jones, the best man, no shit, passed me a wireless microphone. He was skinny and noncommittally handsome in a "plays an evil frat guy in TV movies" kind of way. "Your turn, gorgeous," he said with a wink.

I hated him immediately.

I pushed back my chair to stand, and it screeched in a way that terrorized small children several blocks away. Everyone glared, and I hadn't said one single word.

Nowhere to go but up?

My heart thudded so hard I shook with it. Just say a few words about Jodie. No cussing. No insults, not even about the horrible kale wedding theme, which I fully blamed on Bridget. *Do it for Jodie.* I cleared my throat.

"Hi, everyone." Good. That was good! "I'm…I'm…" I had a name, probably. "Sophie. Sweet. My last name is entirely ironic."

Crickets.

I nodded. "Yup, I am the maid of honor. I've, um, sh-- never done this before. Whew, I didn't say, 'shit.'" I gasped. "Um!"

The entire Edwards clan laughed, MawMaw's cackle sailing over a sea of faces to reach me.

I blurted a cackle and refused to look at Jodie. "Sorry. I'm tr--trying."

Jodie squeezed my free hand. "You're shaking fit to break apart! It's okay." She smiled up at me, warm and wonderful. "It's okay."

A tear slipped down my cheek. I went to wipe it and conked myself in the face with the microphone. The *bonk* echoed through the room. Hey, at least they were laughing with me. Maybe.

"I'm supposed to be speechifying about my best friend on the planet, Jodie. I'm not one much for words. I'm bad at…human…ness." Haaaaaaa. "But the one thing I can talk about is Jodie. Because she's inspiring."

I sucked in a breath that sounded like it'd gone through a desk fan. I heard Mr. Edwards softly groan, "Oh, God."

"My fellow Americans," I began. Accurate if not original. "The internet defines 'maid of honor' as…" Where the FFFFFF was I going with this? I hadn't looked this up! "As…the maid. With the honor. Ha! If you could see my apartment, you would know neither is true."

Crickets.

RKFGJA;LKDGJ;SLKFDJGKLDF;LKGMKDFMVLNSVEOIRFOK

Except…Jodie snickered. And snorted. And shook her head.

I stood straighter. "What *is* true is my love for Jodie." I pressed my hand to my stomach. "I hope all of you have someone in your life who is as amazing. As true. As mighty as Jodie. Someone who, even in dark times, chooses to see and do good. Who inspires me to grow and change, if for no other reason than to try to become worthy of her. Look at her! She's --" I took a deep breath, because it wouldn't do to call someone else's bride "stunning and sexy." Right? I cleared my throat and swallowed down a weird bubble of emotion that would probably come up later in the form of gas, like street tacos. I shook off a chill. "So, anyway, uh, just know that I'd do anything for her. I'd beat up MawMaw for her."

Someone gasped. But it wasn't MawMaw. She cracked up, as did Jodie.

"So behave, MawMaw!" Jodie called. "I can sic her on anyone in this room."

Well, everyone laughed at that.

Except me. "She's right. I'm her bazooka to point. Guess that's what I have to say: Be good to Jodie, or else, because I own a lot of weapons. A lot. I mean, this is Florida, most of them are legal. Plus, I have little to lose and would rule any prison I'd ever be sent to. So remember that, Bridget."

Bridget Jones choked on her champagne.

"I mean everyone." I raised my glass. "To Jodie!"

Every last one of them just stared at me.

I sat, accompanied by a quiet room, except for two people who started applauding: Mr. and Mrs. Edwards. They nodded at me, I nodded at them. I was Jodie's white hoodlum friend, after all.

DJ Happy Mix snatched the mic out of my hand with a, "What the fuck," and stalked away.

I kept grinning, my stomach unknotting, and downed my champagne. Ahhhhhh. I hadn't gotten to threaten a room full of people in *so* long.

The DJ announced, "Now our bride and bride will begin their first dance!"

I swiveled side-eyes to Jodie, who was staring full-face at me. She sniffed, licked her lips, and said, "You would totally be the queen of the women's prison."

Gasp! I clutched my chest. "Thank you."

She doubled over laughing. So did I, but we couldn't enjoy it because Bridget Jones shoved between us, saying, "Come on, wifey! It's time to dance, not do…whatever this is."

Jodie hugged me from behind and left to do the first dance. The married dance. Married. Married, married, married. I fled the nightmarish table at the front where everyone stared at you while you had a breakdown and scurried around the edge of the room. Wonder which car was Bridget's? And how easy it would be to make her tires explode?

Everyone avoided me like the plague, nice, so I found MawMaw, being similarly avoided. The full dancing started, thank goodness. "Let's dance, MawMaw Odessa."

"You're not my type. Too mean."

Wow. Might be the greatest compliment of my life. I wheeled her anyway, like a mean person would. Three points for Sophie. "See, there's your grandson. Mr. Edwards! Come dance with your grandmother!" I screeched it so loud, the man had absolutely no choice whatsoever.

"These people are dancing like whores!"

"Ain't it wonderful?"

MawMawraised her cane, I ducked, and Mr. Edwards saved me. He said, "Let's dance, MawMaw. If you hit anybody, I won't give you the extra cake I stashed."

"Did you make it?"

"No."

"Good. Hoodlum here will stash me another piece, won't you, hoodlum?"

I saluted her. "Yes, ma'am."

Mr. Edwards blinked in confusion. "What's wrong with my cake?"

I shrugged. "I…I've been told to give the lady what she wants. Sorry, sir."

"You can do the same for me, cutie." Davy Jones grabbed my arm and yanked me damn near off my feet. His smile shined dully, like a Ken doll's. "Sorry, everyone, but I need Sophie for a dance. Try to shield the children from MawMaw's blows, will ya, Trevor?"

MawMaw started swinging. "Don't say my name, or my son's name. We don't know you, douchebag!"

She swung, I blocked. *Pop!* Right in my kisser! I stumbled away, shielding my already swelling bottom lip, and thought *well, it's a good thing I'm not kissing anyone.* Game, set, match to MawMaw. Her best play was being too old to hit back.

"Oh, no, sexy lady!" Davy Jones, still manhandling my arm for some reason, pulled me against his body—his whole body—and rubbed a thumb over my bleeding bottom lip. "Poor girl, you're—"

I snatched MawMaw's cane and clubbed him on the shoulder. The *crack!* that sounded chased away my hangover like no coffee or booze had managed all day. Wow, it made me violence-horny, my third-favorite kind of horny, after horny-horny and food-horny. And he finally released me.

Standing at my full five-foot height, I said, "Number one, I am not a girl. Do I have a Trapper Keeper? Am I attending the third grade? No! Second, why was your dick rubbing on me? Why were you touching my friggin' mouth? I don't know you. Do you even wash your hands after the urinal? How about you ask me for a dance instead of commanding me? Am I supposed to swoon because you're in a rented tuxedo that smells vaguely of sauerkraut?"

"Sophie --" Mr. Edwards grabbed the cane from the other end.

I pulled away from him. "I have more questions for this Monkee." MawMaw cackled; the sound propelled me. "Do you keep your good sense in your locker, where you drowned it?"

"What's going on here?" trilled Bridget Jones, swooping in with a Cover Girl grin to save her similarly stupidly named bro.

I sucked in a deep breath to stifle my rage as everyone talked at once. MawMaw snatched back her cane just to prod me with it, for she clearly wanted me to assault Davy Jones some more. Jodie had turned her attention over here, and shiiiiiiit, I could not get in trouble! Not after I'd done so well today with behaving as a human and almost delivering an okay speech!

Though I wasn't drunk, everything slowed down and went wobbly. Davy Jones reached out to grab me—again!—with smarmy eyes. I jerked backward to avoid him, right over MawMaw's chair, *oh, craaaaaaap!*, and kept flipping, butt-over-head. A rip sounded, long and slow, yet I saw nothing but black fabric. *Bam!* I hit the floor with my hip. Every nerve exploded, I screamed, gasps echoed around me. On the fake wood, over concrete, I rolled from side to side. Stunned from the throbbing, driving pain, I cradled my ass with my free arm, and—

My ass.

My *bare* ass.

Where—my pants?—Mrs. Edwards screamed my name—my ass—cold air whooshed across my bare fucking ass!

You know, in retrospect, perhaps my best friend's wedding was one place I should have worn underpants.

Someone jumped on top of me. "I'll shield you!" said Davy Jones, the glint in his eyes even wetter now, probably because I owned a magnificent ass. Round, juicy, firm from a lifetime of kicking. Although from the searing throbbing pain, it had to be half-purple already.

Now was the time to behave with dignity. And calm. These things happen. Into each life, a little rain of ass must fall onto a hotel ballroom floor.

If only I possessed that level of chill.

Instead, I screamed; elbowed that gropey creep off my friggin' body, where his hand had landed directly on my bare ass; and flipped onto that bottom to at least plug the leak. So to speak.

Oh, God, mistake. Mistake! Pain! Throbbing! Armageddon! I might never sit right again!

I peeled one eye open. The entire. Wedding. Circled. Me. Half of them with gleeful expressions and recording cell phones, because what else is there to do in our modern dystopia?

Not one extended a hand to help. Except for Davy Jones, his legs still tangled with mine.

MawMaw cracked him upside the jaw, and that dude went *down*. Her other cane-hits had been love taps compared to this swing.

"Thanks, MawMaw," I groaned.

"You thicc enough to defend."

I giggled. I laughed. I guffawed. It broke the dam, and everyone joined in. My face caught fire, damn it, because I was usually not so easily embarrassable. Once, I'd streaked across the football field to protest cheerleaders. Now, however, I froze in place because my tuxedo pants lay in tatters, one leg torn half off, the corner still caught in MawMaw's wheelchair.

And who should break through the crowd?

"What are you doing?" Jodie whisper-screamed. "Are you kidding me?"

"Hey!" MawMaw raised her cane. "I won't hit the bride, not today, but you need to settle down. This Davy Jones fella was groping the white hoodlum right and left. She tried to get away, tripped over me because she's a clumsy white hoodlum, and her pants tore. If you're gonna blame someone, blame him."

"Excuse me!" Davy Jones said, indignant and back on his feet. "All I wanted was a dance!"

MawMaw swiped at him. "No means no!"

I sat there, my mouth bleeding on my pretty, destroyed blouse, and felt the bruise on my hip spreading to epic proportions. My head fell into my hands, and I gave up on this whole existence. Perhaps my true love was my ass bruise.

Fitting.

"Sophie, honey, I have a blanket for you." Mrs. Edwards! She draped it around me and held it together at my waist. "Okay, slowly stand. That's good. MawMaw, fix her from behind. Everyone, please disperse! Sophie merely fell, that's all. Grow up!"

Finally, I managed to get to my feet and hold the blanket around the bottom half of me.

Jodie's nostrils flared, her eyebrows colliding into one another. "You just had to ruin it."

Panic rendered my bones pure jelly. "No! It was an accident, I swear it. I wouldn't—"

"You wouldn't? Like you wouldn't last night?"

"It was his fault!" MawMaw pointed at Davy Jones.

Jodie threw her hands up. "I don't believe that. His grievous sin was asking you to dance? Sounds about Sophie."

"No, no." I just kept shaking my head, slowly, as if through Jell-O or something. My voice came out raspy. "I-- I tried. I tried all day."

"This is you trying?" She barked a short, snotty laugh. "That's pathetic, Sophie. Most people do not have to try this hard to be normal! Just—leave. Please. You're half-naked anyway. It's embarrassing."

She stomped away, followed by her smug-faced Bridget Jones, and the crowd followed behind.

I froze in place, mouth open, brain disbelieving. My eyes burned, but no tears came out. I was beyond weeping, which somehow seemed worse than all the crying. A hot shame made my chest sweat, and I damn near fell, only for Mrs. Edwards to catch me.

She met my eye and swiped the hair out of my mouth. As I stood there, shaking, I think Mrs. Edwards actually forgave me for last night. She smiled, small and sincere. All of a sudden, I needed to hug my surrogate mom so tight, she squeaked before pulling away.

She brushed the tears from my cheeks and gave me a gentle, odd look. I held my breath for some reason. "I know you love her, Sophie," she said. "But she and Bridget are going to be really happy."

It sure would be nice to know where my stomach kept running away to. I swallowed down every emotion, I was good at that. Like a robot, I agreed, "Yes. Of course. I'm happy for her." Once again, I *smiled, smiled, smiled.* It made my lip split and ooze. *Do it for Jodie, even if she hates you.* I licked at the salty blood and couldn't meet her eye. "I only ever want what will make her life the best it can be."

She rubbed my back. "I know, honey. But you..." She sighed. "It's probably best—"

"I'm going." After my behavior last night, the whole Edwards clan deserved to celebrate without more disasters. I clutched my blanket with as much dignity as my sore, bare ass was capable of and started toward the door, whispers and hisses and mockery following behind me. Honestly not the first time I'd been kicked out of somewhere in disgrace.

But I usually didn't care.

Because it wasn't usually Jodie kicking me when I was down.

CHAPTER FIFTEEN:
CLUELESS

Come along, Sophie." Tiffani grabbed my arm and marched me through the hotel lobby.

Where the hell had she come from? She was always sneaking up behind me! Did she have a transporter and a Scotty? "Where are we going?"

"We have to decorate the bridal suite, silly!"

I yanked away and clutched my butt blanket. "No. Absolutely not. I have to go home! My ass feels like it was pounded by a Mac truck. Uh, so to speak. Leave me alone, okay? Please?" I actually whimpered at her. My whole body sagged. I possessed no strength except to stumble home. I had to get home. To my only friend, my cat, who never snickered at my butt. Or, at least, he did it in a cat language I didn't understand.

But then—I yelled, "Hey, pizza lady!" From a reserve of strength that required grease, I plodded her direction. "That's mine."

The small woman examined me up, and down, and up again. "What happened to you?"

I pointed my elbow at Tiffani the Psychic-Guidance Counselor-Goodwill Manager-Private Secretary-Vagine Examiner-Wedding Planner-Bruise Dispenser. "*Her.*"

"Uh, okay. Would this help?" She lifted her pizza bag. "The last time I ended up wrapped in a blanket in public, a pizza helped." With a faraway gaze, she added. "As did tequila. Of course, the tequila kinda started the whole thing…"

My lip cracked in a new place as I managed to smile. "You get me."

Her eyes went wide, and she nodded in solemn solidarity. "Thanks for the tip, by the way. I couldn't find a nude calendar of Denzel Washington, though. Best I managed…" She slid something out of her pizza bag.

It was warm in my hands, the calendar. I flipped it over to see Don Cheadle. Not nude, but still a cutie. He posed in a fireman's helmet.

Pressing it to my chest, I whispered, "Thank you. Thank you so very much." MawMaw wasn't getting the lovely Don Cheadle away from me. Not now.

I also took my damn pizza.

Tiffani dragged me away from my new best friend, Tequila and Calendar Lady, and toward the elevator bank. Once in the metal box, and away from inquiring ears, I went offensive. On the offensive. Same diff. "So, Tiffani. Great party! I feel like such a heroine right now. Where is my rom-com lover, hmm? I don't think it was Davy Jones, who got a chubby while groping me on the dance floor."

"Ha-ha! You keep trying to be funny!" With a sideways look, she said, "Although, he wasn't very nice, was he? Sometimes, the bit players take on a life of their own."

I narrowed my eyes at her so hard, she actually managed to appear sheepish.

We dinged at the penthouse level. Fancy schmancy. This wedding had been well planned. It seemed that Tiffani's talents knew no bounds. If only she used them for good.

We entered the suite in silence. Wow, it was over the top, in white and golds, with navy blue velvet curtains, and a huge king-size bed in the center of the bedroom. Beautiful. The kind of thing I only saw on TV for the first couple of decades of my life.

I—I couldn't breathe. Couldn't breathe! I clutched my tightening chest and found myself falling to the carpet. On my knees. On my butt.Arrrgggghnoooooooooooooooo! I allowed myself to continue collapsing until I lay horizontal. Was this a heart attack? Yay: death.

But no. I stayed sadly alive.

Only one thing to do. While I gasped for air, I flopped the pizza box down, threw the lid open, and took a bite.

Better.

"Sophie!" Tiffani stamped her high heel. "The room is going to smell like pizza!"

"Yeah, I know. You're welcome." This horrid woman really made no sense.

She sighed. I munched. After several more sighs, she hurried over and pulled my sweaty head into her lap.

I couldn't fight her. I just ate. The room seemed to echo without sound, reverberating through my skull. Even my newfound spring of weakness water had finally dried up.

She smoothed my hair from my eyeballs. "Shhhh, it's okay, Sophie."

I swatted her hand limply. "Stop."

"It's okay, sweeeeeeeetie."

I went hot all over. "No, no." The black hole inside my soul told me nothing would ever be okay again. "What'sh happening to me?" I asked through pepperoni.

"Only you can answer that."

I pushed myself off her, not nicely, with at least one jab landing in a soft place, and rolled across the room until I hit the bed. "Why?" I stayed there, wrapped around one of the bed's feet. Wow, it was so clean under here. "Why are you doing this? I didn't even have a rom- with my -com this time. And I'm not laughing!" Spit flew outta my mouth, but none hit her stupid face. "Come here and let me spit on you! You're giving me a heaping rom-complex." I added with a whimper, "I'm on the floor making sadness puns."

I turned to try to take in the damage to my ass. Once the blanket fell away, I gasped, and Tiffani let out a shriek. A red, purple, and black monster crept across the side of my butt and bloomed down my hip. I couldn't see the whole thing without a mirror. This damn thing had to be at least nine inches long, and, like six wide! A moan escaped me, and I gritted my teeth to roll back over to my pizza. And Don Cheadle. Aw, February had him dressed like a Valentine's teddy bear.

Tiffani's brows came together, and finally, *finally!*, annoyance showed on her face. I sucked in a deep breath for the first time in hours—somehow her actual human emotion made me think I'd broken through the veneer of *Tiffani.*

"Do you really want to know?" she asked.

"Know what?" I arranged the blanket over me. Ish. Even its soft touch friggin' hurt my enraged skin. The air hurt it. "First, more pizza."

"First, we have to decorate the bed, ha-ha!"

Ha-ha, no-no! First, pizza. Pizza was an emotion I understood, consisting of sub-feelings I could deal with. Carb sub-feeling. Pepperoni sub-feeling. Gooey, stringy cheese sub-feeling, the kind that warmed your gut the way life refused to.

I pressed my eyes shut. Why was she making *me* do this? Of all people? I managed to stand; my hip killed me more and more by the minute. I snatched her basket of red rose petals—I was in Instagram hell more and more by the minute—and threw them across the bed in one toss. "Boom, decorated."

The sight of the huge bed, all romantical now and…I fell across it, onto my good hip, so I didn't have to look at it. Munch, munch, munch. Huh, this was an amazingly soft, and somehow firm, mattress. The kind of wonder-bed perfect for a bridal suite. What Jodie would sleep on. What Bridget *Jones* would sleep on.

What they would sleep on together.

Somehow, Tiffani was so psychic, she lifted a garbage can under my mouth for when I puked. Last night's Cosmos, check. Pizza, check. And shame. Stinking, burning shame. Checkity check check.

I flopped over the side and thought: just kill me now, universe. It was my only method of escape…except for murder? Slowly, I turned, and step by step --

"No, the universe will not murder you, ha ha! Come up here." Tiffani sat beside me and yanked me back onto the bed. She propped me on my uninjured side and smoothed back my hair again. "And I can kill you with my brain."

"Yet you never do." *Don't stop the hair thing, though*. Damn her, it was nice.I said, "If you aren't going to end me, bring more pizza."

She huffed, "You just vomited!"

"Yeah. Which means I'm empty of pizza." Wow, she possessed no common sense whatsoever.

"Sophie, Sophie." She actually did fetch it for me, and the calendar, then returned to her hair-playing. "I do this because I believe in love."

Oh, hell. "Lots of people bewieve in wuv," I said as nastily as I could manage through acid-burned vocal chords. "They rent *Casablanca* and post terrible pink Comic Sans poetry on Facebook. They do not kidnap innocent assholes and destroy their lives."

Above me, Tiffani's lips pursed. "See, we do have something in common. A hatred of Comic Sans." She kept playing with my curled, straightened, curled hair. I sank into her, just a little. "My parents are still together. Thirty years of marriage so far, and not a day has gone by when they don't profess their profound love for one another. Their joy at being in the same room. Their wish for the other's total happiness. They were almost like…characters from the movies. Their total bliss translated into them being super fun to grow up with. They let me run wild, ha-ha! They wanted me to be happy."

I squeezed my eyes shut. Again. Must have been nice, as a kid, to see that. I needed more pizza, for my black hole demanded payment. My doting father only ever referred to my mother as "The Bitch."

Tiffani continued, "And yet, I have never been in love."

That caught my attention. I shifted around to almost being on my back; Tiffani put a pillow under my bruise to prop it up.

Her face fell, the smile falling away in fits and starts. I paused, pizza halfway to my mouth.

She sighed. "I've tried. I've dated." Her eyes blinked her huge lashes, which were especially thick and magazine-cover-y today. "It's difficult as a self-made woman in the world. You know. And I'm Korean, mostly. People hold some grossy gross stereotypes about women like me. They see my amazing hair and the devotion to fashion, and they consider me a Barbie doll to play with. Except for you, who considers me a Barbie doll to hate."

My mouth opened to argue, but it wisely snapped closed. Yeah. I had made a lot of assumptions from the jump.

"I don't actually think you judged me for being Korean," Tiffani said, placing a hand on my arm. "But you have judged the crap out of me."

I jerked my thumb toward my chest. "Kidnapped."

She raised one shoulder and flipped her hair. "So says you."

My spite rose. "Wh--"

"Anyway! We were talking about me, not you, shh!" She flashed that sweet smile of hers, and it occurred to me that maybe *she* was actually made of barbed wire.

Just like me.

"I'm 30 years old," she said. "I know I don't look it, but I guess I thought I'd find my soulmate by now. My parents met at 15, high school sweethearts, and have never separated for one day since then." Her expression took on a faraway cast. "So when I see people who *could* love— who are wonderful, who have so much to give, who aren't giving it…I get frustrated!" She went full squeak, and I accidentally smiled. "I have to help! It's my divine purpose! I have to help people stop hitting themselves because I literally can't staaaaand it."

I turned the widest of gazes on her. "Did you just say you kidnapped me because I'm wonderful?"

Oooh, she didn't want to admit it; her face gave her away.

"How many people have you done this to?"

"For. Done this *for*. Ummmmmmmm…none who were as stubborn as you."

Heh. I continued eating my pizza. "Tiffani, I have no doubt you'll achieve your dreams or whatever. All of them. You're determined and relentless." *Understatement.* "Sweet and stunning. He, or she, or they are out there; I'm sure they'll live, love, and 'ha-ha' with you. Forever. You're basically a mascot for the Hallmark Channel."

She stretched out beside me. "I just panic, you know? I want to have kids and be a stay-at-home psychic." I shot her a frown at that one, and the witch smirked. "I want to raise them to have open, kind hearts. To not make assumptions, but to merely live and be."

"You can have all that." The urge to roll my eyes rose…nah. I propped my head in my hand and licked my fingers. "So, do you, like, torture others into love to, sort of, karmic-ly bring it to yourself?"

She bolted up to sitting. "Oh, my goodness. Yes, Sophie. I think I do."

"How's that working out so far? I mean, look where you are right now? Not one eligible person for you here, but there were plenty at the reception. The Edwardses are a pretty people."

Her nostrils flared, and, for once, she got a taste of what I'd been through. It made me smile. Hey, you can take the barbed wire off the girl…

"Okay, okay." She sighed. "And yes, the Edwardses are genetically blessed in many ways."

"So, where's my romance, Tiff?" I crawled onto my knees and spotted the minibar. *Yes.* I stumbled there with a medium-to-large level of ass-hurt. After downing one whiskey bottle and tossing three more onto the bed, I limped back to her. "What the hell was the point of this one? Or did you just have an insatiable need to introduce me to Bridget Jones?"

"Love is the point of all of them, Sophie Sweet."

I flapped my arms and reached for the whiskey. The only true love Tiffani was going to hook me up with was alcohol poisoning. Hopefully, our life together would be hazy and brief. "I don't know what the last day has been, but none of it has been love."

"You sure?" Tiffani cracked open one of the whiskey bottles, sniffed it, and pulled a face.

My stomach went twisty. "What do you mean?"

"It's love that put you by Jodie's side today. When she needed you." She wandered toward the minibar. "It's love that taught you valuable lessons about not being selfish last night. About making new friends. About trying new things. Ooh, champagne!" One *pop!* later, she poured it into a glass. "It's love that's starting to teach you that you must open up or live miserably. You're young, Sophie, and life is looooong when you're so afraid of everyone rejecting you that you choose to live apart."

My knees buckled. The bed caught me, and I rolled onto my side, a fish out of water. The black hole inside me, always beckoning, dimmed with the realization: "I have to give to get."

She rushed to sit next to me. "Yes!"

"But you give, and you haven't got."

Her head snapped away, her face going hard.

"I'm, I'm sorry." Sigh. This day had been a week. I flopped further up onto the bed. "But I guess belief is the first step. Or some shit, right? Like…I believed I could make a kick-ass game of my own. So I went to school, dominated 'cuz I'm awesome, and got the job I wanted."

"That's exactly right. You did those things, you worked in a positive direction, because you knew you deserved them."

Sure, okay. I got where she was going. But. "It's not that simple. Sometimes, the best person doesn't win. Also, love and… and relationships aren't pithy sayings. They're work. Complicated work. And my machinery is broken. Or some other simile."

"Sweetie," she put a gentle hand on my shoulder. "You mean metaphor. And we're all broken. In our own way. Sure, your brokenness was unfair from your awful family and should never have happened. Yet, you still deserve the same wonderful things that people with idyllic childhoods get. There is no line that says you must be this 'lifted up' to get on the ride. Take Jodie."

I swallowed my feelings lump and tensed. "Jodie is perfect. She absolutely deserves a happy ending."

"Of course she does, ha-ha!"

Well, I supposed she'd suppressed her *ha-has* for a while; I could give her one. I regretted that when she added—

"But she's not perfect. She has flaws"

I scoffed so hard, I left scoff marks on the golden duvet. This libel would not stand. Slander? Fancy words for lies. "Look, okay, technically, I suppose she has flaws, per se, but they don't matter. Like—who cares that she snores? It's cute. Except when she keeps me awake, that's annoying, okay, and she refuses to wear that nose-strip thing, but she can't help it."

Whiskey fired my belly. "And she blurts the answer in Final *Jeopardy* when I'm still thinking about it. I've told her to stop it, butthe witch is just damn fast. She likes being faster. She *loves* being right." I laughed, because now we had a contest for who yelled out the answer first. "If you go to her place, there will be, like, 10 pairs of little socks everywhere. They stay wherever she's dropped them until she does laundry, I swear. I have tripped over her socks so many times, in my own apartment, too. One time, I fell on the cat. Who bit me, then went to sleep on her lap."

We laughed together, and Tiffani's open smile made me want to keep talking. In this moment, I didn't hate her. What was that emotion even called? When you almost not-hate your enemy?

My shoulders inched down. "Jodie likes to call me stubborn, but whoa, is she ever. We have arguments from ten years ago still. She hits me in the face with her stuffed animals! Oh, and she sleeps with stuffed animals."

Tiffani giggled. "Really?"

"Yes! She has this stupid, ugly old pig." I snorted and shook my head. "She calls it 'Piggy Bear,' because when she was little, she thought it was a bear and not a pig. It's all matted up and grody. She loves it so much. I'll turn over at sleepovers and have this thing stuck under my butt. Then I pass it to her when she's asleep, and she hugs it like a kid, so happy. It --"

Whooping sounded from the hall, cheers from several people, and Jodie's unmistakable voice sounding joyful.

We froze.

"Quick!" Tiffani said, leaping up. She slapped the pizza box against my chest. "Grab your butt blanket, too!" She tottered to the adjoining living room. "There's an exit from here. Come on, come on! Bring the bottles with us."

I scooped everything into my butt blanket and carried it out like a hobo while Tiffani smoothed the bed and, er, fluffed the rose petals or whatever. Just as we closed the door between the rooms, people entered the bedroom. Well-wishers made adorable winky jokes about the bridal suite, Bridget *Jones* made one back, and then everyone cheered, saying, "Kiss, kiss!"

Tiffani stole a large throw from one of the couches and traded blankets with me so my ass was covered when we fled the room. Nobody was in the hall, and we managed to make it into the elevator without being seen.

Breathing way too fast, I collapsed against the side of the elevator. "That was close. At least I left my pizza smell behind."

Probably for the last time. No more sleepovers for me and my girl.

Jodie was married. Jodie was married. All at once, I overheated and started sweating. I had a flashback, images of the days after my mother left. Feeling sick and hopeless. Certain it was my fault, because I wasn't a good enough kid for her to want to stay. I hugged my queasy belly and slid down the wall.

Tiffani pulled the emergency stop, like we were in a movie. "Why can't you be happy for her?" she demanded, the therapy portion of the evening finished at last.

"I am," I ground out. Crap, I was gonna vomit.

"No, you're not. You're pale and sweaty. You're shaking."

I clutched my head. "Shut up, shut up! I want her to be happy."

"Not like this."

"No!" I pushed into the corner to try to get away. But there was nowhere to go.

She crouched in my friggin' face. "Why not?"

"I --" God, I would die in this tiny box! I shook so hard I might break apart. How was this happening? After many successful years of avoiding any emotion whatsoever, now I was having *all of them*! And they sucked *just as much as I always thought!*

Tiffani screamed, "Why don't you want her to be happy?"

"I'm jealous! Okay?" It would eat me alive.

"Of whom?"

My gaze went blurry with tears. I whispered, "What?"

She leaned forward, until she stood nearly nose-to-nose with me. "Jealous of Jodie? And her happy ending?" Her eyes narrowed. "Or of Bridget?"

Oh, my God.

CHAPTER SIXTEEN:
THE 26-YEAR-OLD SPINSTER

Sophie! Sophie!"

Why was someone always yelling my name in an angry tone? It felt personal.

Beautiful darkness surrounded me, and I rolled over in bed. My butt! I -- oh. I reached under the covers slowly to check the state of The Ass Bruise That Ate Florida, but I didn't hurt. Huh?

"Sophie, rise at once!"

"Be quiet, Tiffani," I groaned. The bed shifted weird—stiff and…weird. I sat up. This mattress was small, with a rugged wooden footboard carved with fat, waddling sheep. Not even a twin size, actually, just some bizarre small bed. Where the hell was I?

Memories of yesterday flooded back. Wedding. Butt blanket.

Jodie.

My body shrunk to the fetal position, and I cradled my head in my hands. My stomach dropped. Oh, hell and disaster, my Jodie was married.

Light spilled across me as a curtain got dragged, and I peeled one eye open.

And laughed my butt off.

"Tiffani! Holy shit, what are you wearing?" I added a "ha-ha!" for extra mockery. She looked like Bob Cratchit's mom in a long,ugly antique dress and a frilly bonnet thing. True to form, she was pink head to toe. And her toes? Clad in the least old-fashioned stilettos I'd ever seen. She might get burned as a witch in those. "Are you doing an imitation of saltwater taffy being pulled over a haunted doll?"

She pinched up from head to toe.

I laughed at Tiffani the Psychic-Guidance Counselor-Goodwill Manager-Private Secretary-Vagine Examiner-Wedding Planner-Bruise Dispenser-Haunted Doll. As always, crapping on Tiffani's ridiculata never failed to pull me from my black hole.

And its many horrible realizations from before I would never admit to.

The haunted doll flapped over to me. "I say, dearest daughter… "

Dearest…oh, no. Dearest…*daughter*? No, no, no, no, I already had one terrible mother—two was plain overkill!

Evil Mother 2.0 kept talking. "…and such disrespectful language will never gain you a husband."

The horrors of our new familial relations aside, why was she talking like that? Like Madonna speaks now, or when Kevin Costner tries any accent.

"Oh, indeedy doo!" I said in my best Maggie Smith. "Curse words are shit fuck bad. Four score and seven craps ago, I don't care." I flopped horizontal again and failed to bounce on the sinky mattress. "Go away."

"But Sophie!" Tiffani sat on the bed. "Nether Regions Park is let at last!"

I stopped dead, because there was something super familiar about what she said. A ghost of English class past. I looked down; I wore a long, white nightgown. The kind popularized by Sophia Petrillo, not Sophie Sweet.

"Wait!" I gasped. "Wait, this is a new one. Isn't it?" I scrambled to my knees. "Where is Jodie? Is she…is she married?" I held my breath.

"Of coooooourse not, silly girl!" Tiffani shoved a wad of her hair under her cap. "Alas and also alack, she is but an old maid. I expect she shall never enjoy the circumstance of blessed nuptials at this late date. She is six-and-twenty, after all. As are you." She poked at me. "And you, recalcitrant child, resist every effort to do your duty."

What kinda child? Sounded like an insult, so I said, "Thank you."

She sighed in pure exasperation. I knew what that word meant.

I propped myself on my arms to take stock of this place. An old farmhouse? It was all woods and chintz and old-timey stuff. Another bed sat right next to this one, and a fire danced nearby. Not only annoying, but annoying *and* cozy.

"Okay," I said. "What fresh hell is this? Hey!" I grinned at her frown. "I just got what that meant. Thanks to you, demon."

"Excuse me?"

"MawMaw called you a demon."

Tiffani sniffed and pursed her lips. "I have no knowledge of who that is. I am not a demon, I speak to angels." Her eyelashes fluttered. "Yes, I'm sorry, Happizzez. I know you're not a demon! There, there." She shot me a huffy look. "Oh, I know she is."

Excuse me? I thought Happizzez was my buddy!

My personal devil stood and smoothed down her ugly, ruffly, floral dress thing. Wow. Maybe she was cosplaying as some kind of wailing ghost. I, for one, would definitely lock her in an attic forever.

She huffed, "I cannot at all decipher your nonsense this morning, daughter."

I choked on my own spit. "Please stop using the 'd' word."

"So come to breakfast!" she trilled. "You've lazed the day away enough already, and it's sooooo shocking. You're supposed to be up when ye olde cock crows."

"If you'd offer me a decent cock, I'd let it crow."

The creaky wooden door opened, and my heart leaped into my throat. "Jodie!" I nearly screamed it.

"Sophie!" She skipped over to me and jumped onto the bed. Her old lady dress was sea foam green and yellow striped, like a dowdy, sexy couch. This time, her hair bounced with ringlets, peeking from under her own white cap. She looked like a beautiful doll. *Not* the haunted kind.

I nearly cried when she pulled me into a fierce hug. God, I squeezed her back so hard. "Jodie," I began, but then I lost my thought. I smelled her hair and sagged onto her shoulder…and remembered before.

What I'd realized before.

Oh, noooooooo. Nooooooooooo!

Ahem.

Best to swallow that realization down. Waaaaaaaay down. Yeah, denial was the way to go.

"Dearest friend Sophie," said Jodie, also all Britishy.

It was *hot*. I swallowed down.

She continued, "Isn't it capital? An Earl has let Nether Regions Park!"

I blinked. "Let it do what?"

"He shall throw a ball tomorrow-eve! Come, let us breakfast this fine spring morning, and, anon, decide what ribbons we shall wear to catch an Earl's eye." She paused and sucked on her bottom lip. "Well, maybe not an Earl." In a winky whisper, she added, "Perhaps he has a sister."

She held out her adorable little hand to me. I took it, not really understanding half of what was going on, yet always ready to follow her anywhere. Especially since I realized I --

Nope. Emotions were for yesterday. Today, I would channel that energy into embarrassing Tiffani in front of every member of the Royal Brigade of Rich Muckety Sucks. Nothing personal; I just hated her.

"Forsooth, what are you smiling about so jauntily?" asked Jodie.

Tiffani huffed and flapped her arms, with their many miles of lace-strewn sleeves. "Something to make a poor mother's heart flutter, no doubt."

"I never got to avenge myself on my mother, Tiffani," I warned, low and rumbly. "But I'm happy to start now. Where are my matches?"

"Thouest jokest so funnily-est!" said Jodie.

"Okay," said Tiffani. "Let's dial it back."

Jodie blinked. Tiffani sighed.

I scratched my head and concentrated on the one thing that made any sense: "So, there's food?"

They put me into something called "undress," which consisted of layer upon layer of bullshit, including a corset, shift under-dress thing, over dress, left dress, right dress, neck kerchief, stockings, cap, and eight maids-a-milking. If this was me undressed, then I would 100% not be leaving the house ever. The Earl could come see my ass in my bed carved with sheep. Heh. That was probably a good way to nab an Earl when all the other women were more locked up than Fort Knox.

At least breakfast was interesting. Apparently, I had sisters. There were several to a lot of them—seven or eight?—but they kept moving around like a shell game, so actual numbers could not be calculated. They were indistinguishable from one another, each one a varying degree of blonde with a distinct lack of chin. And loud. Extremely loud. I also had a dad, who tended to ignore everyone, which made me feel comfortable, as I was used to that level of neglect. Nobody seemed to care that Tiffani would have needed to birth all of us beginning at *her* birth for this family to make sense.

But the food! Bacon and eggs, ham, toast, jams, fruit! Also, mushroom and tomatoes for some reason. Tasty, though. Thankfully, my eight or nine sisters ignored me as I stuffed my face. Fake life was too short to learn nine or ten new names.

Tiffani made many loud screechings forthwith and verily about the ball I would be refusing to attend.

I ignored these horrific sounds and instead talked with Jodie. In this nightmare, Jodie was my "spinster" friend from the next British mud hole over. She often spent time in our—whoever we were—house to hang with me. Score!

Jodie was literally the only one who didn't appear to be a puff pastry made of boring. Somehow, her pretty curls dancing from under her cap were captivating, and I couldn't stop staring. They highlighted her perfect little freckles.

I didn't want to know what I looked like. Maybe nobody had invented mirrors yet.

Wait. I gasped and turned to "Mom." "Tiffani," I began, warning in my tone. "What year is it?"

"It's the year of our lord 1811, what what, ha-ha!"

My fork clattered to my plate. "Why?"

"Why, because of the concept of linear time."

"I'm no science nerd, but that is the opposite of reality." Oh, Tiffani. Why did -- I gasped, "My phone!"

"What's a...phone?" Jodie asked.

I screamed. And dammit, I dropped my ham!

"Enough, Sophie!" Tiffani barked. "You will survive. More time to concentrate on what is important."

"True love!" declared Sister Eight.

"Romance!" saith Sister Two.

"Officers!" screamed Sister Seven.

Officers of what? Army? Star Fleet? If someone threw me in a brig, I hoped it would be solitary confinement.

Sister Seven continued, "As a matter of fact, Mama, I have already met an officer! He is so charming and handsome, and I shall surely dance with him tonight at the ball."

My "father" dipped his newspaper. A pair of bushy eyebrows and watery blue irises appeared. "As long as you don't run away with him and disgrace the family in a horrible scandal from which we shall never recover."

"That sounds fun," I said, which earned me a *look* from Tiffani.

I munched sullenly on a mushroom. With this many vegetables, my intestines would work better than they had my whole life. "So, Tiff, will your bull --" Tiffani shot me a second, spikier *look*. "-- hockey end if I marry this Earl?"

The room exploded into screams. Each of my 10 or 11 sisters shrieked like I'd already set the house on fire, which I inevitably would.

"No, the Earl is mine!" said one sister about a dude nobody had met.

"I deserve to be the Earless!" proclaimed another sister, using a title even I knew to be nonsense.

While they argued, I grabbed Jodie and ran out the front door. Except I got caught in my purple tube sock dress and bit it. I tried not to think about the fact that I seemed to be extra clumsy now that I was a rom-com heroine.

Eventually, we made it through the door while Tiffani hid under the table from her rampaging children. Heh.

Jodie led me to a glen, which turned out to be a pretty little green valley, and not the dude I hoped would rescue me. I didn't need him anyway, when I had my Jodie.

"Jodie?" I asked.

"Yes, dearest one?"

I broke into a grin. My heart did a thing that I thought would murder me for a second. I whispered, "Could we...sit for a while? Just sit in the sunshine. Without this," I dragged my cap off my head and the lace outta my boobs, "stuff. We'll sit and be and...also not be."

She plopped onto the grass and spread out, arms wide, eyes closed. "That sounds like heaven."

I held a deep breath and released it, along with a least a few sorrows. Then, I hitched up my tube sock and lay next to Jodie. We held hands and just existed there. The grass smelled sweet, the flowers, too. Even the dirt made my nostrils happy. Clouds rolled across the sun, shading my closed eyes from time to time. The light of day chased away some of my demons, leaving me feeling like...floating.

Her hand sat light, delicate in mine, but strong, too. Holding on tight, as if she read the turmoil inside me. Could she?

Could she know that the one person I'd be able to find true love with was the one person I would never, ever pursue?

CHAPTER SEVENTEEN: RUNAWAY PRIDE

say, do you hear hoof beats?" Jodie asked.

She sat up, and the loss of her hand was a bucket of cold water.

I sighed. Nothing nice ever lasted in Wonder Tiffani's Emporium of Torment and Pinchy Clothing.

Apparently, it was time to torture the heroine of this flop—two dudes on horseback came trotting over.

"Cover yourself! Your state of undress is quite shocking!" Jodie gasped.

Wasn't the point of "undress" to be "undressed?" Whatever. I stuffed lace across my collar bones, lest some pasty innocent see them and faint. If only they knew panties hadn't been invented yet.

Eh, I probably wouldn't wear them, anyway.

"Good morning, fair ladies!" said one Horsey Man, a redheaded fellow with transparent skin. Yup, there were his bones, and a stray white blood cell floated across his cheek. "I am Lord Richington, and this is Lord Stonewolfrock."

"The Earl!" Jodie squeaked in a loud attempted-whisper. She dipped into a deep curtsey.

I twitched my head into a nod-like formation. Mostly to hide my eye roll.

"Miss Sweet? Is that you?"

Huh? My gaze jumped up, because the voice echoed through many of my familiar places. No. No, that wasn't possible. I shielded my eyes from the sun to actually see his face. Blood flooded my heart. "Earl?"

Jodie clutched my arm. "*He's* the Earl?"

"Yeah." I licked my lips. "That Earl."

"I say," he said, which seemed redundant. He swept off his hat. "You're quite fetching, Miss Sweet! As always."

"Um. Um? Um!" This was it—the Tiffani heart attack. I clutched at my chest. "What's up, Earl?"

Jodie shook her head and stared, hard, at him. "You should address him as Lord Stonewolfrock. One never addresses an Earl as 'Earl.'"

"What?" These stupid British rules were more confusing than Malbolge. "But—his name is Earl."

"I know that!" she snapped. They'd never particularly warmed to one another.

Earl the Earl smiled at me with his smile. That devastating grin— because my smart, sexy, fun, hilarious ex-boyfriend looked as friggin' gorgeous as ever.

To me, he'd been known as Earl Molina. He looked good as hell on the horse, of course, of course. Earl stood five-foot-seven or so, compact, muscular, with light brown skin and deep, mischievous eyes that crinkled at the corners. We'd dated and had hella fun and nerded out about our future games full of diverse characters. For no reason, my game heroine's anti-hero/love-hate interest was a Latino man who resembled Earl enough that he could probably sue.

I stumbled back as he jumped off the horse athletically, his thighs rippling in tight pants like in an awesome book I'd bought at the airport. Last time I'd seen him, I'd dumped him right after he'd asked me to move in with him. About six months ago.

My mouth went dry as vermouth, and a panic sweat broke out. I'd missed Earl, I really had. But relationships with me…well, people left, didn't they? When you got serious, and moved in, and confessed love, and started to rely on them, they bailed on you because everyone leaves. Especially once they figured out Sophie Sweet was a good time, an awesome buddy—yet not worth the price of an engagement ring.

If I hadn't been able to take that step with Earl, how could I possibly try it with --

Tiffani's voice echoed in my brain, telling me to be kind to myself.

Wait—that might be happening for real.

"Daughter!" she screamed from the other end of the little valley. It took time for her to huff her way to us, slowed as she was by her lack of grace and the 20th-century stilettos. They sank slowly into the grass the longer she stood. "Daughter! I didn't know you'd already made the acquaintance of such a super-duper gentleman."

She screwed up her face in a look that told me she did, in fact, know I'd already made the acquaintance of such an esteemed gentleman. And his real-life version, who was a helluva guy but no gentleman. We'd gone to the same CS school and shared teachers; we'd toilet-papered one professor's house because he was racist on his secret Twitter handle. Which we'd found by hacking into his email. A CS guru who didn't use two-factor? Tut-tut.

"Madam," said Earl the Earl, a handsome, if overdone, joke. "Might I beseech you and your wonderful daughters to attend mine ball this evening at Nether Regions Park?"

I yanked Jodie to me. "And also Jo-- er, Miss Edwards, too?"

"Of course. I'm always delighted to see Miss Edwards," he added with a bit of an edge.

Jodie narrowed her eyes at him.

"As am I," declared Lord Richy-Rich. "I pray the beautiful Miss Edwards might save me the first dance of the evening?"

The beautiful Miss Edwards replied, "Perchance, are you blessed with a redheaded sister?"

"We shall be there with bells on!" Tiffani's voice reached new heights of ear-piercing-ness. Somewhere, a dolphin shook its head in confusion.

I warned her, "I am not wearing a bell."

"It's an expression."

"So is, 'you're the worst.'"

Earl laughed, plopping his hand to his chest in a familiar gesture that made my guts go squidgy. "Miss Sweet, as always, you are a comely, witty delight."

"Come where now?"

"He means thou art hot," said Jodie. "I don't know why Lord Stonewolfrock cannot speak in a normalest manner." She smirked and dipped.

Wow. I hadn't realized a curtsey could be sarcastic.

"Well," I said, "I've got to go choose whatever Laura Ashley nightmare my nemes is will stuff me into, so, see you later, I guess." I walked away, only to be overtaken by Earl.

He took my hand, raised it, kissed it. My breath caught. "Until tonight, my dear."

Tiffani let out such a squeak, the poor dolphin thought she was hearing ghosts.

Lord Fartlyrich and Earlthe Earl of Stonewolfrock rode away, and I did not stare at Earl's ass bouncing on that horse. No.

I rounded on Tiffani. "What are you doing?"

This woman yanked off her bonnet exclusively to flip her damn hair at me. "What do you meeeeeean? You have critiqued my romantical choices for you, so I decided to offer someone you actually enjoy."

Jodie huffed and rolled her eyes so far back, we almost had to restart her.

Tiffani came closer, her gaze narrowing with such sharp precision, it slashed straight through to my core. "Maybe," she said, taking another step forward, "things can work out the way they were supposed to."

"What does that mean?" Jodie asked. She kicked an innocent flower. "Why couldn't we get a good Earl? Like James Earl Jones?"

Tiffani couldn't seem to answer that, so she stalked away. The attitude was pretty ineffective, though, because she did it on tip-toe.

We started back toward the house. Jodie groaned, "I thought we'd got rid of that horrible, boring fellow."

Earl was neither of those things. I was smart enough not to say that out loud. "Yeah, I don't really need the ghost of boyfriend past in all this mess."

She stopped and faced me. "What mess?"

The urge to tell her about our real life in the future rose, but I'd gotten whiplash at this point with explaining reality to her. It didn't always go well.

I released a long, pent-up breath. Today the sun shone, not too hot, not too chilly. Just the perfect amount to warm not only my skin, but deeper. Into my dark places. Flowers exploded into rainbows around us. Birdies chirped, and maybe a bunny would leap to my shoulder and start doing my hair or whatever.

Shit was idyllic.

So, I yanked Jodie toward home. "No mess. Just a beautiful day. Honestly, I would rather not think about…anything."

Jodie leaped into the air and skipped around the grass, just like when we were 16. A couple of weeks ago, she'd skipped her way along a beach with me. Or a couple of centuries in the future, I guess.

I giggled, because she was a glorious goddess. Her frowns about Earl went away, and she chattered as we strolled—about the ball, and how beautiful Nether Regions Park was. Guess visiting someone else's house was the ultimate in entertainment in the before times. There were way more fun ways to pass the time.

Nope. I stopped dead. Couldn't think about…*that.*

Hopping over to me, Jodie said, "What's that particular expression?" She touched my nose. "Your freckles are glowing in the sun."

My whole nose tingled. "So are yours."

She wiggled her shoulders all cutesy like. "Yes, I know. I'm rather adorable."

My breath kept catching, and I couldn't—words—brains?—no nono. So, I safely nodded.

We were almost at the crooked little country house. Jodie stopped and leaned against a tree, her gaze downcast. "Do you perchance intend to dance with Lord Stonewolfrock this evening?"

Was she…upset? Angry? Happy? About it? My heart thundered so hard, my dress shook. "I guess I probably have to? In this time, women are auctioned off to the highest-ranking male in the tri-state, right?"

Jodie blinked her giant eyes. "In this time? Auctioned off?" She tugged at her ear. "What is a tri-state?"

I pulled her toward the house. "It's a bad joke."

Her mouth went smirky. "Oh, so you were attempting humor?"

"Apparently."

Shaking her head, she said, "Be wittier next time, foozler."

Huh? "How do you know about Fonzie from *Happy Days*?"

With an even pointier shake of her ye-olde-noggin, she said, "You are most confusing this day, Sophie, although I agree, 'tis a happy one." She flashed me a sneaky smile. "I suppose I must venture homeward—to collect funds so I can win the auction for you."Jodie laughed as she said it, but then…

An expression crossed over her. A look that made me melt inside. It was serious and full of affection. And something else? Our eyes met, just for a second. And I shook.

She waved and sauntered away toward a hill, and I died, the end.

I boiled inside with utter and complete confusion. At the door, I yelled that I was going to walk a little more, by myself. Alone. I needed to be alone. Just the sight of her drove me to turmoil.

Never mind Earl the Earl.

Behind the house, I found what a poet would call a gently babbling brook, and I nearly fell down at the bank. My slipping feet were as uncertain as my brain. Was it possible to murder myself via emotions? I slumped to the ground and tried to put my head between my knees, but I bounced off my tube sock of a Barney-the-dinosaur-looking dress.

I was already having difficulty swallowing down A Terrifying Feeling Named Jodie. That damn thing kept crawling up my gullet like acid reflux.

And now, *now*, here was Earl! He of Another Emotion, One I Ran Away From Once Already. It wasn't in the same league as The Terrifying Feeling Named Jodie, but dammit, I had cared for him.

I crawled to the water's edge and splashed the cold, clear stuff on my face. Heat flicked through my body from deep inside.

The only reason I'd dumped Earl was because of fear.

Yet, as Tiffani said, the only thing I had to fear was fear of love itself. Right?

"Right!" called Tiffani.

I slipped backward. How—how?

How??

H O W ? ? ?

"Why are you still asking *how*?" asked Tiffani, suddenly sitting a few yards away from me.

I anger-crawled to her, over a rock, through some mud, and maybe on a bug; whoops, sorry bug. Dignity be damned, my hands gripped the top of her offensively unattractive dress, and I jolted her. I had to grit my teeth to stop myself from shaking her head clean off. I begged, "Tiffani, please. Let me go. If you want me to call Earl, I'll call him. And not just a booty call. Although, obviously, it will be a booty call."

"He always *was* fantaaaaastic in bed."

"Yes, I -- stop that! Get out of my brain!"

The best case scenario really was a coma, I thought to myself. Yup, right this minute, I languished, splotchy and pale, in a hospital bed. Having delirious coma dreams. If only my coma-mares were about banging the Dallas Cowboys Cheerleaders circa 1978.

Unfortunately, not all comas are fun.

Oooh! But I might just die soon. Wouldn't that be fun? My dad could pull the plug; awww, he'd like that. They probably didn't make you vomit emotions in hell, only spiders. *And no, I don't need your commentary, Tiffani!*

She pursed her lips, then said, light as whipped cream, "Come inside, darling daughter. You must put on your frock for the grand ball this eve."

I released her fabric abomination and slowly stood. With a deep breath, and with great dignity and calm, I said, "It's pink, isn't it.?"

"Oh, Sophie, I would never choose to do that to you."

Whew.

"Except that I psychically predicted you in a pink dress way back in Chapter One, sooooooo…"

CHAPTER EIGHTEEN:
JUST LIKE HEAVEN'T

Well. Being Lord Stonewolfrock was a good damn gig, because Nether Regions Park was splendiferous. See? I could so talk old-fashioned. This place appeared to be a castle, or manor, or whatever word the ultra-rich use for "palaces enormous enough to house all the local homeless, but lol, they would never do that."

Jodie clung to my arm as we entered the party, and to be frank, I was loving her little hands clutching me so much that I blanked on what I actually looked like. Which was a sort of…sea creature comprised of Pepto Bismol runoff and ruffles.

How I would achieve a booty call with anyone in this getup…

She smelled so good. Though quite a few of the attendees did not. Not only did I not have my cell phone in this terrible era, but nobody owned deodorant. My airport novel lied to me, because there was no chapter titled, "Ew, Everyone Reeks of B.O. Shellacked in Perfume."

That awesome dirty book *had* been right about boobs in old-timey dresses, because Jodie's were spilling up over the low neckline of her dress. Dark beauty peeking through an edge of white lace. They swelled, soft and firm, with every breath. And she was breathing. Hard.

Oh, God. The room. I should stare at the room because it wouldn't make my head spin. It was…room-shaped. Huge, and stone-y. With a marble floor ribboned through in green and black. Forest green drapery had been swagged everywhere, and Jodie leaned close to say something funny about one guy's weird hair, and her sweet breath tickled my ear, and - -

I tripped through a fern. As I clattered toward the marble, Jodie caught my arm and yanked me upright. Against her.

"Are you okay?" she asked, pressed up on me from top to bottom.

Oh, God, oh, God, oh, God. My parts—all my parts—melted. And then, she *breathed* again!I emitted the dolphin-squeaking sound.

Her arm still around my waist, her gaze swept down my chest and up to my face. "You look so beautiful. This pale pink gown brings out the color in your cheeks, and the highlights in your hair." She pulled one of my curls taut. It boinged back like the last thread of my sanity. "And the red here." She tapped a single finger on my mouth.

My cheeks went hot, and I really, really could not speak. She just stared at me, a small smile on her lips. Wow, but *she* had the most amazing mouth, her top lip a little bigger than the bottom. Not much of a cleft, so it was just round and always pursed and adorable.

And so wildly sexy, I jerked away. "Let's drink!" I said way too loud."They have liquor in 1811, right?"

She trailed down my arm to take my hand. "Of course. How else do you suppose anyone stands each other? This way." With a naughty wink, she added, "Let's get you tipsy."

I floated on air all the way to the snack table. Jodie did flirt with me sometimes, in real life. Pretty often, if I thought about it. It was always fun because, come on—the world's greatest human being flirting with you? Come *on*! But tonight, she made my bosom heave. Which is an actual thing that happens to bosoms in real life, and not just in airport books.

Nothing of this was real life, though, right? And yet, her arm sneaking around my waist felt pretty real.

Soon, champagne had been acquired; it and the food were the highlights so far. Well, maybe the fact that Jodie had wound her fingers through mine again was pretty phenomenal. Then, when I couldn't hold her and champagne and grab munchies at the same time, she hand-fed me a mini-pie thing. My lips brushed her fingers.

Oh, God, oh, GoD, OH, God.

Just when my tingling mouth began actually twitching, Earl appeared in my vision. "Oh, God!" I declared.

"The Misses Sweet and Edwards," he said, too softly, too intimately. "How I've been looking for you."

Uuurrrghghghghg, I thought in a totally coherent way.

Jodie yanked me closer. "Lord Stonewolfrock," she ground out. "You're here."

Her tone captured my attention; her mouth had pressed into a thin line.

"I live here, Miss Edwards," he replied, smoothly.

My BFF's nails dug into my flesh. "Well, don't you just have an answer for everything!"

Earl's nostrils flared like they always had with Jodie, and he turned to me. "Miss Sweet, may I entreat you for a dance?"

Wut? "I literally have no idea."

He laughed, rich and full, and I couldn't help but smile. I knew that look. That look said he'd rather dance horizontally.

"We're eating right now," Jodie said. "Come back later. Or not at all."

I swiveled from Jodie to Earl, staring one another down, and my knees nearly buckled. What the heck was Tiffani playing at? I pried Jodie's claws outta me, ducked between her and Earl, and grabbed a glass of champers. I drank it in one, quick swallow.

"Come, Miss Sweet." Earl tucked my hand into the crook of his elbow. "Let us dance."

Before we escaped the buffet's orbit, I snatched another champagne to help me cope. That one didn't last long, either. Hey, at least they had something good in the past! Earl led me away, Jodie huffed, and I experienced a kind of brain spasm that left the colors of the room blurry.

People formed two columns, facing one another. Earl deposited me opposite him, and the quartet started a song. Wonderful. More public mystery dancing! If I ever got outta this, I vowed to randomly kidnap Tiffani exclusively to force her to polka in public with her exes.

Around me, people jumped, turned, clapped. I went right, they veered left. Earl clapped, and I hopped. They zigged, I crashed! Whoa, Sister Seven was pissed I'd stepped on her dress. With a grin of glee, I stomped on random feet, just to feel alive.

The lines came together, and Earl grabbed my hand so we could, um, *prance* to the end of the room. In general, it's safe to say I was not a *prancer*.

"Miss Sweet," said Earl, "do you not know this dance?"

"Unless it's the Electric Slide, I don't know shit."

Everyone around me gasped. I said, "Oh, blow it out your top hat."

Sister Seven shrieked, moved a few paces to the right, aimed, and fell into some dude's arms. Ah, probably the officer she wanted to bang. He was pretty cute, and less unpleasant from downwind.

The lines moved apart again. I kept backing away, my heart pounding, trying to escape. But the officer fella lifted Sister Seven upright… and straight into me. "Ack!" I gasped as we landed in a heap on the cold, hard floor.

People laughed, gossiped, and Sister Seven slipped on my hair on her way up. "You're a disgrace!" she screamed. "I shall never be able to marry until you do, you horrible old maid!" She placed a hand to her forehead, took stock of where her bright-red soldier stood, and fainted dead away into his arms. Wow, she had great aim. The guy had no choice; he carried her out the side door. Guess this counted as interesting before TV, for half the room followed.

Not Earl.

Earl picked me up in his arms. I flailed and protested, yet he strode with manly steps out of the room and further into the house. Not gonna lie, his display of muscles did not leave me unmoved. Soon, we arrived at a library, and he set me on my feet in the darkness.

A single candle flickered just enough to let me see him flash a smile. "I thought we might abandon the experiment in, oh, let's call what you did 'dancing,' before you injured half the landed gentry."

The urge to argue rose, but."Yeah. I hate to land on gentry-men, especially when they're as smelly as those guys." His mouth twitched into a grin, which I matched. Oops. "Anyway, I never was much of a line dancer. Or whatever that was."

"A reel."

"A real what?"

He laughed, not maliciously. Then, a shadow passed across his face, and he shifted onto one hip. "I've missed you, Sophie."

I pushed my hair behind my ears. "I've missed you, too," I said before considering I oughtn't. "Sometimes. You know."

Earl chuckled; yeah, he knew. "I'm quite glad you're here. I --" He walked closer to the giant wooden desk, the candle on it illuminating more and more of him. The light turned his skin warm. Golden. "We had a great thing."

I closed my eyes. Tiffani had probably brought me here to force me to have this conversation. My stomach felt gross, like after too many funnel cakes, if there was such a number. "We did?" I cleared my throat. "We -- we did."

"But you freaked out."

My eyes flew open.

Earl's expression went wry. "You think I don't realize why you dumped me? Right after I suggested taking our relationship to the next level?"

He'd often seen right through me. The only other person who did that even more reliably was Jodie. I gave a shrug I knew was cowardly. "I was saving us both time. It wouldn't have worked out."

"Why not?"

I raked a hand through my hair and grabbed a bundle. Several pins went flying. "I'm not… marriage material."

Earl stepped closer. "Why not?"

No, no. His eyes went dark and seeking, and he came closer. My whole body told me to bolt, but nothing would obey. "Look, it's sunshine and roses when signing up for the thing, and a lot nastier on the way out the door."

"Who says anyone will be exiting the door?"

"Oh, come on!" I finally forced my limbs to move, and I passed him by to steady myself against the desk. "This isn't a fairy tale. I don't know hardly anyone who hasn't been divorced. Your heart gets smashed, and, and your life is ruined—for what? Greeting-card slogans and sex and being forced to do all the dishes?" I scoffed. Hard. "I can get sex without having to do my dishes. And the day I put 'live, laugh, love' on my wall will be the day I give you permission to run me over."

His eyebrows collided. "How long has it been since you did your dishes?"

Um… "That's not the point!"

Hell, he came right over and ran a hand down my arm. "Soph," he said, softly. Too softly. I shivered. "I guess I always figured you left me because of Jodie. Here I see the two of you together again, and I --"

Panic replaced my blood. "What do you mean?"

"Oh, you come on." He brushed one of the curls off my forehead. "She never liked me. The longer we dated, the more she hated me. I heard her say little things to you, about me. Negative things. She would interrupt in the middle of dates. She would invite herself to weekends away. It was clearly jealousy."

My mouth fell open to deny, to defend Jodie. But… suddenly a lot of things clicked into place. She had done those things. Called at 11 or midnight when I spent the night at Earl's. Usually in the middle of sex. I would answer, because it was Jodie. She might need me! Earl and I had taken a long weekend to go to Jamaica, and Jodie dumped her girlfriend just then. She'd cried that she'd be sad and alone forever. I'd never allow that to happen, so I'd purchased her a ticket to the resort with us. And a couple of new bikinis. Plus a spa day.

Earl had been hella angry, and *why* had only now occurred to me.

Wow, I was not a great girlfriend. A series of hot and cold *yikes* ran through my spine.

He stepped closer, his scent invading my good sense. With a soft look, he cupped my face. "Soph, are you with her?"

I shook my head, but I couldn't feel it. I felt nothing. Except for everything.

No, no, no, I wasn't made for this kind of emo-gency. I started shaking, from my knees to my lip, which went full quiver.

"Stop," he whispered, before he kissed me.

Oh, God, it was good. He lifted me onto the desk and pressed against my knees. My arms fell to my sides. I couldn't fight. Not him. Not Tiffani.

Why would I? Earl was clearly my escape hatch.

A scream sounded, and the door flew open. Earl broke away just as one of my sisters— Sister Eighteen?—flew in the door. "Our beloved sister has run away with an officer! He is a scoundrel of the highest order!"

"What's wrong with a little sexcapade?" I asked.

Sister Eighteen shrieked and held her hands over her mouth. Guess that had been the wrong thing to say. Then she uncovered her mouth, which made everything loud again. "'Tis a scandal! We'll be ruined!" She collapsed to the floor to wail at it with snotty abandon.

I hopped off the desk and closed the gap. "Nope, no side stories!" I gripped her arm and yanked her toward the open door. Damn, this wood floor was smooth; good for draggin'. "I'm trying to be ruined all on my own here, so piss off!"

She managed to flee before my foot connected with her ass. Although this dress really hampered my ability to kick people. I guess women in the past weren't allowed to kick their family members. Or spread their knees on a desk with their ex-boyfriends. No wonder feminism had been invented.

I slammed the door shut and fell against it. "Now, where were we? You got a bedroom in this mausoleum?"

Something propelled me forward, *splat!*, onto the floor. Ow, my knees, argh! I flipped over to see Jodie, backlit in the doorway. My heart leaped into my throat.

Jodie's eyes bored into my ex as she grinned and said, "Your sister hast disgraced herself, Sophie, and you must run away in shame." Her head cocked to a dangerous angle as she leaned down to offer her hand. I took it. "Isn't that just too bad, Earl."

Damn. She said his name the way I said "Brussels sprouts."

"That's Lord Stonewolfrock, madam." Earl shot forward. "As a matter of fact, Sophie needs not leave."

I turned to Earl. "I need to leave?"

"Yes," replied Jodie, yanking me toward the exit.

"No!" Earl grabbed my other hand. "You need not."

Huh? "Sure, okay. I definitely understand all this stupid old-fashioned talk."

Earl yanked me close. "We were having a private discussion, Miss Edwards. You are not required."

Jodie tried to pull me from Earl, but he was strong, and she collided with me.

I was the creamy filling in a Jodie-and-Earl rage-sandwich. Reminded me of this amazing porn I'd seen once that had featured two ladies, tear-away Velcro corsets, a stable boy, and the acrobatic use of hay bales. Damn, that dude wore a corset better than I ever had.

Jodie stood on her tip-toes and jabbed a finger in Earl's face. "She daren't be alone with you, wicked man. It is against the mores of the day! And since we are cursed to live in *this* day and not some *other* day…" Her gaze took on a faraway cast. "Some other day when women can be left alone as happy spinsters. Together. Maybe in a little cottage in town with…sheep."

"Sheep?" I asked, my eyes wide.

"Or cats, maybe."

"Nice."

She pressed my hand to her chest. "I would get you so many cats. We spinsters would thrive without anyone bothering us with their," she hissed, "unnecessary handsomeness."

Earl said, "Thank you for the compliment, Mi --"

"I will take my friend out of here to save her reputation!" Jodie snatched me so hard, she won the tug of war. She jerked my dress into place and smoothed my hair. "There. Come along, Sophie."

"Not so fast." Earl grabbed my elbow again and pulled me the other direction. "Do you want to leave, Soph?"

"Stop!" I -- I couldn't catch my breath. Too fast! Too much! *Cat cottage!* I gasped and started for the door. I had to get out. Outside.

I ran.

CHAPTER NINETEEN:
SHE'S JUST THAT INTO YOU

What was I supposed to do? What did all this mean? I kept running. Should I go with Earl? Maybe he was the jailbreak from Tiffani I needed! It might not last, but he seemed to be willing to try. I'd wave the white flag at this point. Or the white, lacy thong, whatever it took.

I lost both of my stupid wallpaper-pattern shoes; I kept fleeing anyway, toward what appeared to be a low-walled garden.

The best part? Losing Earl wouldn't shatter my soul the way losing Jodie would.

I skidded to a stop just inside the hedge opening. All of a sudden, gravity got the better of me, and I collapsed onto my hands and knees, struggling to catch my breath.

"Barfy!"

"Buffy!" I gasped.

She came skidding up, gravel flying, and then sank next to me. "Are you quite alright? What did Earl the Earl the Jackass do to you?"

I shook my head. "Nothing! Nothing."

Jodie helped me to standing and guided me over to a little bench, recessed into the rose bushes. An arch sheltered us, with roses climbing over it, blocking the stars and enveloping us in velvety darkness. She slid her arm across my waist and tucked me into her.

My head fell on her shoulder, where her curls tickled my nose. I giggled.

"That's better." She set her head on mine while her hand traced lazy circles on my waist.

It wasn't unusual for us to cuddle. We did it all the time. Yet tonight...tonight the roses filled the air with luscious fragrance. Tonight, the moon beamed in flashes through the swaying trees. And tonight, I finally realized that my best friend had always been jealous of anyone I dated. Just like I'd been jealous of her pretend-wife Bridget.

Also: Suck it, Bridget.

A tear slipped down my cheek, and my body shook with it.

She immediately turned. "He did do something to you!"

"No, I --" I inhaled a deep, shaky breath. "Jodie, do you think…"

"What?" Her eyes shone with worry as she cradled my hands.

It took all my might to resist the urge to pick up hers and kiss them. "Do you think I'm capable of… of love?"

Her shoulders fell, and she flashed that heart-piercing smile. "Of course you are!"

I squeezed my eyes shut; the tears hanging on for dear life escaped anyway. "How...how does someone do that? How do they justput their heart out there and say, 'Please, hold this,' knowing the other person might drop-kick it at any moment? I've been drop-kicked by so many people, I --"

"Oh, Sophie." She pulled a pin from my hair, and the whole dark mass fell down. She slowly ran her hands through it.

I shivered straight through to my soul.

Jodie continued, "That's why we have to choose our person carefully." She licked her lips. "We have to choose…" Her gaze lifted to meet mine, and she released a slow breath. "Choose someone who will be our best friend."

My eyes would follow her anywhere. She was truly the most beautiful thing in this godforsaken world. My mouth hung open, but no words came out.

Jodie took my hands again. "Sophie, are you in love with Earl the Earl?"

I shook my head.

She released a held breath, a half-laugh. "So you are…available?" Her voice dipped. "For other interested parties?"

I nodded. My heart thundered. I could not have moved for any force on earth.

"Well, then." She paused, uncertainty chasing across her face.

I squeezed her and held my breath.

"Why not me?" she asked in an unsteady whisper.

This was it. Oh, my God, this was it. I grinned. I couldn't help it, my body had begun to move without asking my brain. I giggled, breathless and giddy. Like a total girl.

She tucked my hair behind my ear with a shaky hand. "Sophie." She leaned in close. Closer.

My beautiful Jodie was about to kiss me! I'd never wanted anything so much in my whole life. Elation pierced my chest. Chased by terror. She was my best friend. My life. My happiness. My everything. My *everything*.

I leaped to my feet and ran a few steps away, tiny rocks pressing into my stockinged feet. A safe distance away. "But it won't work!" I blurted, facing the roses instead of her.

"What?"

Oh, no, she sounded so –

I spun around.

Her everything had fallen.

I whispered, "I mean…we might lose everything, Jodie."

We froze, facing off. She turned her gaze to the ground. And then she nodded. When she finally looked at me again, I stumbled backward into a gathering of thorns.

Rage. She shook with it. "I should have known. You are too trepidatious to live life with anyone else, why should I think I'm special enough to be the exception?" She stepped forward and jabbed a finger in my direction. "You're a coward. You need to work through your past, Sophie. Honestly, I wouldn't even allow you to be with me if you didn't commit to that. And true to form, you're throwing me away because you're beholden to fear above everything else. You're paralyzed by it!"

I sank to my knees. Because she was right. She was so right. After all— who knew me better?

"It saddens me most grievously to tell you," Her shoes sent dust flying when she turned, as if she couldn't stand to look at me anymore. "But you have lost everything. I can't do this anymore. I deserve someone who has the courage to believe in us. To fight for us! I'm worth that!" With tears running through her voice, she added, "I can't believe in you more than you believe in yourself. Goodbye, Sophie."

That's when I collapsed onto the ground and had a heart attack.

CHAPTER TWENTY:
LEAP FEAR

First thing I did in hell was sigh, because, naturally, everlasting damnation ended up being pink. And full of Tiffani.

I kneeled on squishy ground I couldn't quite see, in the middle of what looked like Tiffani's psychic tent—or, at least, a version dipped in cotton candy. Fuzzy edges. Vague shapes. Or maybe that was the inside of my head.

"So," said Tiffani, sneaking up behind me *yet again*. I turned to face her. She wore a glittering pink dress. The skirt bubbled around her like a Christmas ornament. Like you'd see in a Sixties movie or something. I'd always figured hell would be ugly, but I had no idea how much.

She put her hands on her hips. "Is this rock bottom? Are we done running amuck?"

"I don't think I *can* run on this squishy floor. Besides, aren't I dead?" I broke into a horrible laugh. "I hope so."

Tiffani hauled me to my feet like the sack of potatoes I was tonight. Push, pull, haul, drop, kiss, kiss, scare, scare!

She patted my shoulder. At least I didn't want to kiss one of the people pulling me into unfamiliar places this evening. "So, Sophie. It's time to make a choice."

"Oh, God." I tried to fall over. The witch wouldn't let me.

"I have stuff going on in my own life, you know," she began. "This is just my day job. And I guaranteed Jodie a true love. As Fromm said, love is an act of faith, and whoever is of little faith will die alone, so make a decision already!"

I started. "Wait, what?" Memories of Halloween night burst into my brain. Tiffani had promised Jodie a true love. Within the month, or her money back.

Jodie. Not me.

Tiffani's pretty, annoying little face drew closer. "Yes, Sophie. I guaranteed Jodie her one, true love. She was the one who asked for a reading. She was the one who paid me. You sat there looking like you poop scorpions; I haven't been doing anything for *you.*" She flashed me a smile so smug, it had its own pompous and circumstance. "The moment I met her, I knew poor Jodie was stuck. Watching you flail about. Denying her emotions. Knowing you could not handle an adult relationship and would probably destroy a decade of devotion because of your soul-shattering self-doubt and --"

"Feelings of inadequacy as a byproduct of my abusive childhood," I finished. "Damn you."

"So, I had to pound you into a new outlook, like a metal-maker person would do with crappy old metal that they heat up and hammer on to make something useful. I don't know about construction things." She rubbed her hands together, like an actual Bond villain. "It's been fun, abusing you. You really shouldn't mock beautiful psychics who are just trying to spread the messages of love and pink through the world." She gave a short, bitter laugh. "Most people learn their lesson in one scenario. But not you! You can't even admit what your hair color is!"

My stomach dropped. "Wut?"

She hissed, "You're a *blonde.* A natural blonde!"

I clutched my fake-black head and started hyperventilating. Oh, God. My secrets!

"Yet I pressed on! While looking amazing." She patted herself on the back. Literally. "I needed to make it happen for Jodie, who is so lovely. What she sees in you, I doooooon't know…" The face she pulled!"But you know the old saying: The heart wants what it doesn't realize is a snarky jerk."

"Jodie just…she just left me on the ground!" I attempted to stand and fell. It was like balancing on the back of a moving elephant. With a point, I added, "Exactly how I knew this disaster would end."

"Oh, you mean when she bravely put everything on the line to confess her feelings for you, and you immediately said it wouldn't work out?" She pursed her pink mouth. "Please don't go into writing greeting cards, ha-ha!"

My brain slid down my spinal cord. "Oh, shit."

"Yes, oh shit." She kneeled and took me by the scruff of my antique dress. "Listen, you stubborn, cowardly moron. You can either gather your ovaries, go to the woman you love, and give it a try, or you can continue this nonsense and be alone. Also, you look fantastic as a blonde, okay? Almost no one has that natural silvery hair color."

I looked past Tiffani. All at once, my pink fog gave way to crystal clarity. Fear was a death, wasn't it? Bad things can happen whether you fear them or not. How many things had I feared that never came to pass? My car might wreck, but I still drove. I could choke, yet I still ate Doritos Surprise. And as a kid, no matter how bad tings got, I had never considered that my mother would abandon me.

It had happened anyway.

It happened. And I hadn't died. I'd kept going, half to spite her. My dad barely fed me, but I went to school anyway, even when I smelled. Even when I had no pads for my period, only wadded up toilet paper from the gas station. I'd gone to CS school and graduated at the top, even though some of my classmates had been outright hostile. I'd gotten a baller job, plus I'd kept creating on my own.

I'd managed to make friends with the most amazing woman in the world, and keep her, even when I was the worst sometimes.

Jodie Edwards had lifted me up through everything. And I had lifted her, too, because she was a goddess who deserved it. I'd punched bullies for her. Charged into the fray. Spoken up, gotten suspended when her teachers treated her badly. Always answered the phone. Always came running!

I would never hesitate to step in front of the bullet for Jodie; I would gladly die for her. Shouldn't I at least stand tall and work to come to terms with my damaged parts so I could *live* for her instead?

Tears crowed my eyes. Snot ran from my nose. I met Tiffani's gaze.

She smiled, and a tear slipped down her cheek. No snot, though, because I was pretty sure Tiffani didn't put anything on her face that wasn't attractive. "Yes, Sophie Sweet, you super-duper pain. It's time to *live*."

"But—but she left me. It's too late," I sobbed. "And I. Have. Black. Hair!" My shoulders fell. My voice squeaked. "Throw me a bone, you evil --
"

"Ha-ha, shut up! This is my universe, Sophie Sweet. And I say it's never too late for love." She fanned her hair in a truly magnificent flip. "Now, get out of here. This is my personal relaxation fantasy area, and Harry Styles is on the way."

She snapped her fingers.

CHAPTER TWENTY-ONE:
LOVE, DEFINITELY

Morning sun burst through the windows. I found myself in my bed. In my 1811 bed. But who cared? Even if I had to live without cell phones and video games forever, it would be worth it to live with Jodie.

Although that would not be ideal, Tiffani! I knew she heard me, the nosy brat.

Sister Seventeen bolted through my door. "Our sister has eloped to Gretna Green!"

"Good for her. I hope she elopes to Great 'n' Purple, too. Which way is the dad's room?"

She wailed and flopped to the floor like a dramatic fish. Geez. Wouldn't catch me dead collapsing constantly. I stepped right over her, shook her hand off my ankle, and tried doors until I found the master bedroom.

My pseudo-dad looked up from reading to object to my being in there.

I shook my head, with its gorgeous naturally raven black hair. "I don't care what you think. You are a damaged man who, in turn, damaged me. But I refuse to emulate your miserable life any longer. You stay alone and angry—I'm going to get my lady."

His bushy brows twitched. "If only I *were* alone."

"If only you were my father."

He shrugged and returned to reading.

I ransacked his drawers. Grey pants, white shirt (ooh, piratey), decent socks, check. Next, I searched through the boots in the house until one of the maids brought me a pair of men's boots without any stupid heels. They must have been some kid's, but they fit!

"Wait, did you say *lady*?" the dad asked.

With a wide grin, I said, "Yes, not-father. I'm super gay."

He nodded. "I do want my daughters to be happy. Go, be as gay as you like."

Wow. Who would have thought 1811 dad would be way cooler than the modern version?

Back in my room, I stripped off my ridiculous dress, yay, and yanked on the shirt and pants over nothing. Heh. Maybe Jodie would be into that.

And I finally got to burn something when I threw that ugly damn dress in the fire.

No time to admire my arson, though. Boots on, coat on: Time to steal a horse. I ran around the house to the little stables, where a horse and a donkey resided. A sliver of fear shot through me. Damn, horses were giant, and I'd only ever sat on one once. But I would not *fear* anything this day.

I put my foot in a stirrup.

I would be brave!

I swung over the horse to sit astride. I gasped from the rather, er, firm way I'd landed. I'd need those lady parts, thank you very much. Hopefully, anyway.

Sophie Sweet's It-Has-to-Work Plan for Declaring Terrifying Feelings, Fuck Shit Fuck

- Ride a horse dashingly

- Don't die

- Say appropriate mushy things to perfect woman

- Don't call them mushy because you are an adult

- ????

- Profit!

"Onward, horsey!" I told him. He did not move. I leaned over; where was the "on" button? I lightly kicked my heels in. Didn't want to hurt the fella, but we needed to get going before Jodie met some sexy, mentally healthy woman!

The stable boy wandered in. "Where yagoin'?" he asked.

"Um, where does Jodie Edwards live?"

"Next village over the hill. In Plopshire."

I squeezed my eyes closed. Plop. Shire. She'd told us from the start, *damn that Tiffani.*

But I could damn her later. And I *would.*

Now, I needed to make the horse go. I thought about my beloved Satan, and how I got him to do anything. "Hewwo, sweetie horsey-kins! Yes, you're the pwettiest horse in pretend-land, yes you are! So handsome! And your penis is alarmingly big. but that's coming from a human. I bet the sexy lady horses think you're --"

Horsey whinnied and *went.* I didn't need to tell him to go faster, for he'd already achieved a full gallop, and I was busy saying, "Aaaaaahahahahagagagaghahahahahh!"

All penis-people enjoy being told their dick is the biggest. That's a fact.

I bounced and freaked and hurt my vagina and peed a little, but I held on! I would not give up no matter how horrifically terrifying this nightmare hell beast was. Pretty metal, honestly. My screams echoed off the hills we passed, so my arrival would be a surprise to no one.

By the time I arrived in Plopshire, population: dozens (of cows), my noble steed had beaten the nerves outta me. Pure excitement bubbled through my veins, and wow, I just wanted, needed, to see her perfect face.

Rando side characters told me where the Edwards' cottage was, and soon, I galloped up the pretty path to the medium-sized house. It looked like something out of a fairy tale. All beige and straw-roofed, with bright green shutters decorated in hand-painted bouquets. Real flowers and roses twisted everywhere, like a secret garden. It was the perfect frame for my beautiful Jodie, who sat on a stool to one side of the house, doing…something? Beating? Pumping? With a stick and a big bucket.

"What are you doing?" I asked.

Her gaze rose up, up to me on the horse. Shock froze her eyebrows. "Churning butter, of course."

Tiffani the Very Accurate Psychic's words echoed in my brain. I whispered, "Romance cannot happen without butter." I released a burst of laughter. I was meant to be here. Right now. In this ridiculous time, in a pirate outfit, on a horse, ready to finally do the thing.

Jodie stopped, er, bashing the butter and pursed her lips.

I swung off the horse and landed perfectly on the muddy ground. In my fantasy. I actually slipped in the mud, grabbed for the horse, damn near got bit, and finally found my footing.

Ahem.

Oh, she tried to keep her lips in a straight line of disapproval, but one end betrayed her. It floated upward as I flailed. I could work with that. I hurried to her and found a dry patch of grass.

Here goes nothing.

Here goes *everything*.

I fell to my knees. Jodie had forced me to watch enough rom-coms that I knew when to commence the groveling.

"Jodie," I began. And immediately welled up with tears. Uuuurrrgggghhh, I would never forgive Tiffani for turning me into a crying machine. "Jodie. You're right. Absolutely right. I have been a coward for a long time." I swallowed. Every cell in my body told me to bolt, but I refused.

Do it for Jodie.

No.

Do it for *me*. Because I deserved to be happy, too.

Jodie stood. "Go on," she whispered with a smile. She put her thumb to her forehead and wiggled her fingers.

She wiggled for me!

I wiggled back!

The sun broke through the clouds to sparkle across her face and everything!

"Steady, Sophie" she said. "I love your outfit, by the way. Very comely."

I squeaked. "Is that good?" I looked down. Damn, the neck hung low; maybe that would help. "I want you to know that I'm ready to…grow as a person and shit. Stuff. I shouldn't cuss in the middle of this, whoops."

She giggled. "It's bloody okay."

I matched her giggle. "Thanks. You're right about my…damage. I want to work on it and improve my outlook. Not just bury everything under leather jackets and being awesome. I'm gonna," *deep breaths*, "go to therapy."

Her jaw dropped. "Holy bloody shite."

"Yeah, it's time. I've been holding myself back. And, and maybe holding you back too? Because—because I love you." This was it! I closed my eyes because seeing her was one input too many. "I love you. I love you! Not like a friend, but, I mean you are my best friend. I love you, I mean like…my love. My heart." Gaaaaahhhhh. My head fell back. "Er, emotions. And sexy stuff. You are very beautiful, and you make me feel lady feelings. *Strong* lady feelings. Keep-me-up-in-the-middle-of-the-night lady feelings!" I peeled one eye open. "Not only because you're the single most gorgeous human ever invented on planet Earth, no matter what year we're in, but because you're funny, and smart, and loving, and, and, and, all the things!" I spread my arms wide. "You're all the things! You're all *my* things. And I want to worship the ground you walk on for as long as you'll let me."

My horrible speech ended in a croak because I would surely burst into flame.

I kneeled there, arms out, like the finale of *Hamilton* or something.

She blinked. And did that friggin' sexy lip thing she did, pushing the bottom under the top. My heart thudded, because all I wanted to do was --

Jodie rushed forward, fell to her knees, and kissed me.

Books talk about explosions. Or fireworks when you find your person. I finally knew what those purple prose people were talking about. Kissing Jodie was not kissing other people. Kissing Jodie was why I had been born.

I took her face in my hands and pressed my lips to her softness, her warmth, the amazing, sweet taste of her. God, she felt incredible! I pulled her bottom lip between mine, she made this little moaning sound, and I about died, my heart bursting with total joy. When she tasted me back, the shiver shattered me. Everywhere. I wanted to eat her up.

So to speak. And also very, very literally. How gay was a gal allowed to get in 1811?

Jodie pulled away with a huge grin. "Finally!" she gasped.

I set my forehead on hers. "Finally."

We kneeled there, leaning on one another, breathing each other in.

"Oh!"

I opened my eyes to see what was wrong.

"No, no, don't look like that." My love smoothed my forehead with her fingers. "I just forgot to say I love you back."

I gasped, my soul in my throat. "You did?"

She nodded. "So I'd better do that, huh?"

"Well, you were the one Tiffani promised. I'm the tag along."

"What?"

"Nothing, nothing." I held my breath. For so much of my life, I'd longed for the love that had never come. Love for me, for the person I was: good, bad, and petty. I'd called this longing my black hole because it sounded metal. But from now on, I would work to heal that hole. It was time.

She lifted my hands and kissed one, then the other in turn. "I love you, Sophie Sweet."

A bright light shone. Blinding! I shielded Jodie's eyes and strained to find the source, but it appeared to be coming from everywhere. A sudden falling feeling overtook me, and soon all I saw was...

Pink.

CHAPTER TWENTY-TWO:
ALWAYS BE MY LADY

W hat?"

I bolted up. Gah, this continuous alarmed waking would give me angina. Whatever that was. The sun shone straight through to my brain, and I blocked it with a hand. My bedroom shone around it with a yellow glow.

My bedroom!

I rolled outta bed and ran to the window to throw it open. My street! There was the vacant lot full of garbage and needles. The payday loan place across the street never looked so sweet! I leaned out. "Hey, you there, kid!"

The boy one story below on the sidewalk stopped. "Who you calling 'kid'?"

"Well…how old are you?"

"I'm 10, motherfucker!"

I bit my lip and nodded. "Ohhh-kay. Young man, then. What day is it?"

The kid shook his head, his mass of blonde hair flopping about. "Don't you got a phone?"

"I don't know, that depends on what year it is."

"You need to stay outta the vacant drug lot, lady."

"Probably. But I'm getting therapy!"

He flipped me the bird and walked away.

Shit. That had not been helpful whatsoever.

I closed the window and turned back to my very own bedroom. "Jodie," I whispered.

She sat up and rubbed her eyes. "Hey, Barfy."

I held my breath. What—how—did she remember? Had it really happened? My lips still tingled from hers. And the rest of me…let's just say I was a puddle from head to toe.

On my nightstand, exactly where it ought to be, I saw my phone. My heart thundering, I ran that way—and tripped over a pair of Jodie's socks. I damn near scooped them up and kissed them. But love has *some* limits. When I got to my phone, the date was November 1. Of the current year! The day after the Gator Riviera Autumn Carnival.

The day after we'd met Tiffani.

My Jodie—I hoped she was my Jodie—smiled at me and held out her hand. Immediately, I rushed to her and took it, cradling her tiny fingers against my chest. "Hi," I said, breathlessly, like Julia Roberts in one of those movies.

Er, *not* a rom-com, dammit.

"Hi," Jodie whispered. "So…I had the craziest dreams. That felt really…real."

My palms over hers went clammy.

"I dreamed we were back in high school, when you would go after anyone who hurt me. Then, it changed, and you were a real-life princess. We ran away together." She grinned, and giggled. "After that, I got married to a blonde lady, and you were," she sucked in a deep breath, "super jealous." With a pause, she looked down. "In the end, we were in a Jane Austen book? I guess? That guy Earl was there." Thunder rumbled across her features. "I never liked Earl."

"I'm sorry."

"But you threw him over. You rode up to my house." Her eyes went very wide, as if she played a movie in her mind.

I kneeled in front of her again. Hey, it had worked the first time.

"And I said I loved you. While wearing a sexy pirate shirt. Because I do, Jodie. I love you. In a more-than-friends way." My breath caught as I waited for her to say something.

Her big eyes went even wider. "Was it a dream?"

"I -- I don't know. It may have been. Or Tiffani might literally be a magic psychic witch from hell who could bend space and time to her infernal will. Either way, my feelings are very, extremely real."

She grinned, huge, and adorable. "You said you're going to go to therapy so you can be happier? Because you deserve that, Sophie."

I nodded. "I will. I promise. Because I *do* deserve it."

Jodie nodded. "Well. I guess there's nothing else to say. Except that I love you, too."

I did the most horrifying rom-com thing of all: I burst into tears.

And then she did the most wonderful rom-com thing of all: She kissed me.

After several minutes of the hottest freaking making out of my life—oh, my God, Jodie was an amazing kisser!—I came up for air with great, *great* reluctance. Mmmmmmm she looked all soft and sexy and turned on mmmmmmm.

"What's wrong?" she whispered.

"Nothing! Not one thing in this whole world. I just..." I blew out a breath. "I want to take this slow." I held her hand. I couldn't hold both because one was on my ass. Heh. I had an amazing ass. "I want to do this right."

"Oh, I'll do it right. Where are your nail clippers?"

This woman would give me a heart attack! I laughed through my sex haze. "Let's get brunch. Like, have a date or something. And then, " my eyes narrowed, "I have questions for Tiffani."

Even though we were fully clothed, we had an incredible brunch. I kept smiling at her, my heart so full it threatened to explode and make a real mess of the pancakes. And she just grinned, grinned at me, like I was amazing or something.

You deserve her, I told myself. One of these days, I'd believe it without Tiffani's voice running through my head.

I picked up the tab, for my *date with Jodie*, aaagdahidhdhuhediudhwudh!

Hand-in-hand, we returned to the Autumn Carnival and made a beeline to Tiffani's tent. After a brief stop for fried bacon. For me. And only me.

Jodie skipped the whole way, never letting go of my hand.

Tiffani the Psychic-Guidance Counselor-Goodwill Manager-Private Secretary-Vagine Examiner-Wedding Planner-Bruise Dispenser-Haunted Doll-Love Expert seemed to be waiting for us. She perched on her ugly orange armchair, facing the door to the tent today, and wore the most self-satisfied smile ever to say *I'm the shit, peasants*.

And, well, with my fingers woven tight with Jodie's, maybe she freaking was.

"Ohem gee, Jodie!" Tiffani clapped and bounced in her chair. "What do you think of my guarantee?"

Jodie clasped her chest. "Tiffani! You were right." She threw an arm around my shoulders. "I have a girlfriend."

"Damn right you do," I said. "But, Tiffani, you guaranteed her a girlfriend within the month." I tore myself away from Jodie and loomed over Tiffani. "It's now November."

Her face fell. "You know what I meant. Within a month!"

I crossed my arms. "Somebody owes Jodie her money back."

Tiffani stood and stomped her pink-clad foot. Jodie put her hands on her hips.

With a laugh, I added, "And that someone is me." I pulled a wrinkled 20 out of my back pocket and offered it to my lady love. "I would be honored to pay for your trip to the tunnel of love, eventually. We seemed to have happened overnight, but," I glared at Tiffani, "it's been a *long* time coming."

"It doesn't usually take that long," Tiffani said. "You're the most stubborn jerk I've ever met."

My spine stiffened with pride, pure pride. "Aww, thank you!"

Tiffani came in for a group hug. I allowed it.

Jodie pulled back and hit Tiffani with a searching look. "So… what *are* you? My great-grandmother says you're a demon."

"MawMaw's right," I confirmed.

"Ha-ha, no!" Tiffani smoothed today's caftan, a fluorescent pink leopard print number, the kind you'd find at an international bazaar located in Las Vegas. "I'm not really interested in labels. I'm just a girl, searching for true love, hoping I can help others along the way."

Jodie pursed her lips. "You into boys? Girls? Both? Everyone?"

"Boys."

"That's too bad. I've got several girl friends who could do with a bit of hot girl magic. But I do have a dude teacher friend…"

Jodie promised to pass on the guy's info via text, and I loved her for her kindness. I loved her for her everything. I especially loved her tight jeans and off-the-shoulder sweater today. Loved her for the fact that she clearly wasn't going to make me fight through a bra later on.

I pulled her close for a kiss. A delicious, brain-breaking kiss that made my whole being burst into fireworks. The black hole shrank a bit, and not just because of Jodie.

"Hey," I said, "I want to say something to Tiffani alone. Can I meet you at the funnel cake stand?"

Tiffani squeaked in alarm.

Jodie shook her head at me. "I'll see if I can find an antacid vendor for you." With a smile that melted my deep, dark places, she slipped out of the tent. Then peeked back in. "Holler if you need help, Tiffani. I understand how to soothe the savage beast."

Once Jodie had left, I turned to my tormentor. "Tiffani," I began, "you're still the worst. I mean, you tried to get my vagina examined by a bunch of gross old men."

She waved her arms. "Oh, I knew you would never go for that. I needed you to run away." With a blink that might have been an attempt at a wink, she added. "With *her*. And I gave you a secluded cabin. Like in every sexy romance. You're welcome."

"Except you burst in on us!"

"You should have sealed the deal quicker. You know what they say: Among all paths leading to a woman`s heart, rain is the shortest one."

Uh…sure. I nodded and continued my little speech. Which I had intended to be nice except she was terrible. "Anyway—I just want to wish you…good luck." I held out a hand. "With your quest for true love. I fully believe you'll find him. Just don't psychic him into an aneurysm."

She shook my hand, firm and fast. "Thank you, Sophie Sweet. I always knew you had it in you. All because of me. Ha-ha!"

"Yeah. All because of you. Thanks, jerk."

"You're welcome, bitch."

With a laugh, I tossed back the tent flap and emerged into the sun. Jodie waited there for me, her eyes loving and welcoming. "I have a better idea than funnel cakes," I said.

"Oh, no." She held my hand and started walking. "Not Doritos Surprise."

"What's wrong with Doritos Surprise?"

"Everything!" My Jodie tugged me along and added, "But since you've had a magical epiphany about life and personal growth for me…I can eat some disgusting glop for you."

Wow. It really was true love.

ACKNOWLEDGEMENTS

I'd like to thank my beta and sensitivity readers, who include the wonderful Kayla Dunigan of Black Sensitivity Reader, Paige Bainbridge, Orla Egan, and The Amazing Freedom Kim.

ABOUT THE AUTHOR

Martti Nelson is a humor author, specializing in comedy, satire, parody, and general nonsense. She lives with her husband, cat Otis, and a little lemon tree she is way too proud of. Her dream job is to write filthy skits for Rupaul's Drag Race or to cuddle baby elephants. In the meantime, she writes funny feminist books in the hope that every reader will feel like a superheroine by "the end." Because we all are! She lives in LA to try to pick up Mel Brooks.

www.ingramcontent.com/pod-product-compliance
Lightning Source LLC
Chambersburg PA
CBHW061235210726
48293CB00003B/780